HIS RANCH REDEMPTION

LAURIE WINTER

Recycling programs for this product may not exist in your area.

ISBN-13: 978-1-335-46043-1

His Ranch Redemption

Harlequin Enterprises ULC
22 Adelaide St. West, 41st Floor
Toronto, Ontario M5H 4E3, Canada
www.Harlequin.com

HarperCollins Publishers
Macken House, 39/40 Mayor Street Upper,
Dublin 1, D01 C9W8, Ireland
www.HarperCollins.com

Printed in U.S.A.

"I've missed you, Sarah."

She rested her head on his chest and breathed him in. "I missed you too." Being close to Pete was like returning to a familiar place. Their bodies swayed with the gentle rhythm of the song.

"I found out I can't start in Phoenix until I'm released by a doctor, which won't be for at least another four weeks." He cleared his throat. "I could stay a little while longer and build more social media content. And help around the ranch as much as my bum arm allows. Only if you want me to. If you'd rather I didn't stick around, then I'll head south and hang out in the heat until I can start work."

Her head spun. Pete staying longer was her dream and nightmare combined. She'd already felt her heart slipping and he'd only been here less than a week. What if she remembered all the reasons she'd loved him?

Dear Reader,

Imagine the most ideal place to live. For Sarah Carmella, nothing compares to her beloved ranch. Who could blame her? The beauty of the mountains and rivers in the Cascade Range region of Washington State is truly unmatched. Waking up every morning on a property filled with horses and other rescue animals is a dream come true. For Sarah, her purpose is found in taking care of those entrusted to her.

Peter O'Keefe returns to Carmella Ranch as a lost soul, unsure of where or when he will settle down. The only certainty he has when stepping foot back on the ranch is that he can't stay. But will fate prove him wrong?

I thoroughly enjoyed researching the intricacies of a horse ranch. Animal rescue is an expensive undertaking, and Sarah's concerns about finances reflect the struggles many organizations face in providing food, medical care and housing. Please consider donating your time or money to one of these deserving organizations.

Visit my website, lauriewinter.com, and sign up for my newsletter to stay updated on my latest releases.

Peace and love,

Laurie

Bestselling author **Laurie Winter** creates authentic characters who overcome the odds to find true love. She keeps her life balanced with yoga and binge-watching true-crime shows. Laurie enjoys time with her family and three dogs, all of whom inspire her every day.

Books by Laurie Winter

Love Inspired Suspense

Hunted by a Killer

Love Inspired The Protectors

Safeguarding the Witness

Visit the Author Profile page at Harlequin.com.

To every reader who shared their enjoyment of my stories. You are the reason I stay lost in fictional worlds.

CHAPTER ONE

"I CAN'T BELIEVE he's coming!" Sarah Carmella paced back and forth across the plank floor of the front porch. With each step, the hard soles of her boots rapped on the wood. She spun around to face her friend, or at least she had considered Jacob Wood a friend—until now. "Why did you wait to tell me?"

Jacob retreated down to the top porch step. He rested a hip on the rail and crossed his arms over his body. "Pete told me he couldn't be here for the wedding. Then he texted a few days ago. The start date for his new job was pushed back and now he can make it to the wedding in Fern Hollow less than a week from now. He's a good friend, Sarah. I'm not going to tell him to stay away."

She huffed at the logic, fighting to stay reasonable. Her history with Peter O'Keefe made her irrational—and irritable. Positioned directly in front of Jacob, she prodded him in the chest with her index finger. "But *your* wedding is on *my* property. I won't be able to avoid him."

Swallowing hard, Jacob broke eye contact. He stared at the flowerpot filled with pink petunias resting at the foot of the stairs. "Perhaps the time has come to *stop* avoiding him. I care about you both. Don't forget—I was there after Pete left for basic training."

"And you brought me brownies and held my hand when I didn't have the willpower to get out of bed." Her heart ached. She sighed, humbled by Jacob's kindness, and instinctively pressed it over her belly. The dark days of her past hovered around the edges of her mind since the news of Pete's return. She didn't want to relive them, not even for a moment. "I cried on your shoulder when the annulment went through." She exhaled a long breath, as if she could rid herself of every painful memory surrounding Pete. Falling in love with him had been her biggest mistake. Traveling from Fern Hollow, Washington, to Las Vegas at the age of seventeen to marry the eighteen-year-old young man had been her most reckless act. The one time she'd let her heart rule her head. And the reward for such a risk? Her life shattered into a million pieces. It took her a long time to stitch herself back together.

She refused to allow herself to fall apart again because of his return. "You're right. I'm overreacting. Maybe it won't be so bad seeing him again." Or better yet, she'd hide the entire weekend. But she'd miss Jacob's wedding if she buried herself under a blanket and watched movies all day. As enticing as avoidance sounded, she owed it to her friend to be there.

"That's the spirit." Jacob skipped down the remainder of the stairs like he didn't want to give her a chance to fire back up. "Don't allow your mind to spiral and come up with the worst-case scenario."

"It's just that I don't want to ruin your special day with an awkward reunion." And when she faced Pete again, she'd be lucky if it was simply awkward. As long as they didn't rehash old hurts, Pete could leave Fern Hollow after his short stay without any drama and she could get on with her life.

"I trust the both of you to act like adults and not throw wedding cake at each other." He gave her a cheeky grin.

She bounded down the stairs after him. Just because she thought of him as a little brother didn't mean she'd allow him to act like one. "Don't think you can say something like that then run away."

Standing his ground, Jacob laughed. "I'm sorry. You know I love teasing you. Kay will be over later with the wedding planner to bring some of the decorations. The number of flowers my soon-to-be bride has ordered could fill up a cathedral. We may not have room for the guests." His playful expression faded, now hinting at pre-wedding stress.

"Take a breath. We'll make sure everything fits, including the wedding guests." Hosting weddings at Carmella Ranch and Orchard was new this summer but she had faith in the staff hired to run the events. Jacob and Kay's would be the fifth ceremony and reception held inside the remodeled barn now aptly called the Big Red Barn. The two made a beautiful couple, and Sarah was determined to make everything perfect, despite the new wrinkle of her ex attending the affair.

After waving goodbye to her friend and neighbor, Sarah retreated into the house. How would she react to seeing Pete again? She conjured up his image in her mind. Her chest grew tight. She stood in the foyer and followed her own advice—take a breath. The sheer curtains in the living room fluttered in the afternoon breeze. Pete was coming back to Fern Hollow. They hadn't seen one another in twelve years. What would she say after all that time? If only Mike was still here to serve as a buffer. But his heart had failed after years of intense medical care. He'd died shortly after their daughter

Chloe's second birthday. Her eyes and throat burned at the memory of his funeral and how completely alone she'd felt after losing the man she loved. Chloe never got to really know her father's deep commitment to them. He'd done his best to beat the odds and live. Now, Sarah did her best without him.

She continued into the kitchen and filled the kettle with tap water. Once the kettle was placed on the stove, she turned on the burner. A cup of tea would help soothe her frayed nerves. A rap on the screen door that led outside from the mudroom made her heart jump. *Not helping with my peace of mind.* She checked the time. How was it two o'clock already? "Come in," she hollered to her guest.

"I was wondering where you were." Milton Monroe swaggered into her kitchen with a bow-legged gait. He acted like Sarah's house was his second home. It kind of was. The older man had spent many years on the back of a horse. Once age hindered his love of riding, he traded in his saddle for a truck and horse trailer. Milton picked up horses in need of rescuing and transported them to Carmella Ranch. He also volunteered with every other aspect of the rescue, from feeding to arranging farrier visits to figuring out creative ways to pay the never-ending bills.

"I'm making tea. Want some?"

He scoffed. "Do I look British to you? You got any good whiskey?" With a flash of a grin under the scruff covering the lower half of his face, Milton pulled out a kitchen chair and got seated. He leaned back, legs stretched out. "What we really need is a good rain. It's been a dry spring and the ponds are shrinking too much for my liking. There's nothing like a good rainstorm to put the world right."

She'd need more than water to balance her world. "Don't get too comfortable." She shook her head. The problem with Milton being a volunteer was he didn't *have* to listen to her. He was a hard worker when he felt like it, but sometimes his breaks lasted half the day. "You know I don't keep whiskey. Plus, it's too early to start drinking spirits."

"Never too early for spirits in my book." His eyes sparkled as he watched her prepare her tea. "I heard that ex-boyfriend of yours, Peter O'Keefe, is coming to Fern Hollow for the wedding. Arriving tomorrow according to my sources."

Sarah fought back the snappy reply poised on the tip of her tongue. *Just breathe.* "You have sources?"

Milton nodded, and part of his silver hair flopped into his face. He smoothed it back. The man likely hadn't gotten a haircut this decade. "I got plenty of sources around town for all sorts of things…fishing reports, who's mad at who and what flavor pie they plan on serving the next day at the Columbia Diner. The hot topic at the diner is Peter O'Keefe's return and how you'll react."

Embarrassment caused heat to flush through her chest and up her face. When would people in this town learn to mind their own business? A small chance of that happening. Like a Yeti learning to love the beach. "I'm glad my personal life is giving the community something new to talk about." She loved living in Fern Hollow, with the exception of the small-town chatter, which flew from mouth to ear with supersonic speed. If something sensational happened in Fern Hollow, everyone in town knew about it within the day.

"Your personal life is always of interest to the community." Milton coughed, covering his mouth with his fist. At least he had some manners. "Don't let the talk bother you. People around here care. Want to see you happy again after Mike." He snapped his mouth closed. "Sorry. I know you don't like me bringing him up."

The sorrow she thought was under control reappeared in a rush. Threatened to rupture. Was it that obvious that she avoided talking about her feelings? In the months after Mike died, she worked nonstop. People found it hard to check in when she never stopped moving. "It's okay. I like to remember Mike but it hurts to think about losing him." Their love had been safe and comfortable. They'd had a good life. In the end, both men she'd married had left her. Pete by choice. Mike due to illness. At this point, she felt content as a single woman. Since becoming a widow, she'd refused every request for a date from interested men. After a year, Aaron, her most trusted farrier, had finally given up asking her out after each visit. Sarah had no interest in starting a new romance. Why go searching for more heartache?

"I miss Mike, too. He was a good man. Died way too young." Milton stared down at his stocking feet. "You've always done good for yourself, even in the middle of grief. He'd be proud of you."

Tears pooled in her eyes, and she blinked to clear them. Her horses had helped her survive grief—over and over. "Mike was a good husband and father." She couldn't let herself become lost in the dark hole of missing him. She'd known about Mike's health issues when they'd started dating. Still, she'd expected more years together. Her mind drifted back to Pete. That wasn't any better. *Think about work.*

Milton coughed again, then cleared his throat. "The town gossips will move on to someone else soon. I heard Missy Farmington is getting a divorce."

"Missy Farmington threatens to divorce her husband every other month." The kettle hissed with steam. Sarah went to retrieve a mug from the cabinet. She turned off the stove top, then poured hot water into the cup with a tea strainer resting on the bottom. The scent of peppermint promised to soothe her churning stomach. Thinking of Milton, she grabbed a glass, filled it with water, then set the glass down on the table in front of him with a clink. "I hear water is good for the body."

Milton eagerly downed the glass of water in one gulp. "*Ah.* Not as good as whiskey but it will do."

"How's the new rescue looking?" she asked, hoping to change the subject. The more she dwelt on Pete coming to town, the more overwhelming her anxiety grew. They'd have no happy reunion, just a pleasant greeting, and then she'd keep working. She had a business to run. Pete had groomsman duties. With any luck, she'd barely see him. Why did the prospect of a brief and insignificant reunion leave her glum? She did not want to see Pete again.

"The new mare is scared but she's a real

beauty. Definitely neglected judging by her looks and temperament." Milton pushed up to his feet. Break time must be over. Good. There was a lot to do. "I think she'll be fine after some time to decompress."

"Then we can evaluate her personality," Sarah said. "I'd love to have another dependable riding horse in the stable." Their newest rescue was a bay-colored American quarter horse who'd been put up for auction. The photos posted online showed a skinny horse with terror in her eyes. Sarah recognized a spark of something else in the pictures—pride and resistance. The mare didn't appear willing to easily accept her fate. So Sarah made arrangements to purchase the horse, taking it off the auction market. At the ranch, the mare could recover and find purpose again. Maybe make a friend or two.

Her stable was full, her bank account thin. Which meant she had to make smart decisions on which horses to rescue. She dreamed of possessing the funds to save every single horse in need. Too often, she saw herself in the horses that came in—unsure and frightened. If they could overcome their trauma, then so could she. Fundraising money remained sparse. The investment account she inherited from her grandparents grew smaller every year. The apple orchard and event hosting business helped supplement her finances but there was only so much she could take on without hiring more people. She didn't have a limitless number of hours in a day. Being a good mother to six-year-old Chloe was always her top priority.

With the cup of tea in hand, she followed Milton out the back door. Behind her, the screen door banged closed. The weather today was perfect, sunny with an easy breeze. Fingers crossed the good weather would hold for Jacob and Kay's wedding, which was less than a week away. She paused to take a test sip of tea. The water was still hot, so she blew across the surface.

A braying sound from the direction of the field caught her attention. Horace, an old donkey rescued four or so years ago, came dashing toward the fence. More braying followed—Horace's way of saying hello. He had knobby knees due to arthritis and was missing several teeth. Horace and Chloe had taken to one another immediately when the donkey came to live at the ranch. Mike had been the one to bring in Horace. A final gift to his daughter. If a little girl and a donkey could be best friends, then Chloe and Horace were that pair.

"Chloe will be home from her grandparents' house soon." Sarah wandered over to where Horace stood with his head extended over the fence. She rubbed his velvety nose while Horace flicked his tall ears. "I don't have any treats but I'll make sure Chloe brings carrots for you."

Horace shook his head in assumed exasperation before strolling away, returning to the pair of horses he'd been grazing beside in the field.

She turned to the sound of Milton grumbling by the horse trailer as he attempted to open the stuck latch. No wonder she felt as if some days she spent most of her time around grumpy gray-haired men. "Let me help," she said at the same time Milton unstuck the latch. Earlier, he'd backed the truck and trailer up to the gate of the quarantine paddock. The horse could unload without assistance and stretch her legs. Sarah entered the paddock and glanced around to make sure the space was ready to host a new guest.

Milton motioned to Sarah. "Block the opening. Don't want her to bolt." He swung open the doors, then rested a hand on his hip. The horse inside snorted and stomped her hoofs against the metal floor. "She'll settle as soon as she understands she's safe."

She moved to the entrance of the paddock. "I hope so." Sarah didn't feel like getting kicked today. Her entire mission revolved around bringing animals to a place they could be well cared for and loved. Saving horses in need had been the drive behind her grandparents starting Carmella Ranch. Her grandad originally inherited the property as an apple orchard. He'd eventually married her grandma. They were a young couple with dreams of growing apples and a family. Saving horses came later. The buildings and land, along with caring for the trees and animals, were left to Sarah, who'd spent as much time on the ranch as she could while growing up. Her parents had no interest in ranch life. She believed in her grandparents' mission after witnessing their selfless work, day in and day out. Their actions showed the true meaning of love—to care for creatures who had nothing to offer in return. Although that wasn't completely true. She'd found animals had a lot to give, just not things the world often valued.

"Hey, girl." She spoke in a soothing voice to the horse. "Welcome to your new home." She crept cautiously up to the side of the trailer, then stood on tiptoes to peer in by the mare's head. Ribs poked out from the horse's side. Regular healthy meals would fix that.

Milton brought over a stool to the other side and reached in to unhook the tether securing the horse to the trailer.

As soon as the tether was free, the horse took several steps backward, then unloaded herself out of the trailer. After a few shakes of her head, she raced off to explore.

"Welcome home," Sarah said again. Her eyes misted. Tears always came with the arrival of a new animal. With every horse rescue, she saved herself as well. The new mare would spend time in the quarantine paddock. They'd run various tests for issues such as strangles, a highly infectious disease that could transmit to the entire herd if an infected horse got close enough. A new horse wouldn't be introduced into the general population until both Sarah and her vet felt confident the horse was healthy.

"Sarah," a female voice shouted. "Sarah, there's a problem in the barn."

She spun to find her event coordinator speed-walking in her direction, fisted hands swinging at her sides. *This can't be good.* "What's the problem?" Sarah moved to the fence to meet Helen.

"There's a leak in the women's restroom and several inches of water on the floor." Helen huffed out a breath. "I called the plumber. He'll be here as soon as he's able. I could use some help with the shop vac and mop."

Sarah turned to ask Milton if he'd be alright handling the mare alone.

Before she could ask, he waved her away. "Go and help Helen. I'll watch her for a while, then make sure she's good on food and water. Vet will be here later to check her over."

"Thanks, Milton. Don't know what I'd do without you." Truly, he'd saved her too many times to count. He'd stepped in to help at the ranch when her grandfather grew ill, and thankfully he'd never left. A friend of her grandparents, Milton was now a trusted partner to Sarah.

Once out of the horse paddock, Sarah took a gulp of tea before following Helen to the barn. By the pond, one of her livestock guardian dogs, a Great Pyrenees named Beaker, bathed in the sun while indulging in one of his favorite pastimes—monitoring the ducks. Even the ranch's duck population needed his protection.

The barn had recently been renovated with vibrant red exterior paint, sanded hardwood floors and a wide-open area for dinner and dancing, along with a new kitchen and added restrooms. The Big Red Barn was now the town's best venue for weddings and other events. At least in her mind. Along with Jacob and Kay's wedding later this week, they had a baby shower booked for tomorrow evening. Hopefully they'd get the bathroom plumbing fixed in time.

The reminder of the upcoming wedding and Pete's arrival made her stomach flip. Maybe he wouldn't make it after all. But she'd prepare for the likelihood that her ex-husband would be standing inside this barn very soon. She'd be forced to do something she'd avoided so far—face him and the tragic history of their short-lived marriage.

PETE O'KEEFE STOOD at the bank of a crystal blue lake, taking in the fresh country air. Mountains rose in the distance; their peaks aspiring to touch the heavens. His last month had been filled with the hustle of New York City while gaining experience with their elite SWAT team. His new job would bring him to Phoenix, and the SWAT team he'd join there promised a challenge. A step in his post-Army career. His father had wanted Pete to stay enlisted longer but after a lengthy discussion, he'd conceded the SWAT position provided new opportunities to use Pete's combat skills and even develop new ones. The arid Southwest wasn't a stark difference from the deserts he'd once served in. At least this time he'd be based on US soil.

He selected one of the smooth rocks covering the beach and tossed it over the water. It struck the surface and skipped twice, creating ripples that pulsed outward—similar to his exit from Fern Hollow twelve years ago. He hadn't known Sarah was pregnant then. They'd only been married for a few days before he delivered her back to her furious parents. With the clock ticking, he left for basic training. While saying goodbye to his new bride, he'd been filled with optimism. Their future stretched out before him, bright with potential after Sarah had told him she was pregnant over the phone from the other side of the country. Then she miscarried and everything crashed—ripples in the water that left his heart scarred.

Pete should have advised Sarah his schedule had changed and he was coming to the wedding. Instead, he chickened out and left the task to Jacob. Not a great start to his arrival. *Stop hiding and face your mistakes.* He wished to prove he'd grown over the years and was now a different person from when he'd visited in his youth. His parents brought Pete and his brother to the Cascades region of Washington state every summer for family time. They rented a cabin in the area around Fern Hollow, neighboring Jacob's ranch and the Carmella property. His mom stayed for the summer with the boys while his dad traveled back and forth from Southern California. Once Pete reached thirteen, Giorgio Carmella hired him as a stable hand and subsequently instructed him in horsemanship. When he heard about Giorgio's passing from Jacob eight years ago, he'd felt the loss as if he was still a teenager training a horse beside the older man.

Tossing another rock into the lake, he steeled himself for seeing Sarah again. His first love. His only love. No one he'd dated since compared. Sarah wanted stability and safety. Marriage to Pete provided neither. The opposite, actually. Since Sarah had been underage when they'd married, an annulment cleared the slate, as if their marriage never happened. But their love had been real.

A strap tightened around his heart. His eyes burned with tears he fought not to shed. Pete had less than a week in Fern Hollow. He'd survived tougher missions. He had five days to make things right between him and Sarah Carmella.

"Dinner's done." Jacob stood on the porch of his log cabin, hands cupped to his mouth to project his voice. "Do you need a few more minutes?"

His old friend understood. Pete put on a relaxed expression, the opposite of the storm brewing inside him. "Just admiring the view. I haven't seen water this clear in a long time." His mind directed him to go inside for dinner. His heart asked for more time to bask in beauty and peace.

Jacob descended the porch steps and joined Pete at the water's edge. "I want to thank you again for being my groomsman. It means a lot to have you here."

"Of course." Pete slapped Jacob on the back. "Sorry I declined at first. I'm glad they gave me another week. Once the new job starts, my life won't be my own for a while."

"Kicking in doors and busting bad guys." Jacob laughed. "You were always one to run toward danger."

Except when it came to facing his ex-wife, apparently. From what Jacob had mentioned, Sarah was happy in Fern Hollow. She'd married again and had a daughter. Though her husband had passed away. Sarah's life in Fern Hollow hadn't been perfect but it had likely been better than following him around the world at the Army's discretion. He didn't blame Sarah for not wanting that life in the end. His reckless personality had gotten him into more than one near-death experience. But he loved the risk. And his continual rise in rank had pleased his father. The more dangerous the assignment, the greater Pete's desire to be a part of the team.

Sarah hadn't been able to come to his graduation from basic training and he recalled his disappointment with stinging clarity. Then he received orders to deploy to eastern Europe. He hadn't been able to get back to her. After the shock of receiving the annulment request from

Sarah, he had signed off without a fight. If that was what she wanted, then how could he convince her otherwise when he was stationed on the other side of the world? Letting go of her so easily was the biggest regret of his life.

"I should probably go see Sarah before the festivities begin." His skin prickled. Would she take one look at him and kick him off the ranch? Was an amiable reunion possible? "I don't want things to be strained between us."

Jacob cleared his throat. "You both are very capable of putting the past behind you. Go down to her place tonight. She'll be working with Chloe in the stables. Just make sure she doesn't have a pitchfork in hand when you approach."

Pete swallowed hard. Tonight? Nothing like jumping in without a chance to consider too deeply all the ways things between them could go bad. Just rip off the Band-Aid. Or should he continue to work out the right words to say and go over tomorrow? "Let's eat first." The anxiety swirling in his stomach extinguished his appetite, even after inhaling a whiff of the smoked brisket Jacob had been working on all afternoon.

After dinner, eating less than his normal serving despite the meal's delicious taste, Pete helped clean up the kitchen. His stomach was full of food and dread. He was stalling. Stalling to make a decision. Stalling to do what he knew was right: go take a walk along the fence line to the Carmella Ranch and face Sarah.

Jacob found Pete seated on the porch bench, tying his shoelaces. "You going over?" He didn't need to indicate where.

"That's the mission." He secured the shoelace, then stood. "I've never been this nervous, not even heading into a firefight. What's the matter with me?"

"You loved her." Jacob didn't need to say more.

Pete still loved Sarah. Always would. But they were too different to ever fit comfortably. He should have known that when he'd asked her to marry him. Set to leave for basic training, with the pressures his father had placed on his shoulders, Pete had wanted to keep Sarah in his life. He'd assumed if they were married, their love would never falter. Yet reality knocked him down.

Before leaving for an uncertain reception, Pete stole another moment to take in the view. He pictured options in his mind for some videos he'd shoot here. His social media accounts, which he'd placed under a pseudonym, had started as a hobby. He posted videos about his explorations and non-military-focused experiences. Over time, they gained traction and now he had hundreds of thousands of followers.

The valley Fern Hollow resided in was tucked into the Cascades. Pastures stretched unhindered across the landscape until they reached the root of the foothills and mountains. With the Columbia River nearby, the area was a hot fishing destination. His mouth watered at the memory of the salmon he'd enjoyed in Fern Hollow restaurants over the years. Due to its location, the small town and surrounding farmland remained remote—unspoiled by the outside world. *I understand why Sarah didn't want to leave.*

He strolled down the driveway and onto the well-worn path that led to Sarah's house. Might as well get it over with. Then he'd turn his complete focus to Jacob and Kay's wedding—the reason he'd come. The sun had another few hours before it completed its descent. Summer days here were long and warm. A light breeze helped relieve some of the heat building in his body from walking and stress.

When he arrived at rows and rows of apple trees, his pulse increased. He was close. The spring blossoms were long gone, and golf ball–sized green apples adorned the branches. The air carried a sweet scent. By autumn, large red apples would be too numerous to count. Pete had never been around for apple harvest but surely it was amazing.

Too soon, a large red barn came into view, no longer the deteriorating structure he recalled. His heart pounded and his ears rang. No amount of turning over thoughts in his head had prepared him.

A dog barked when he reached the pond. The group of ducks that had been resting on the grass scattered into the water with a chorus of annoyed quacks.

"Hey," he greeted the dog. "I've come to see your owner." *The woman who was once my wife.*

The dog continued barking until a whistle sounded from the direction of the horse stable.

The sight of Sarah when she appeared out from the shadow of the stable almost knocked him to his knees. Emotions deeply buried rushed up like a geyser in Yellowstone National Park. He pressed a hand over his heart, attempting to keep it from exploding out of his chest. She'd been beautiful at seventeen. He'd stared at their wedding picture enough times to have that version of her burned into his brain. But the woman marching toward him right now took his breath away. Her red hair was darker, and her frame had been gifted more curves. She wore faded blue jeans, boots and a pink V-neck T-shirt with a streak of dirt running down the middle. Stunning. He was so transfixed that he almost missed the scowl pulling down the corners of her mouth and the spark in her gray eyes.

"I wasn't expecting you to come around until the rehearsal." She stood before him, hands on hips. No pitchfork. Good.

His throat worked down a swallow. He hadn't imagined speaking would be so hard. "I wanted a chance to say hello before the rush of the wedding. It's nice to see you again, Sarah." He longed to wrap her in a hug and recalled the feel of her in his arms. Instead, he shoved his hands into the front pockets of his jeans.

Her eyes traveled down his frame, then returned to his face. "There's not much to say. Ancient history."

Her cool tone stung. For Pete, his past with Sarah felt like yesterday. If he could go back in time and do things differently, he would. He'd do a better job convincing her that his love was worth leaving Fern Hollow. "I hope we can catch up. I'll be around until the day after the wedding."

"Let me guess—then you'll leaving for some high-octane job that involves explosives and bulletproof vests." She glanced over her shoulder at the noise coming from the stable. "I still have chores to see to and then Chloe needs a bath before bed. I appreciate you stopping by but—" Her voice faded.

Pete understood what she couldn't say. He was her past. Maybe the edges weren't as raw for her as they were for him. "Understood. I'm staying with Jacob if you change your mind." At least he'd tried. Though his feeble attempt didn't satisfy his desire to reconnect and heal. Could he even think of Sarah as his former wife if in the eyes of the law they'd never been married? They'd each committed to a faithful love. But did the words of their vows hold any meaning if they could be erased by the signature of a judge?

"Mom," a little girl called out. "Horace is asking for more oats." A miniature version of Sarah darted from the stable and skidded to a halt by her side. Her cherub face was framed in a halo of wild red curls. "He said you didn't give him any treats today." She stomped her little foot.

Gazing down at the ginger-haired girl, Sarah sighed. "Honey, donkeys can't talk."

"But Horace talks to me and he said he's starving." The girl glanced at Pete before turning her pleading eyes back to her mom.

Must be Chloe. Pete's chest squeezed so hard he struggled to breathe. Fatherhood might be a dream not destined for him.

"Give him an extra cup of oats, then tell him

that I don't appreciate being swindled." Sarah ruffled the girl's hair.

"What does swindled mean?" Chloe asked with pure curiosity. "Who's that?" She pointed at Pete.

"Swindle means to trick." Sarah bent at the knees to bring herself closer to eye level with Chloe. "This is Mr. O'Keefe. He's an...acquaintance. That means we knew each other when we were younger."

"Like when you knew Daddy?" Chloe stared up at him. "Did you know my daddy?"

"I did not." Pete struggled with the right answer. He could talk with hardened criminals but apparently conversation with a little girl stumped him. "I was friends with your mom before she met your daddy."

"Oh." Chloe bit her lip. "Did you come for Uncle Jacob's wedding? It's at our barn. See. Right over there. There will be a band and dancing. Do you like dancing? I got a new dress with butterflies on it."

Pete chuckled. Conversation with this little girl was definitely entertaining. "I *am* here for the wedding. And I love to dance. Will you save a dance for me?"

"Sure. If it's okay with Mom." Chloe bounced on her tiptoes and wrapped her little fingers around the straps of her overalls. "Horace needs his oats. Bye." She darted back into the stable.

"Sorry about that." Sarah shook her head. "Sometimes, I think they really do talk to each other."

"She has your love of animals." Pete struggled to control his emotions, which threatened to wash him away like a tall wave racing toward the shore. Time to leave before he embarrassed himself. "I'll let you get back to your evening. Sorry if I disturbed you." He turned to leave, not wanting Sarah to witness the strain on his features.

"Wait." She reached out to touch his arm, then immediately pulled back. "I appreciate you coming over. I shouldn't be rude. I have no reason to act like that."

The spot where her hand rested tingled. "It's alright." He felt fortunate to lay eyes on her again; he didn't regret their love. "I caught you off guard. I just didn't want our past to overshadow Jacob and Kay's happy day."

She folded her arms across her body. "Of course. I don't want that either. Plus, you're only in town for a few days. Surely we can be gracious to one another for a short time."

He wanted more than modest politeness. But he wouldn't push. He'd accept whatever Sarah offered. She might have moved on, but they'd been madly in love when they'd eloped. And that type of love didn't just disappear like it never happened. Of that he was sure.

CHAPTER TWO

HER DRIVE INTO town felt longer than normal. Chloe sang in the back seat. Her cute voice normally lifted Sarah's mood. Today, all she wanted was quiet. Which she would not get for the foreseeable future. Not with a full schedule of events at the barn, animals in need of care, apple trees requiring spraying and a little girl who hadn't stopped talking about the nice man who'd visited last night. Chloe had made Sarah pinky-promise to introduce Pete to Horace the next time he came over. Great. Although Horace was known for biting people he didn't like. He could do damage with his few remaining teeth. She didn't want to disappoint her daughter with the news that Pete wouldn't be showing up at the ranch for another social call. Why had he come by last night anyway? Didn't he want to avoid conflict as much as she did?

Sarah braked at a four-way stop and then turned left. The town's water tower loomed overhead as she drove by. Soon, her parents' two-story house came into view. The home she'd grown up in wasn't as large as the farmhouse Sarah had inherited. And her parents' three acres seemed small in comparison to the ranch. Her father had never wanted to follow in his parents' footsteps and run the ranch, and he married a woman who considered animal poop her kryptonite.

As soon as Sarah parked and turned off the car, Chloe's voice rose to a crescendo with the concluding notes of her song. Sarah exited the car, then released Chloe from her booster seat. Her daughter ran excitedly to the front door and went right in. Her parents had transformed when they became grandparents—from strict and unyielding to soft and indulgent. Chloe got the best version of her mom and dad, and for that Sarah was grateful. They watched Chloe during the day now that school was out for the summer, freeing up Sarah to focus on work. A good deal all around.

When Sarah entered the foyer, the sound of happy voices drifted from the kitchen. Her mom had mentioned baking cookies was on the agenda for today. She hoped they'd bring over a few for her when they dropped off Chloe later this afternoon.

"Sarah," her dad called out from his office. "Got a sec?"

Her stomach dropped. Tim Carmella owned Fern Hollow's only accounting firm and he served as the CFO of the Carmella Rescue Foundation, set up by his parents to sustain the rescue. When an accountant asked to talk, there was a good chance it wasn't about the weather.

"What's up?" She stepped into the walnut-paneled room and took a deep breath. A row of tall windows took up most of one wall, taking advantage of the southern exposure. Book-lined shelves were recessed into the wall behind his desk. Sarah found none of the titles enticing, unless she was looking for something to fight insomnia.

Tim Carmella reclined in his leather office chair, glasses resting on the tip of his nose. He lifted his chin to meet her gaze over the lenses. "I wanted to run over the financials quick. I have some concerns."

"When don't you have concerns?" She plopped down on the upholstered chair at the other side of the desk, steeling herself for uncomfortable news.

"As the rescue's numbers guy, my job is to make sure the foundation stays financially sound." He typed on the keyboard of his laptop. "The stock market has not been kind to our accounts. To be frank, our funds took a big hit."

Rubbing her forehead, Sarah mulled over how big of a hit. Did she even want to know? The lives of her rescue animals depended on her ability to pay the bills. "Whatever the numbers, I'll deal with it."

"The debt from the barn renovation and new hires isn't helping. Too much is going out."

"And not enough coming in." Her vision of bringing in extra income via event rentals would take time to come to fruition. The debt she'd taken on was significant and kept her up at night. "We have the barn space booked through the summer and into the fall. And then the apple harvest should bring in some money. The square dance fundraiser is next month."

"Even all that isn't enough." Her dad tapped the tip of a metal pen on his desk. "You should consider expanding the boarding program. Add more training options. People will pay good money for your skills. You have too many rescues that are all cost and no income."

She pushed to her feet, frustration surging. "The rescues are the reason for everything I do."

"I know." He held up his hands. "All I'm recommending is to put a freeze on acquiring more rescues until the balance sheet is more…balanced. You can rehab horses with owners willing to pay for your services."

Sarah reflected on the mare they'd welcomed yesterday. The horse had started relaxing. From her experience, she anticipated that by the end of the week, the horse would show her true personality. How could she put a price on a horse's well-being? All the animals on the ranch counted on her. An obligation she accepted with honor. "Email me the account information and I'll look it over. But I won't turn away an emergency situation."

"If you're not wise in your decisions, you won't have a ranch to bring them to." Tim stood and wrapped her in a gentle hug.

Her dad was hugging her. That bad, huh? He hugged Chloe all the time but rarely his own daughter. "We'll think of something." Investments rose and fell in value. Her grandparents had struggled to pay the bills back in their day. Sarah vowed not to allow the ranch to fail on her watch.

Carmella Ranch was her family's past and future. She'd kept her maiden name in honor of her grandparents. There had to be a way to ensure the ranch's survival. Mike's life insurance money sat in an account, untouched and gathering interest. But Sarah was safeguarding that money for Chloe's future—she refused to use it for herself or the ranch.

She poked her head into the kitchen to say goodbye to Chloe and her mom before heading out. As she walked to her car with a head full of new worries, a voice called out Sarah's name. Mrs. Bryan had lived across the street since Sarah came home from the hospital as a newborn. Dubbed the unofficial queen of Fern Hollow, Mrs. Bryan knew everyone and everything that happened within the valley.

"Hi, Mrs. Bryan." Sarah met her at the end of the driveway.

"I baked chocolate-glazed doughnuts and thought you'd like some. Fresh out of the fryer." The older woman passed a container into Sarah's hands.

Despite the sealed lid, the smell coming out of the container was heavenly. Her stomach grumbled with a reminder that she hadn't bothered with breakfast. "That's very kind of you. Is it okay if I share with the ranch workers?"

Mrs. Bryan nodded. "Yes dear, except for Milton. Kenny MacAfee told me that Milton complained at the church picnic that my cherry pie was too tart. Ever since, I refuse to let him indulge in my sweet treats." She waved her hand with a sense of finality.

Sarah smiled at the indignant expression on

Mrs. Bryan's face. The rumor around town was Peggy Bryan and Milton had been sweethearts a very long time ago. Whatever had broken up their relationship remained a wedge between them. Sarah was confident a slight to Mrs. Bryan's cherry pie was only the latest dispute. "I'll make sure Milton doesn't get one." She'd stop by the diner and pick up something else for her faithful volunteer.

"I heard Peter O'Keefe is back in town." Mrs. Bryan tsk-tsked, patting her arm. "He was a wild one…and handsome. Broke your heart, he did. I wish you strength while dealing with him."

As Milton had warned, the word was out. "I think we broke each other's hearts, but they've healed." Not completely true in her case, given how unbalanced she'd felt since word of Pete's arrival had reached her ears. "Thanks for the good wishes and the doughnuts. I'll see you around."

"You'll be seeing me at the wedding on Saturday. Got my good dress cleaned and pressed for the occasion." Mrs. Bryan bid her farewell, then strolled back to her house.

Jacob's wedding appeared to be the event of the summer, perhaps eclipsing the upcoming square dance fundraiser. She wouldn't want anything less for her friend.

A stop at the Columbia Diner proved that if the entire town didn't already know Pete had returned, they soon would. The diner's owner, Lauren, didn't hold back her curiosity. The two women had been friends since high school, and they kept few secrets from one another. Except Lauren didn't need to know the depth of feelings Pete's return had stirred in Sarah. She didn't even want to admit the truth to herself.

"Can I get an apple fritter and a cup of coffee?" Sarah asked Lauren as she leaned against the counter. "Both to go." The Columbia Diner, named after the great river that flowed not far away, was the place to go for a hearty breakfast and the best coffee in the state of Washington. And that was saying a lot, given Seattle's prominence in the coffee market. When Lauren purchased the place, she overhauled the interior and menu. Long gone were the mounted rainbow trout covering the walls. All those eyes staring down while she ate used to give Sarah the creeps.

"You bet." Lauren grabbed a paper cup from off the top of the stack, then pumped steaming coffee from the carafe. "Promise me that you and Pete will make time to sit down and have a real heart-to-heart about what happened between you."

A meaningful conversation with Pete was the

last thing she wanted. She'd rather go back and continue reviewing the rescue's finances with her dad. At least that was productive. Sort of. "Talking isn't going to change the past. Pete has lived a full life since our breakup. I'm sure he doesn't even think about me." Not like Sarah, who struggled to banish him from her mind. During her romance with Mike, she'd been able to pack away memories of Pete. She'd been happy with Mike and Chloe. Then Mike's heart no longer had the strength to sustain him. No one could promise forever.

"Pete didn't forget about you." Lauren snapped the lid on the coffee cup. "Anyway, here's the most important question…how does he look?"

Sarah snorted out a laugh as a slow smile crept over Lauren's face, brushing the cobwebs of grief from Sarah's thoughts. "Good. He looks really good." Incredibly so. Too handsome. His short beard and slightly overgrown dark hair made him appear more sophisticated than she remembered. And older. While away circling the globe, he'd grown into a man. Long gone was the lanky boy she'd fallen in love with. "I wouldn't be surprised if he has a wife or girlfriend." An idea that dampened her mood.

"Pete looked like a movie star back in the

day. I can't wait to get a glimpse of the grown-up version." Lauren's eyebrows wiggled.

Shaking her head, Sarah grabbed the coffee cup and the bag holding the apple fritter. "You're not a good influence." The man was a distraction Sarah did not need.

"Lauren, dear, are my pancakes almost done? I have a meeting at nine." A dark-haired woman questioned from her seat at a table by the window.

"I'll check." Lauren glanced over her shoulder at the opening to the kitchen, which was empty. She turned to Sarah. "I should see to Mrs. Eastman's breakfast order. Promise me that I'll be the first to know if anything happens between you and Pete."

"Nothing is going to happen. He's here for the wedding. That's it." Pete wouldn't stick around. Sarah left Lauren to wait on her customers and exited the diner, shaking her head. Pete's arrival had disrupted every aspect of her life. Even a stop at the diner left her dodging questions. His stay in Fern Hollow couldn't come to an end soon enough.

During her drive back to the ranch, she mulled over her to-do list. No more brain function dedicated to men and the problems that came along with them. By the time she parked next to her house, the list was a mile long. Better get moving. But the sight of Pete standing outside the stable left her frozen in place. What was he doing here? Again. And why did he look so good? Wearing snug blue jeans, a black T-shirt that highlighted his biceps and a black Stetson, Pete appeared ready for a Western-wear photo shoot. Place him on the back of a horse and his image would grab anyone's attention. Instead of going into the army, he'd have made one heck of a cowboy. Sarah had always thought he was too striking for the good of any girl's heart. Studying him right now, she maintained that opinion. The first time she'd seen him when his family returned to Fern Hallow the summer after her freshman year, her head filled with daydreams of Pete O'Keefe. For weeks, they'd worked closely together to nurse one of her favorite mares, who'd hurt her front leg trying to jump a fence. Everything changed that summer. Pete had been her first real crush. Her first kiss. Her first love.

After a minute of stunned inaction, she got out of the car and debated. Run inside and hide? Confront him and demand he leave? The decision was made for her when Milton walked out of the stable, hands waving in Sarah's direction.

She gritted her teeth, considering if she could race into the house before Milton caught up.

"Sarah," Milton shouted. "Look who's come over to see you!"

What if I don't want to? Her feet refused to move.

Pete's feet didn't have the same problem. He strode alongside Milton, who hobbled to keep up while clutching his lower back. That wasn't good.

"Jacob asked me to bring over a sign for the wedding. I left it in the barn." Pete ran his fingers through his dark hair. "I saw Milton struggling with a horse so I offered to help."

Her gaze moved to Milton. "Did he fill out the volunteer liability form?" The last thing she needed was a lawsuit because one of the horses kicked Pete in the head.

"Nah," Milton huffed. "You know I don't do paperwork. Plus, there's no time. That new mare didn't want me putting a halter on her this morning. She's a spirited one. I'll give her that. She liked Pete though. Let him walk right up and give her a kiss on the muzzle."

Sarah whipped her head to Pete. "Really?" Was she jealous of a horse? "Thanks for helping Milton and bringing over the sign. I'll let you get back to Jacob's place. I'm sure he has more for you to do." Sarah spun on her heel, ready to make a clean getaway.

"I'm free for the rest of the day," Pete said before she could get far. "Milton was saying you needed extra hands. You know I love horses. I haven't had a chance to work with them for years. I'll sign any forms you need." Was his wide smile an attempt to charm Sarah or Milton? She couldn't be sure.

"Milton?" She pinned him with a narrowed gaze and balled her hands into fists. "Why do we need extra help?"

While rubbing his lower back, Milton shook his head. "Dylan called in sick. I think he stayed out too late last night. Teenagers. And my back's been acting up. All the horse stalls need mucking. I was wondering how I'd get everything done when Peter showed up. Like all my prayers had been answered."

While Sarah's were being ignored. The conversation with her father still rang inside her head. If she didn't make smart decisions, she risked the ranch's future. Turning away free help was not smart. If Pete stayed in the stable, she'd steer clear. "Fine. But you will need to sign the waiver. We require it of our volunteers, even if it's just for the day." She waved for Pete to follow her to the house. First, she stopped at her car to retrieve the doughnuts and apple fritter. Sarah considered not telling Milton about the fritter but couldn't fault him for accepting assistance. Should she hide Mrs. Bryant's doughnuts from him to try to not hurt his feelings? She slid the container behind her back.

"What do you got there?" Suddenly, Milton's pace improved as he walked toward Sarah. "Are those Peggy's chocolate doughnuts? I can smell them from here."

Too slow. "Mrs. Bryan gave me strict instructions not to share them with you. Something about you complaining that her cherry pie was too tart at the church picnic." She secured the box under her arm. "I picked up something for you at the diner."

With a snort, Milton accepted the small bag and peeked inside. "That's kind of you. Can't believe Peggy's still holding that grudge. Her cherries *were* too tart. The woman won't listen to reason." After a bite into the fritter, he made his way back to the stable.

"He's a character." Pete chuckled. "Am I allowed to have a doughnut? No complaints about cherries by me. They smell amazing."

"Yes, since a doughnut is my only method of payment." She fought the smile creeping onto her mouth. *You can't fall for him again.* How easy slipping into loving him would be. "We rely a lot on volunteers."

"Doughnuts are the only payment I'll accept." He held open the screen door, then trailed after her inside and through the mudroom. Glancing around the kitchen, he turned in a circle. "I'm having a flashback. Everything looks the same."

Images appeared in her mind of Pete seated at the kitchen table, their heads together, sharing an apple pie and dreaming of their future. They'd been so young, with no idea of the realities of life. Sarah gazed at the man, now grown, and felt an overwhelming sense of remorse. If only she'd been wiser at the age of seventeen. She would have understood their young love didn't have the strength to bridge the canyon of differences between them. Tightness squeezed her chest with a rush of memories. Ones she'd worked hard to lock away. The door to her past had cracked open but she quickly slammed it shut.

"No time or money for kitchen remodels." She thumbed through a file folder, searching for the liability form. It had been a while since she had a new volunteer. After pulling out several of the wrong sheets, she found the one she was looking for. "Here. Take a seat, read it over, then sign if you agree."

Pete took the paper and pen Sarah handed him. A glance toward the container on the counter hinted at what was on his mind. "Can I try one of those doughnuts while I read?"

"Sure." She gestured for him to sit. The sooner he left the house, the sooner she could breathe again. Sarah plated a doughnut, then placed it on the table. After inhaling the scent of chocolate and pastry, she took one for herself. Her taste buds sang with the first bite. Milton was missing out. Never criticize Mrs. Bryan's baking. Not ever.

"Good, huh." Pete wiped a spot of chocolate frosting off the corner of his mouth.

"Mrs. Bryan loves to bake but has no family around to bake for. She lives across the street from my parents." She caught herself staring at Pete and forced herself to look away. "It's one benefit of living in a small town." Something Pete had declared he'd never do. Why hadn't she recognized his statement as a giant red flag? Young love had blinded her. She'd been ready to follow him anywhere. Instead, fate kept her feet planted in Fern Hollow. Although she mourned the losses loving Pete had brought her, Sarah was grateful she hadn't chased after Pete. She loved her life on the ranch. She had a purpose. Which she reminded herself of over and over while fighting a growing attraction to her ex-husband.

SIGNING HIS NAME on the waiver form brought back the day he signed the annulment agreement. A deep sense of failure returned. He could have done more to prove his love. Instead he let her go after only a handful of communications and they moved in separate directions. Pete had pursued his goals in the army. Sarah had stayed and worked on her grandparents' ranch. His vision of the future had always included adrenaline and adventure. And for a brief moment in time, it had included Sarah.

"Here you go." He stood, overwhelmed with the urge to run brought on by too many uncomfortable emotions. Ones he hadn't felt in a very long time. The harvest gold refrigerator against the far wall taunted him with the reminder of the many times he'd opened its door looking for a pitcher of lemonade or sandwich fixings. His current connection to Sarah, though weak, was still there. "I see you still like crossword puzzles." He pointed to the book on the desk that sat snug in one of the corners of the kitchen, flipped open to a page with a half-completed crossword. Way back when, they'd had competitions to see who could finish the same crossword first. Ever since, he thought of Sarah each time he did a crossword.

"I like to do them when I have some down time. It's one of the few things that I find relaxing. I'm waiting for the day when I can play Scrabble with Chloe." Another competitive activity Pete and Sarah had enjoyed together. She glanced over to the puzzle in progress with a hint of sorrow in her eyes. "Let me walk out with you. I'll find Milton." She tossed the liability form on a desk by an ancient desktop computer. "I'm surprised Jacob doesn't have you playing golf."

Pete stepped outside into the sunlight and fresh air. He needed to clear his mind. His relationship with Sarah was history. There was no going back. He'd enjoy a few days with her and then return to his normal life. "I'm not the golfing type. The pace is too slow." Plus, he could only stand being around a lovestruck Jacob in small doses. Spending time on the Carmella Ranch provided a welcome break, with the added bonus of seeing Sarah. He used to hang around the ranch with Sarah for days on end in the summer during his youth. After chores like mucking the stalls, they'd take off on hours'-long horseback rides. Then lose track of time and not come home until dusk. She'd made him feel welcome at the ranch and invited him into her world. Her laughter always produced smiles. She made people happy. She'd made him happy. Was it too much to ask to be a recipient of her smiles again? Perhaps nostalgia was getting the best of him.

She shook her head. "Will you ever slow down?"

Her question made him hesitate. After turning thirty, Pete's body didn't recover the way it used to. He'd wake up with cracking joints and tight muscles. Someday, he'd take a desk job or something less physically demanding. But that day wouldn't come until after he caught up to his older brother. Chris, a Navy fighter pilot serving in the Middle East, was a true hero. Could Pete ever live up to the standard Chris had set?

"I start a new job next week. SWAT team member with the Phoenix Police. I'd like to lead my own team someday. Slowing down isn't in my immediate future." The call of a new challenge always excited him. Since joining the military, he hadn't stayed in one place for long. Seeing Sarah on the ranch had him questioning if he'd be happy settling down someday. Or would his feet always itch to move?

"Mucking stalls is slow and monotonous, remember. You may wish you were golfing." Sarah's pace quickened, as if she wanted to get away. "Look for Milton in the stable or over by the south pasture. He'll give you directions on what needs doing."

Her change in mood hung over him like dark clouds. "I'm sorry if my being here makes you uncomfortable."

"No." She glanced away in the direction of a

pair of black horses grazing. "Okay, it is kind of weird to be honest."

"It is kind of weird, isn't it?" He studied her while her attention was elsewhere. So beautiful. And proud. His respect grew after witnessing everything she'd accomplished with the property she inherited. His gaze drifted down to her stomach, and his chest tightened. What if he'd insisted she join him after basic training graduation? *Don't play the game of* what if. *You always lose.*

"Where's your mini-me today?" He hadn't seen her little girl around. When did school go on summer break these days? He recalled counting down the days until his school year ended and the family packed up and headed north.

"School just wrapped up for the year. She stays with my mom and dad during the daytime hours over the summer. That way I can work and then focus on Chloe in the evenings." She released a breath. "Or at least I try to focus completely on her. Some days I don't feel like I do that well enough."

The last time Pete had seen Sarah's folks, they'd been fuming mad about their elopement. He was sure they'd influenced Sarah to seek the annulment, not approving of her exploits—including altering her birth certificate to show she was eighteen in order to marry Pete.

"Chloe looked very happy helping you yesterday," he said. "She's adorable. You must be proud." His heart ached, imagining the family he'd dreamed of raising with Sarah. The children they might have had. Trips to the beach or days spent at an amusement park. All those dreams had started to collapse once he'd learned about Sarah's miscarriage from her grandma. Sarah had been too distraught and depressed to tell him herself. The pain he'd felt during that time approached like a dark fog. He'd mourned for the loss of his child. He'd mourned for the loss of his wife. He'd mourned for being thousands of miles away with no power to get to Sarah.

"Chloe is the best." A warm smile lit Sarah's face. "She wants to introduce you to Horace." She pointed to the donkey currently kicking up his heels in the pasture. "Maybe if you're still around after she gets home."

"Absolutely." The idea lightened his spirits. "I'm looking forward to getting to know both of them."

After a nod, Sarah left for her next task.

Pete headed off to find Milton and find out where to begin. Turning to catch one more glance of Sarah before she disappeared into the barn, he sighed like the lovestruck teenager he used to be. She'd changed—was less carefree.

She carried the weight of the rescue and orchard on her shoulders. What other burdens did she carry? Raising a daughter without a partner must be a struggle. Could he heal their damaged relationship? Perhaps. Mucking out horse stalls looked like as good a place as any to start.

CHAPTER THREE

PETE LEANED BACK against the split rail fence. The sun warmed the skin on his arms and face. The muscles in his arms and thighs ached. A good feeling. His body needed the physical exertion. Since leaving the Army six months ago, he kept in shape by going to the gym at the different places he'd traveled to. He'd taken the small window of freedom to visit places he never had a chance to see while in the service. Lifting weights was no replacement for moving straw and manure with a shovel and pitchfork or carrying bales of hay and buckets of oats. The work was stress-free and not mentally taxing. Carmella Ranch offered an easy freedom.

"Almost time for a lunch break." Milton strolled toward him from the other side of the fence. "My favorite time of the day."

Pete chuckled. "You sound like some of the guys I served with." A black horse nibbled on grass about ten feet away. *Is that Black Beauty?*

He remembered a black mare from before he'd left Fern Hollow, but he wasn't sure if it was the same one. He'd ask Sarah later, if he saw her again today. He took out his cell phone and noticed a string of texts from his father. Nothing that couldn't wait. He dismissed the notifications and then made a thirty-second video of the horse and surrounding scenery.

"I have a lunch pail in the barn's kitchenette but Sarah said she'll bring you out something since you didn't expect to stay." Rubbing his nose with a checkered cloth square, Milton stepped closer. He rested his forearms on the top rail. His arms were tan and well-muscled for a man his age. Though Pete wouldn't dare guess what that age was.

Pete glanced over his shoulder at the house, willing Sarah to appear out the back door. After several seconds with no appearance, he turned back to the field. He shouldn't want to see her. Yet, disappointment settled inside him. She very well could have someone else bring him lunch. "I forgot how peaceful it is here. When I was in Fern Hollow before, I was young and didn't appreciate the beauty." He inhaled a deep breath that carried the scent of grass, then exhaled the anxiety that brewed every time he thought about Sarah and their past.

"A body needs peace and quiet every once

in a while. Even an adventurer like you." Milton stared off into the distance and sighed. "I used to be more adventurous, believe it or not. I wasn't in the military or anything that impressive. But I did love to travel. I left home in South Carolina at the age of sixteen. I got bored in the small town where I was born and raised, and headed west. After a few years of moving around, I arrived in Fern Hollow. I met Giorgio Carmella shortly after. Did he ever tell you the story of how this place came to be?"

Pete shook his head. "Not in detail. He told me on more than one occasion that he fell in love with his wife underneath an apple tree." And Pete had gone and done the same. His first kiss with Sarah had been under one of the orchard's apple trees. He hadn't planned on kissing her. One minute they were sitting in the shade, talking, and the next his lips were pressed on hers. She had tasted so sweet, like the lemonade they'd been drinking. After the kiss, he'd floated on air the rest of the day.

"Well, we've got some time now." Milton checked the hour on his wristwatch. "The boss can't holler too much since we got most of the chores already done. Wish I could keep you around. You do more than three of those high school helpers Sarah likes to hire."

The black horse lifted its head and looked

their way before shaking its mane and running deeper into the pasture. Pete was struck by the majesty of the animal. And to think Sarah enjoyed these sights and sounds every day.

Milton cleared his throat. "Giorgio had immigrated from Italy when he was twenty and lived in New York for a few years before getting word a relative had left him land in Washington state. He packed up his suitcase, bought a train ticket and made the trip out west. When he arrived at the land, which was the very dirt we're standing on, there was nothing but a dozen or so half-dead apple trees. I met him after he'd been living here for a year. Giorgio visited another apple orchard to ask for help on getting his trees back to health. That's where we met, and he convinced me to come work for him. In those early days, Giorgio's English wasn't great and I didn't know a lick of Italian, but somehow we made it work."

Pete pictured a young Milton and Giorgio standing in what would become Carmella Orchard. He had a hard time imagining either man without wrinkles and gray hair. The last time he'd seen Mr. Carmella had been a few days before he'd eloped with Sarah. The man had been good to Pete, and Pete had repaid him by stealing away his granddaughter—if only temporarily. "How long did you work at the orchard?"

"Almost ten years. It was hard work but we got those trees producing again." Milton adjusted the brim of his cowboy hat. "Giorgio was about five years older than me. He was like a big brother. I was best man at his wedding to Lucille. They were made for each other, no doubt. After a while, I got the traveling bug again and started working as a long-haul truck driver. Then I got a job at a cattle ranch in Texas. The years finally caught up to me and I couldn't ride a horse like I used to. When I got word Giorgio was sick and Lucille wasn't doing good either, I came back to do what I could."

"I'm sure you've been a great help to Sarah." Unlike Pete, who'd been long gone. Sarah must have struggled after her grandparents' death. If only he'd reached out to her at some point. He might have been able to offer his condolences if nothing else.

"The horses did the real work of helping Sarah through her grief. First after Giorgio and Lucille died and then her husband, Mike. I just made sure the horses had clean stalls, food and water." Milton sniffed. "I wasn't around when you broke her heart the first time." He pinned his gaze on Pete, who fought not to visibly squirm. "You seem like a good man, but I want to be clear—don't go breaking her heart again or, son, you'll never be able to step foot in this town again."

"Understood." Pete swallowed, not underestimating the threat from the wiry man who cared for Sarah very much. "I'd like to make peace with her. Apologize and hopefully earn her forgiveness."

Milton slapped him on the shoulder. "Good luck with that. I'll let you get started right now."

Turning his gaze, Pete startled at the sight of Sarah marching in his direction. She held a paper bag in one hand and a thermos in the other.

With a chuckle, Milton traveled with his swaying gait toward the barn.

He had to stop going all gooey every time he saw her. Pete bent over and moved under the fence rail to the other side. "We were taking a short break. Milton was telling me the story of how your grandpa started Carmella Orchard."

She snorted a laugh as she approached. "Milton has a million reasons to take a break." Arms outstretched, she offered him the bag and thermos. "It's not fine dining but should fill you up. I made a cold meatloaf sandwich with chips and an apple. Oh, and I tossed in another doughnut as a bonus. There's ice water in the thermos."

"Thanks." He took the items and peered inside the bag. "Did you make the meatloaf?"

"Using my grandma's recipe. I remembered you'd devour an entire pan by yourself if she made it when you were here for dinner." Her cheeks flushed, and she looked away. "The bread is from a new bakery in town."

"Do you want to join me?" The offer was a longshot. She surely had too much to do. But a guy could try.

"I can't. Jacob's wedding is only three days away and there's been an issue with the linen supplier. Please don't tell him or Kay. I'll get it straightened out." She reached up and tightened the band holding her ponytail.

The mention of the wedding jiggled something loose in his brain. He was forgetting something. Something important. He'd purchased a gift and even had it wrapped. He'd prepared a few words in case he was asked to speak. What was he forgetting? Pete gasped at the realization.

"A suit." How could he have forgotten he needed a suit to wear to the wedding? "Jacob asked his groomsmen to wear a gray or black suit. When I told him I was able to make the ceremony, I completely overlooked that I brought nothing to wear. I own one suit and it's packed away with the rest of my stuff, heading to Phoenix."

Sarah's lips pressed into a firm line. "That's a rookie mistake."

"I've worn my army uniform to the other weddings I've been in." He scrubbed his hands down his face, feeling foolish. All he had were jeans, shorts and T-shirts. And one flannel shirt in case the evenings grew cold. "Where can I go to buy a suit?"

"In Fern Hollow?" She raised her gaze to the sky. Either she was thinking, or praying for a suit to fall from the heavens. "Blue Bar Outfitters is the only spot in town that sells clothing. But it's mostly Western wear. You'd stand out looking like a rodeo cowboy."

"I'm sure Jacob and Kay do not want me to dress like I'm heading for a shoot-out at the OK Corral." If he wasn't mistaken, there was a twinkle of humor in her gray eyes. And the corner of her mouth twitched ever so slightly, as if she wanted to smile. "Go ahead and laugh. I did it to myself."

"You can drive to Brewster. They have a few more stores. But check out the Blue Bar first. Maybe they have something tucked in the back for a special occasion."

He sighed. "Blue Bar it is. Do you mind if I eat lunch and then head over there? If I can't find anything, then I'll have to take a drive tomorrow."

"Of course." Her voice cracked. "You're a volunteer. Leave whenever you want."

On instinct, he stepped toward her, then stopped himself. *Best keep your distance.* "I'll come back if I have time. And tomorrow, if I don't have to go on a shopping field trip."

"That's not necessary. It was nice of you to help out Milton." A horse in the pasture neighed, drawing her attention. Her face immediately softened.

"You're happy." The statement was both observable fact and an inquiry.

She returned her gaze to Pete. Her eyes studied him. Did he hold up to her scrutiny? If only he had a window into her mind in order to learn what she thought of him now, as a grown man with over a decade of new experiences that didn't involve hurting her.

"I am happy," she finally replied. "Most of the time. Look around. How could I not be? I'm living my dream. And Chloe is the best thing that ever happened to me." Sarah sucked in a breath, perhaps considering the joy and pain that Pete had brought into her life.

Their child. The remembrance pierced his heart. "You deserve the world." She really did. "Thanks for lunch and the suggestions for suit shopping. Where is the Blue Bar Outfitters?"

A flock of birds sailed overhead, heading in

the direction of the grove of apple trees. Their calls carried in the air.

"Fern Hollow has one main street, if you recall. When you drive through town, you can't miss it. Look for the ten-foot cowboy boot. It's between the ice cream shop and the general store. Good luck." She spun away and had taken a dozen steps when she turned back. "I need to head into town anyway and pick up an order from the tack store. I can drive you—that way you don't have to walk back to Jacob's place for your car."

More time with Sarah—definitely. Maybe he would work up the nerve to speak what was on his heart. An apology. An agreement to put the past behind them. A renewed friendship. Anything to not feel as if he was being ripped apart every time he was with her. He had to find a way to compartmentalize, like he did while serving in the army. Somehow, separating logic and emotions proved more difficult while with Sarah than when heading into battle.

"I'd appreciate that, if you don't mind." The weight of the bag in his hand prompted his stomach to clench in hunger. "If you need to leave now, I can eat on the road."

"There is no eating in my truck, Pete. Unless you're volunteering to vacuum out every crumb when we get back." Her smile seemed to brighten the sun.

"How could I forget how militant you are about tidiness?" Sarah was the only teenager he'd known who enjoyed cleaning their room.

"It's one of the few traits I inherited from my mom. I have a phone call to make and then we'll go. You can eat on the front porch." She motioned for him to follow her.

Pete trailed along beside her, keeping everything he wished to say locked away. Now was not the time. If he pushed too hard, Sarah would shut the door in his face. In her youth, she'd been headstrong. Observing her now, fully in control of all facets of the ranch, he determined that trait had not dulled over time. And he liked it as much now as he had back then. An unnerving thought.

What were you thinking? Sarah's hands clutched the steering wheel a little harder. Her trip into town could have waited. But no, she had to offer to drive him. Now, she'd enter the lion's den with Pete—willingly. She could almost hear the buzz of conversations about them. Most of the residents of Fern Hollow had witnessed Sarah and Pete's young romance and the subsequent fallout. Guess she was offering the town season two.

All she needed to do was treat Pete like any other rescue volunteer. If he was anyone else, she wouldn't have thought twice about giving him a ride. Pete wasn't anyone else, though, and the quickening of her pulse each time she glanced over to the other side of the truck cab served as a reminder.

She'd simply point him in the direction of the Blue Bar and carry on with her own errands. If she was lucky, no one would see them together. Who was she kidding? She wasn't that lucky. Curious eyes were everywhere.

"This was your grandad's truck, right?" Pete asked from the passenger seat. He looked odd sitting there. Pete took up a lot more space than Milton, the only other person who rode in the truck with her. Her other vehicle, a practical and safe sedan, was used to transport Chloe.

"Yes. I didn't have the heart to sell it or send it to the junk yard." After her grandparents died, she couldn't stand the thought of losing another piece of them. "It was at the mechanic's for weeks to get it running reliably again but the cost was worth it."

"It's a great truck. I've sat in this same spot several times with your grandad in the driver's seat." Pete ran his hand along the dash. He lifted his hand to inspect his palm. "Not a speck of dust. You do take vehicle care seriously."

"Grandad taught me right. And I'm sure there is some dust up there. We live in the country and I don't have time to wipe down the interior every day." During his final years, Grandad had cleaned his truck every day for as long as he was physically able. Sarah would exit the barn to find him with his top half stretched inside the truck cab with a cloth in his hand. Or he'd pull out the hose and spray down the truck's body and tires. Sarah's job was to take a bucket of sudsy water and a sponge and wash clean the exterior. "Don't miss a spot," he'd always say with a smile. She missed her grandad so much. He'd always supported her, no matter what. The Carmella Ranch was her safe space all through childhood and adolescence, continuing into her adulthood. In high school, as soon as she learned to drive, she'd leave school and head over to the ranch. No time for after-school activities when horses needed tending. Indulging in her grandma's apple pie fresh from thc oven was an extra bonus.

She came to a four-way stop, braked and then proceeded since no other cars were in sight. Only a few more miles and they'd be in town. *You can make it that long.* Although she had to drive him back. But she'd worry about that later.

"Milton is a character." Pete tapped his foot to the beat of the song playing on the radio.

"He sure is." A smile grew while thinking about some of Milton's stories she'd heard over the years. "Did he tell you that the orchard was started by magic apple seeds?"

"No." He snorted a laugh. "Did you believe him?"

"Yes, and for too long." She purposefully focused on the peaks of the mountains on the distant horizon, never taking for granted the grandeur that surrounded her daily. Several mountains still sported snowy caps. "Milton used to visit my grandparents once a year, around January or February. When I was little, he'd sit me on the hearth in front of a warm fire and tell me the story of how he'd gifted my grandad the magic apple seeds he'd carried with him from South Carolina. Of course I believed him since my grandad and grandma never contradicted him." Sarah flicked on her blinker, then turned onto the town's main street. A stoplight had been placed at the center of town three years ago, which had been a big deal at the time. Many a town meeting was held to discuss the pros and cons. Some worried a stop light meant Fern Hollow was morphing into a metropolitan city. No chance of that ever happening. She'd never want it to.

"When did you finally figure out he was spinning a tall tale?"

"Sadly, not until I turned thirteen," she admitted. No getting lost taking a stroll down memory lane. She had to keep her wits about her. Regrettably, Pete's sunny personality made liking him too easy. "He gave me two magic seeds of my own to plant. And I did. When nothing happened, I asked my grandma why the magic didn't work. She felt sorry for me and admitted the truth. I'd never been so embarrassed."

"You always had a dreamer's imagination. I'm sure you wanted it to be true."

"I really did. How many other kids could say they had magic apple trees?" Sarah found an open spot on the street and parked. Yes, she had been a dreamer. Reality had forced her to put away the belief that anything was possible. But every once in a while, especially when Mike was in her life, she'd let her mind soar. Once he died, her dreams had crash-landed and remained a heaping pile of ash.

"There's the Blue Bar Outfitters." Nothing like stating the obvious. Still, she pointed to the large sign spelling out the name of the store in block letters that bracketed the biggest cowboy boot she'd ever seen. "I'll pick up my order at the tack shop, then come over to see if you got lucky."

Pete strode into the store looking like every cowgirl's dream. He carried himself with a swagger that couldn't be faked, only earned. His clothes were slightly dusty from working in the barn. His unruly dark hair only added to his attractiveness. Catching herself staring, she yanked away her gaze. *Get a grip, Carmella.*

As Sarah turned to walk to the tack store, she caught several townspeople on the sidewalk across the street taking in what would surely be the town's latest gossip.

Twenty minutes later, with the supplies loaded into the bed of her truck, she went to check on Pete. She found him exiting a changing booth, a stack of clothes slung over his arm. "Any luck?"

"Do you think Jacob will be fine with me wearing a rhinestone vest, shirt with mother-of-pearl–covered buttons and Wrangler jeans?" He held up the potential wedding outfit.

"Absolutely not." She covered her mouth to quiet a laugh. "Is that the best you found?"

"Unfortunately." Pete hung the jeans back on the stand.

She took the vest and held it up. The material was thick and unyielding. Embroidered horseshoes decorated the back. Rhinestones sparkled across the front. "It's very flashy. As much as I'd like to see you wear this to the wedding, I agree that it's a bit too much. It would be great for the square dance fundraiser we're having at the ranch in a month. The store's owner always bumps up their stock of Western wear in the weeks leading up to the dance." Thankfully, Pete would be long gone by then.

"Well, guess I'm taking a drive tomorrow. I'm still kicking myself for not remembering a suit." After he returned the clothing to its proper place, they left the store.

"Guess we should get back." Sarah slid her truck keys from her back pocket, then froze. All she could think of was to hide. About a half block down stood her mom, who currently had her back to them. No Chloe in sight. She must be home with Grandpa. Her mom was chatting with someone but the conversation could end any second. Then she'd turn and see Sarah with Pete. Not good. "Come with me." Sarah grabbed Pete's arm and yanked him in the opposite direction. Her mom could not know she was spending time with Pete, in town no less.

"Where are we going?" He struggled to keep his balance as she pulled him along.

"In here." After opening the door, she pushed him inside. The Timeless Treasures Thrift Store was as good a place to hide as any. Actually, it might be the perfect spot. Looking around, she found the area with men's clothes. "They might have a suit for you here."

He scrunched up his nose. "You want me to

wear a used suit? I still have time to drive to a few other towns."

"No." She placed her body in front of the door. "Just take a look. There's no harm in looking."

"Okay." An eyebrow arched as he peered down at her. His expression was a mix of humor and bewilderment. "If you insist."

"I insist." Directing him to the men's clothing, she periodically glanced over her shoulder. No appearance of Mom so far. "Thrifting is good for the environment. You want to save the planet, don't you?"

"Sure. I love the planet, but running in here doesn't have anything to do with your mom out there, does it?" His gaze moved from Sarah and ran over the interior of the tightly packed shop.

Drat. He had seen her too. "I don't want to deal with my mom right now. We're both in a hurry." Guilt tugged at the edges of her conscience. Pete definitely knew Sarah's intentions had nothing to do with saving time and everything to do with not wanting to be confronted over being with Pete.

"My options here might be worse than at Blue Bar Outfitters."

He was correct. Timeless Treasures Thrift Store held an odd assortment of goods donated by folks in and around Fern Hollow. No fine

Italian suits had ever been donated here. But it was worth a try. Plus, she had time to kill until her mom left the vicinity. While Pete browsed through the racks of men's clothing options, she approached the home goods section, reminding herself that nothing on these shelves was something she actually needed. She was a sucker, though, for a unique trinket and a good bargain. When she found a pair of wooden bookends that had been carved to look like horseshoes, she was tempted. Her willpower held firm, and she walked away without them in her hands.

Ten minutes later, Pete appeared holding a gray suit. "I can't believe it but I found something. It's a few sizes too big, though."

The suit he discovered appeared relatively new and made of decent material. She took the coat and looked at the label. Not a brand she recognized but then again, she didn't know much about men's formal wear. Mike had only worn a suit three times during their marriage. Once for their wedding—a family affair at the ranch. The second and third were for Grandad's and then Grandma's funerals. She'd donated most of Mike's clothes to a store far away from Fern Hollow. The last thing she needed was to bump into someone walking down the street wearing a shirt of Mike's. Sarah hadn't donated Mike's suit. It still hung in the closet in her bedroom.

There was no way she'd offer it to Pete. It would be too small, for one. And her heart wouldn't withstand the sight.

"Go try it on." She placed her mind back in the present. "I'll wait."

After Pete disappeared into the changing room, Sarah looked through the shelves of books. She selected a mystery by an author she liked in the rare chance she ever found a few free minutes to read.

"I liked that one." Jill Durst, the owner of the thrift store, came up beside Sarah and pointed to the cover. "How are you holding up, sweetie?" She whispered the question.

"Um." Sarah floundered for a response that wouldn't set the town's phone lines on fire. "I'm fine. Pete forgot a suit to wear at Jacob's wedding. The pickings are slim in Fern Hollow. Thought maybe he'd find something in your shop."

"He's fortunate to have you as a guide, whether he finds a suit or not." Jill glanced at the closed door of the changing room. "Is he in town for long?"

"Only until Jacob's wedding." *He can't leave soon enough.* And then again, part of her wished he'd stay longer and not run off to his next big adventure. If she was truthful, she had missed him over the years. When he'd first left for basic training, Pete was all she thought about. After her miscarriage and the annulment of their marriage, she'd worked to purge him from her mind. Easier said than done. Finally, she accepted that the boy she'd loved would always have a small but permanent spot in her heart. Like a tattoo that may have faded over the years but still marked the skin.

Nothing in her life up until the point of her miscarriage had prepared her for the ensuing emotional turmoil. The future she'd dreamed about had been ripped away and her new husband was not present to provide love and support. Comfort had been found with the horses, her grandparents and the ranch. Eventually, she realized Carmella Ranch was her home, and an adventurous life with Pete would not bring her peace.

"That's too bad he's leaving so soon." Jill shook her head and removed her red-framed eyeglasses, placing them to rest on top of her head. "I remember his folks bringing the boys to town for summer-long vacations all those years ago. Pete was my favorite of the family. Don't tell him I said that." She patted Sarah's arm. Jill, a lifelong resident of Fern Hollow, had opened the town's only thrift store thirty years ago as a way to promote reusing items instead of throwing them in the landfill. An ex-hippie, with long silver hair and outfits made up of flowing skirts and chunky jewelry, Jill had a way of helping her customers find things they didn't even know they wanted.

"I won't tell him." Pete had been Sarah's favorite as well, obviously. The O'Keefe father, a veteran who'd been wounded, hadn't projected warm and fuzzy vibes. She'd never seen him crack a smile or even display a hint of humor. Had Pete been shown affection by his father? Likely not. His mom, on the other hand, had been warm and welcoming to Sarah. She made up for her husband's coldness. Pete's brother, Chris, had been friendly enough. Chris was four years older, and had outgrown their family summer trips by the time Sarah and Pete really started spending a lot of time together. From what Pete had shared, Chris went to the Naval Academy after high school and, then enlisted after graduation. No wonder Pete felt inspired to follow in his big brother's footsteps, in his own way.

"Well," Pete said after he appeared from the changing room. "It's a little big."

Sarah stifled a laugh. The gray fabric hung on him like he was a kid trying on his father's clothes. "I'd say."

"That's nothing that can't be fixed." Jill hustled over and assessed the situation. She pinched fabric and folded the cuffs of the jacket. "I can make it fit. Nothing I could do if it was too small. Stay here. I'll get my pins and then mark where it needs to be taken in."

After Jill disappeared into the back room, Pete peered down at his feet, which were hidden by the too-long pants. "I don't think this can ever be made to fit me. Did this suit belong to a giant?"

Good question. Pete wasn't a small man, with a height of over six feet and broad shoulders and chest. "Could have belonged to Mr. Kramer. He was a college football star back in his day."

Jill popped back out of the back room with a tape measure and red pin cushion. "This won't take long and I'll have it all ready for you by Saturday morning."

"You don't have to do all this." Pete put a hand up, like the gesture would stop the speeding train of Jill. She was a woman on a mission.

"Nonsense." She waved his hand away. "Now stand still so I can get this pinned up. Don't want to stick you by accident. Then you can be on your way."

Apparently having grown accustomed to following orders in the military, Pete did as he was instructed, standing still for the thirty minutes Jill took to prepare the jacket and pants for alteration.

While they worked, Sarah found a nice white shirt and tie that matched well with the suit.

After paying for the clothing, Sarah's book and the horseshoe bookends Pete had found and insisted on buying for her, he left with a promise from Jill that she'd drop off a clean and tailored suit to Jacob's house first thing Saturday morning.

Sarah had no doubt Jill would come through. And if not, the rhinestone cowboy outfit was still available in an emergency. Picturing Pete wearing the ensemble brought a smile to her face.

"What's so funny?" he asked while holding open the door.

"Nothing," she fibbed. "You've been saved a long drive and more shopping."

"Thanks for bringing me in." He halted on the sidewalk and waited for her to notice.

She paused and glanced back. "Are you coming? I need to get home. My parents are dropping off Chloe in less than an hour."

"Sarah." He hesitated. "I understand why you don't want to be seen with me. At least by your folks. I don't want to cause you any trouble."

"You're not causing trouble." Not exactly true but if her parents balked, then she'd handle them. "We're adults not teenagers. Plus, they don't have anything to worry about. You're only in Fern Hollow for a few more days." And then he'd be off again. There was no danger of her falling in love with him again because he wouldn't be around long enough.

"It's just that I want to make things right...between us." He stepped forward until he reached her and then met her gaze. "I'd like for my visit to go well. No parental drama. No more hurt feelings."

Her insides softened at his thoughtfulness. She'd never considered Pete the sensitive type. How easily she could get lost in his dark brown eyes. His thick black eyelashes flickered as he blinked. "I appreciate that. I honestly only wanted to avoid a possible scene with my mom on Main Street." Yet she heard in her head the words her mom pronounced the summer before they ran away—*that boy is no good for you. He'll only break your heart.*

CHAPTER FOUR

SARAH TOOK A seat at her favorite table. She'd arrived fifteen minutes early for her meeting at the Columbia Diner with Lauren to discuss the plans for the Carmella Ranch Annual Square Dance. Her skin prickled with excitement. The event was less than a month away and could be the biggest one yet.

Her grandparents had hosted square dances in their barn, back when gasoline cost less than a dollar a gallon. When Sarah took over, she revived the tradition and added a fundraiser element. It was always held the Saturday after the Fourth of July and brought in much needed money to the rescue.

"I'll be over in a sec," Lauren called out from behind the counter.

"No rush." Sarah lifted her mug of coffee and sipped to prove she was enjoying a moment to relax on a Thursday morning. Chloe had fought about going to her grandparents' house so they'd compromised. Sarah promised to pick her up at noon and they'd have a picnic lunch at home. Chloe was six, old enough to help with the small tasks that needed doing before the wedding rehearsal tomorrow night.

Her friends were getting married in two days. Joy bloomed at the anticipation of Jacob and Kay reciting their vows and slipping on wedding rings. Their love would last. They weren't eloping as teenagers. Sarah must have been delusional to believe her marriage to Pete would stand the test of time. In reality, it broke at the first test. Yes, that test was a tough one, but a strong marriage could have survived. Circumstances hadn't allowed their marriage enough time to harden. Sometimes when firing ceramics, a vessel cracked when it couldn't withstand the heat. A good analogy for her relationship with Pete.

Lauren set down her order pad and pen before joining Sarah. She lowered herself into a chair and exhaled. "You have my full attention for thirty minutes."

"Okay." She removed a copy of the flyer she'd worked on. Clicking around on a computer, putting together graphics, didn't come naturally but she'd cobbled together a decent advertisement. At least she thought so. "I'd like to print these off and hang them around town. I know it's late and most people already know about the square dance but it's a good reminder."

"Nice." Lauren's gaze scanned the paper. "Give me a stack once you've printed a batch and I'll hand them out at the shops on Main Street. The site for ticket sales is up and running. We've sold thirty so far."

"That's low." Biting her lower lip, she ran last year's numbers in her head. "I was hoping to up the attendance this year."

"We have time. Remember, people came to the barn on the day of and asked to buy tickets in years prior. They have no sense of urgency."

"What if we offer a discount for tickets purchased more than a week before?" she suggested. "Having a solid number helps with planning seating and food."

"Agree. Let's keep the ticket price fixed for now and advertise the price will be five dollars more if they purchase the week of the dance."

"And ten dollars more if they come without a ticket and want to buy one there." Sarah scribbled down their plans on her legal pad. Her excitement grew while picturing her barn filled with music, dancers and long tables covered in food and drink. A shame Pete wouldn't be able to join in the fun. No. No, it was *not* a shame. A worldly man like Pete O'Keefe would surely consider a small-town square dance hokey. It was hokey, which was one of the reasons she loved the square dance and all the other town festivals.

The scent of chocolate hit her nose, and she turned her head to find one of the diner's servers slicing into a pan of brownies over by the counter. Then, using a serving spatula, she removed a huge brownie square and placed it on a paper tray to be housed in the diner's bakery display. "Can I have one?"

Lauren followed Sarah's gaze. "It's only nine in the morning. Do you really want a brownie?"

"It's as healthy as a doughnut for breakfast." Sarah sniffed again, and her stomach rumbled. The slice of cheese she'd devoured before running out the door this morning was long digested.

"You're right. What's the point in being an adult with adult responsibilities if we can't indulge once in a while?" Lauren stood and walked over to the counter. After grabbing two brownies, she disappeared into the kitchen.

Sarah looked down at her notes. *Wonder what Pete is doing right now?* The second the question popped into her mind, she swatted it away. Why did it matter what he was doing? He'd talked about finding time to fish. Perhaps he'd borrowed a pole and tackle from Jacob and was currently sitting on the banks of a river or lake.

She had to stop thinking of him. Ever since Pete had shown up at the ranch two days ago, her insides felt like they'd been shaken and jumbled up—like a living snow globe. Once he left on Sunday, things would settle back to normal.

Normal was good. Predictable. Stable. After her grandparents' deaths and then losing Mike, she'd assumed she'd never feel good again. Returning to a sense of peace had taken time and it wasn't easy. Each morning, she reminded herself to be grateful for the blessings she had—her daughter, the ranch, even her parents. The brief return of Pete wouldn't upset her hard-won harmony.

Lauren reappeared holding a white bowl in each hand. She set them on the table with a grin. "If we're going to be naughty, then let's do it right."

"Oh yeah." The bowl before Sarah was filled with a dream come true. The brownie she'd craved was covered in two scoops of vanilla ice cream and drizzled with fudge sauce. "I won't tell if you don't." She took her spoon and dug in. "Being an adult isn't all bad."

Lauren had been her friend for a long time. In high school, they'd both dreamed of ditching Fern Hollow for bigger and brighter places. In the end, they'd both settled in their hometown. Along with Jacob, they'd been the three musketeers, running around town and causing as much trouble as three kids could while knowing someone would see them and tell their parents.

"Can I get a brownie and ice cream every morning for breakfast?" she asked with a chuckle.

"Only if you come visit me at the diner." Lauren wiped away a dab of hot fudge from under her chin. Still a messy eater. There was a picture in their senior yearbook of Lauren with a face covered in chocolate ice cream after eating a cone. She'd pleaded with the yearbook staff to never let it see the light of day. Unfortunately, the head of the student yearbook committee had a mean sense of humor. "Now back to business. I have an idea for a way to raise additional money. We hold a pie auction."

Sarah considered the suggestion. Any additional dollars coming in during the fundraiser were welcome. "How do you picture the auction? The pies are lined up on tables and people bid?"

"Not exactly. Those with a pie would stand up with their donation and we'd have a live auction. There'd be an auctioneer. The winning bidder would win the pie and a chance to share a slice with the baker." Lauren leaned back in her chair, grinning. "What do you think? If Travis from the Redroot Ranch donates a pie for the auction, I'll outbid everyone, no matter how much it costs."

Shaking her head, Sarah took another spoonful of ice cream with a hunk of brownie and considered. "I imagine the pie will go for a lot since he's very popular with the ladies. I'm not sure about the quality of his skill in the kitchen though, not that it matters. There's a possibility for some real bidding wars. Imagine the money Kallie Kulper could raise no matter what she bakes. She matches Travis's popularity."

Kallie was the most eligible bachelorette in town. No local guy had snagged more than one date with her. She was like the elusive trout that was rumored to live nearby in the Columbia River. Sometimes sighted but never caught. Every local fisherman had a story about the giant trout. Most men of a certain age in Fern Hollow had a similar story about their failed attempt to land Kallie.

"I think it's a good idea. We can hold it during the first break in the dancing. People can get a drink, sit down for a while and bid." Plus, the more money raised, the better chance of this year's Carmella Ranch budget breaking even. Last night, she'd had a nightmare about shutting down the ranch and watching her horses being taken away. After waking in a sweat with her heart racing, she had to look out the window to assure herself everything was where she'd left it. Then she could turn in again for the night. The pastures had been quiet and covered in moonlight. The barn closed and still. All the animals were tucked into their beds and safe. If a predator came too close, her dogs would bark and chase it off. Beaker and Gonzo lived in the barn with the smaller animals. They took their jobs very seriously.

She and Lauren spent the next minutes going over the musicians, decorations and food.

"Hank will deliver his smoker the day before and start the beef brisket," Sarah said, reading from her notes. "The baked beans, cornbread, and macaroni and cheese will be delivered a few hours before the dance begins. My parents are providing lemonade and sweet tea. Those who win a pie will enjoy dessert. Do we want something for everyone else?"

"How about brownies?" Lauren raised her full spoon. "No ice cream. I can bake a few pans. What are we missing?"

Sarah scratched her chin. The title of this year's square dance was "Hollow Hoedown." Not superoriginal but she hadn't been feeling creative when making the decision. Most of the decorations they recycled from year to year, and she was growing tired of the dusty donkey statue set outside the barn door to welcome dancers. Although Chloe would protest the donkey's removal since the statue looked like Horace. They could reuse the donkey but set it in an open-style photo booth with a Western backdrop and other props. "I'd like some new decorations this year. Keep your eyes peeled for anything pretty and cheap."

"Will do. I'll ask Jill to let one of us know if something good comes into the thrift store donation bin. I'm sure she'd love to help."

With their business wrapped up, Lauren left to check on the kitchen.

Sarah scraped the rest of the ice cream and fudge out of the bottom of the bowl and enjoyed every last drop. With a challenge to her willpower, she did *not* lick the bowl clean. Once she gathered all her things, she waved goodbye to Lauren and exited the diner. She had some time before picking up Chloe. Maybe she should head home and work on chores. Her phone pinged with an incoming text. It was from Jacob.

is it okay I give Pete your number?

Good question. Finally, she replied: Sure great.

Not great. Seconds later, another text arrived. This time from Pete. He didn't waste any time.

Can I visit the ranch and take videos of the horses? I like posting clips of interesting places I visit on social media and the ranch fits the bill.

Reminder—he was here for a visit. A tourist passing through. While she had no problem with him taking videos on the property, she did not want to be around when he was there. Guess she was staying in town until she picked up Chloe.

Yes, you can. Don't let Horace get too close. He bites.

Pete replied with a scared face emoji.

She placed her phone back into her purse, smiling as she imagined Pete and her cranky donkey.

PETE HIT POST on the screen of his cell phone, feeling a deep sense of satisfaction. He'd taken close to thirty video clips of the horses and various other animals that resided at Sarah's ranch. After selecting five of his favorite videos, he edited each and then uploaded them onto Instagram. He added audio and a description before letting them out for public viewing. His followers had had no new content in almost a week. Videos from his time in New York City didn't pull the same level of engagement as the ones he posted from more unique places. Not that NYC wasn't unique in its own way but most people were already familiar with the sights and sounds of crowded streets, lines of taxi cabs and hordes of pedestrians navigating the sidewalks. He'd been uninspired.

The Carmella Ranch and Orchard provided a fresh setting. Milton had assisted in sharing some of the animals' stories. Some were very compelling. The poor creatures arrived in horrific condition and found paradise under Sarah's care. Pete was rightfully impressed. The ranch, which had done well while her grandparents managed the operation, had grown under Sarah's governance.

Milton had also given Pete a tour of the barn and stable. Horace, the feisty donkey, had given Pete some good content. While Pete stayed safely behind the fence, he caught Horace playing with an inflatable ball and attempting to build a friendship with the ducks that wandered into his enclosure.

He and Milton had spent hours together wandering the property. The interior of the remodeled barn looked incredible and could clearly accommodate any type of event, including the square dance coming up next month. If only he'd still be around.

Now, Pete stood on the porch at Jacob's house,

watching the likes and comments on his new posts.

"Are you coming?" Jacob called out from the driveway. "I'm only single for forty-eight more hours and there's no point having a bachelor party after I'm married."

"I'm coming." Pete put away his phone, then tightened up the laces of his boots. The men in the wedding party were going hiking this afternoon before coming back to change clothes and then hit the town. He had no idea what that entailed in a town as small as Fern Hollow. There must be at least one bar.

He joined the two other groomsmen and Jacob, then climbed into the back of Jacob's Jeep. The bumpy drive up the trailhead didn't take long. The pull-off was empty so parking was a breeze.

After getting out of the vehicle, Pete fixed his baseball cap on his head and grabbed his metal water bottle. "What are Kay's plans for her bachelorette party?" he asked Jacob as they began their ascent. The trail started at a slight incline but up ahead the elevation rose at a sharper rate. He looked forward to a good sweat.

"She's having the ladies over for movies and manicures," Jacob said. "I'm sure a wine bottle or two will be opened at some point."

Kay had mentioned the names of her bridesmaids and Sarah wasn't included on the list. She'd likely be too busy working with the event coordinator, ensuring the wedding and reception ran without issue.

"Sounds like fun." He'd rather hike a thousand miles than sit at home for a night and watch movies while painting his nails. He pictured Sarah snuggled next to him on the sofa as the movie played—on second thought, the sacrifice of sitting still might be worth it.

"How about you share some of your action and adventure stories," Jacob suggested. He was growing out of breath already, his blond bangs damp with perspiration. "That way, I can pretend to be a fit soldier while trying not to pass out during the hike."

Pete laughed at the joke that probably wasn't too far from the truth. "I can tell you about the first time I rappelled out of a helicopter over open water. The water spray hit so hard, it felt like the skin on my face was ripping off." Pete went on to share the fun and interesting parts of a few of his training missions. He added in extra details like the sore muscles after hours of marching during the night when he'd keep moving though every cell in his body cried out for rest.

"Were you always training for something?" Greg, another groomsman, asked. He worked as an insurance agent and appeared to regularly work out given he was taking the hike in easy stride, at least so far.

"The Army loves to invent ways to disguise torture as training. But it wasn't all agony. I made lifelong friends and did some good around the world. I helped build bridges and dug wells for clean water." He missed being a part of his group of soldiers. But the time had come to move on, which had displeased his father. He had no interest in moving any further up the line in rank. Making high-level war decisions was for other officers, not him. Plus, he dreamed of having a family someday. Wanted to try marriage again and add a couple of kids to make things interesting. It was hard enough dating as a regular guy, so he heard. Finding a woman who would put up with him being deployed on a constant basis or relocated to a different base year after year was nearly impossible. He understood the reluctance. After giving dating a shot in his mid-twenties, he'd put the brakes on finding love and focused on work. Now out of the military, he hoped he had a better chance.

His brother had met a great woman while at the Naval Academy. They'd married before his graduation. Ashley was a rare person and a saint for supporting Chris's crazy schedule. She'd pretty much raised their kids on her own with the help of her parents. They somehow had made it work despite the difficult times. *What if Sarah and I had stuck it out?* But they hadn't and there was no going back.

The two other guys moved ahead while Pete kept pace with Jacob. "You ready for your big day?" Pete asked.

"I'd marry her today if Kay would skip the big wedding with our family and friends and run away." Jacob paused. "I can't wait to start the rest of my life, you know. We've known each other for years, and many of those I was stuck in the friend zone. I want to make the most of all the time we have together going forward."

"I'm glad you made it out of the friend zone." Pete slapped him on the back. "There's nothing worse when you really like a woman."

"You're telling me," Jacob said with a chuckle. "Thanks for making the effort to come. It means a lot. I know we sometimes struggled to keep in touch over the years, but I've considered you a good friend since we were eight-year-olds, borrowing the Marchionni kids' bikes and taking off to try and find the buried gold Old Man Miller had told us about."

"My mom was so mad when she found out what we were doing." Warm memories flooded in. He and Jacob had become fast friends the first summer his family had rented the cabin next door. While Jacob wasn't a natural troublemaker, Pete had convinced Jacob on many occasions to break the rules in order to have a little fun. Since Pete didn't have a bike with him on vacation and Jacob's was too small, one day they found an open garage with two neglected bikes inside. They'd only borrowed them for the day—occasionally—riding up and down hilly trails similar to the one they hiked today. Jacob would pack food and drinks. Pete was in charge of bringing a radio. The fun lasted until they were eventually caught inside the Marchionnis' garage with no good excuse.

"How are things with Sarah?" Jacob asked. "You were over at the ranch this morning, right?"

"Yeah, but she wasn't around. I took videos of the place for social media. Her animals have a more comfortable life than I do." The fact Sarah had collected a variety of animals didn't surprise him. She'd been the type of person to rescue the stray dog found on the side of the road or guard the baby birds placed inside a nest that wasn't in a sheltered area. She was a nurturer. A protector. Someone who didn't turn her back when she saw a creature in need. So why had she given up on their marriage so easily? Yes, she had been too young to legally marry but they could have fixed that once she turned eighteen. He'd been confident she loved him as much as he loved her. Why let it go as easily as dandelion fluff in the wind? Guess the same could be said about him. If he'd been a better man, he would have sent the annulment papers back unsigned. He hadn't understood Sarah's deep grief over the loss of their baby had caused her to shut him out. If he had, he'd have found a way back to her. They could have comforted each other. Perhaps, after some time, they could have tried again for a family.

"She's done well with the rescue and the apple orchard is going strong. But you didn't answer my question." Jacob nudged him in the ribs with his elbow.

"It's fine. She's been welcoming and hasn't threatened to stab me with a sharp object." He'd keep secret his internal struggle every time he was with her. The emotional turmoil wouldn't last much longer. "I'm glad to have a chance to see her again and hopefully I'll leave on friendlier terms."

"Any hope of a reconnection? Wouldn't it be great if you two fell in love all over again?"

"Slow down. Your soon-to-be bride has put stars in your eyes." Pete stepped over a rock that had tumbled onto the trail. Up ahead, the path twisted around a bend and hugged the side of a twenty-foot or so rock wall. "I'm not looking for anything other than forgiveness. We were too young when we ran off to Vegas. I should not have given in to my impulse to marry her. Instead, I left her to deal with the fallout alone." He scrubbed his face with his hands, feeling every ounce of the shame he carried. If only he'd acted like a man instead of a boy with a fantasy that he could shape his life into whatever he wanted without consequence.

"After Mike died, I didn't see Sarah smile for two years." Jacob took a long drink from his water bottle, then screwed the cap back on. "I think now she's settled into a good place. Chloe is great. Motherhood gives Sarah purpose. As does the ranch. Be kind to her, please. You'll leave in a couple of days, and I hope you'll both feel better after having a chance to heal."

"I hear you, man." A very subtle warning not to break Sarah's heart again. "I'll tread carefully with her." He came to a stop beside the wall and gazed up at the invitation. The rock wall rising before him was covered with beautiful crags and crevices, begging to be climbed. "You don't have to wait on me." He set down his water bottle, then rubbed his palms together. "I should have brought chalk."

"You aren't thinking of climbing that?" Jacob stepped backward and lifted his gaze. Shielding his eyes with his hand, he whistled. "You didn't bring any gear."

He fit one hand onto a piece of rock jutting out. "It's not that tall. I'll be fine. This has a great surface that will be easy to climb."

"If you're sure." Jacob swallowed. "But we're not leaving you."

In case you fall and break your neck. Pete finished the sentence in his head. "Okay, thanks. I won't take long." He pulled himself up onto a ledge about two feet above the ground. The climb wasn't challenging, and he made it to the top in minutes. Standing on the rise, he reserved a moment to take in the view. This far above, he could see what waited ahead for them on the trail—a steep rise that would take them higher than he was currently standing. Not wanting to delay the hike any further, he lay prone on the ground and swung his lower body over the side of the cliff. His feet slid back and forth until finding purchase. He moved thoughtfully, each position secure before changing. Once he reached about five feet off the ground, his moves quickened. Big mistake. His foot slipped off a ledge while only one hand gripped a small pocket in the rock. Before he could make a sound, his fingers slipped and his body slid down the side of the rock wall. He landed hard and awkwardly with his left wrist taking most of the initial impact.

Jacob and the other guys came running to check on him.

After a second or two to catch his breath, he crawled onto his knees and then stood. “All good.” The fiery pain in his left wrist declared Pete a liar. Not his first broken bone but a very inconvenient injury.

CHAPTER FIVE

SARAH WAS RETURNING the bucket for oats into the barrel when her cell phone rang. She searched for Chloe, who she found looking at a book while curled up on a hay bale with a pink blanket and at least three kittens. Her child had a really good life, and Sarah felt blessed to provide it for her.

When she saw Pete's name on her phone screen, hesitation paused her finger. She should have never let Jacob give Pete her cell number. No getting attached. Finally, she answered. "Hello."

"Hey, Sarah. It's Pete."

"I know." She rolled her eyes, grateful he couldn't see her over the phone. "What's up?"

"Not up but down." He chuckled. "I went hiking with Jacob and crew and decided to rock climb."

She pressed a hand to her forehead. "Let me guess, you fell and now you're at the hospital."

"Bingo. You know me so well."

Used to know him well. Now, he was practically a stranger. Though didn't this accident prove he was still the same wild Pete she'd mistakenly fallen in love with? She hadn't heeded her head then but she would now. "What do you need?"

"A ride." The sound of voices and chiming of a machine sounded in the background. "I insisted Jacob and the guys head out to finish the bachelor party. I didn't want my stupidity to ruin their fun. I thought I'd hire a ride share to get me home."

"You're not in the big city, champ." She glanced at Chloe, still absorbed in her book and stroking the back of a black kitten on her lap. "I think we have one driver who covers a seventy-mile radius."

"Yeah, I discovered Frank takes Thursdays off for bowling."

If the injury needed imaging or an emergency room, Jacob had likely taken Pete to the nearest medical center, which was thirty miles away. She checked the time. Chloe would be asking for dinner soon. Who else could he ask? Milton had left for the day, saying he wanted to get some fishing in before sunset. Not her parents. Both Jacob and Kay were busy with their respective parties. "Have you been discharged yet?"

"Yes," he said. "Sent me off with parting gifts of a handsome brace and sling. Fractured my scaphoid. Not displaced, so that's a positive."

"Why were you rock climbing?" The question had to be asked. "Did anyone else rock climb?"

"No one else was reckless enough to join me. It was a nice climb and had a great view at the top. Anyway, about that ride..."

She blew out a breath. What other option did she have? Or she could leave him there, which would solve the problem of Peter O'Keefe suddenly reappearing into her life. "Fine. I need to finish up a few things and then get Chloe wrangled into the car. Text me where you are and I'll let you know when I'm leaving."

"Thanks, Sarah. You're the best."

She was a sucker, that's what she was. Her dad had told her over and over that her heart was too soft. Of course, Tim Carmella was right. Fathers knew best. So why hadn't she listened to him all those years ago when he ordered her to end her relationship with Pete? Instead, she'd run away and married the guy. The one and only time she'd rebelled, and look where her defiance had gotten her.

After finishing her chores and ordering Chloe inside the house to use the bathroom and wash up, Sarah went inside and checked the social media accounts she'd set up for the rescue and orchard. Rarely did she post because who had the time. Plus, she wasn't good at creating content anyone would be interested in. Still, she added a photo of a horse or the progress of the apple trees every now and again. She opened up Instagram and grew confused at the number of notifications. Strange. After scrolling down, she understood. The handle for Carmella Ranch and Orchard had been tagged in a half dozen posts by a user @easyghostrider. The videos the user posted were taken on her property. One featured Horace playing in the field with his ball with a voice in the background that sounded like Milton. Was this what Pete had been doing here this morning? Was he @easyghostrider? Each video was set to engaging music. Some had text on the screen explaining the mission of the rescue. The number of likes, comments and shares for each post had hcr cycs growing widc. *Wow.* Imaginc if a small percentage visited her page. Judging from the new followers, many had clicked over and decided she was worth a follow.

She'd thank Pete. Above and beyond picking him up from the hospital and driving him back to Fern Hollow. Maybe he could share some tips on making content people engaged with instead of swiping past, like most of what she uploaded.

Since Chloe was taking forever in the bathroom, she looked at more of Pete's posts. The most recent were of New York. Kind of boring in her opinion. Further down were clips from foreign places, like Japan and South Korea. At some point, he'd been in Central America. The videos he posted from a jungle hike blew her mind. The snakes alone would have made her run away screaming. The videos taken in the foreign cities were fascinating. She viewed a short one set in Guatemala City and instantly got the itch to travel. Not that she'd be traveling anytime soon. Her time was tightly tied to the ranch. When she heard the bathroom sink faucet run, she closed the app. More proof she'd made the right decision to end their marriage. She'd never wanted to be a hindrance to his aspirations. At seventeen years old, she'd assumed she could have everything. Reality had been a hard teacher. The memories of when she'd made the decision to end their marriage made her heart sink.

Pete had lived a full and interesting life since they'd split. He'd toured the world while with the military, unencumbered by a wife. She recalled lying stretched out beside him on a blanket in an open field. Pete reclined on his back with his hands propped under his head while gazing up into the blue sky. That day, he shared his dream of seeing every corner of the planet. He wanted to meet different people and experience other cultures. Since her dreams included him, she imagined going with him. Silly to think about now. Her home was in Fern Hollow. That was where her roots were planted. If she had followed Pete, surely she'd have grown homesick in no time and returned. That was what she'd always believed. But after looking at some of Pete's videos, she questioned if their story could have ended differently. Would she have enjoyed the travel as much as he had, given the chance? It didn't matter. Her life was perfect now just the way it was.

Chloe burst out of the bathroom, declaring that she was finished. She skipped to the back door to slip on her shoes.

Her sweet daughter. Sarah's relationship with Pete had ended for a reason. There was no other ending to their story. Because she let Pete go, she had had her marriage to Mike. She had Chloe. She had the ranch, which offered a safe harbor for all the animals she'd rescued over the years. Just because Pete was in her life for a few days didn't mean she'd engage in a game of *what if.* Pete ended up living his own dream and so did Sarah. Going their own ways gave them the space to find their happy endings.

Sarah texted Pete right before she left, telling

him she'd be about forty minutes. The audiobook playing during the drive helped distract her mind and made the time fly. She pulled up to the main entrance of the hospital to find Pete seated on a bench, waiting.

When he saw her, he stood and walked over to the passenger door. His left arm was tucked in to his side supported by a black sling. Once inside, he thanked her with his trademark lopsided grin. "Thanks a lot. I really didn't want to drag Jacob away from his party."

"No problem." She put the car in Drive and pulled away from the curb. "Chloe and I enjoy a car ride to a different town every now and then."

"How did you hurt your arm?" Chloe asked from the back seat. "Did you cry?"

Another handsome smile. Sarah forced her gaze to remain fixed on the road ahead and not the man sitting in the seat beside her.

"I climbed up onto some rocks and fell. I cried a little at first but the doctor made it better."

Pete was a natural with kids. Or at least her kid. That came as a surprise. Her traitorous gaze slipped over to him and her heart fluttered. Either she gained control of her emotions or she'd be wrecked on Sunday when he left town.

"Broken wrist, right?" she asked. "This is why we don't climb on rocks, right, Chloe?"

"Mommy won't let me climb up on big rocks when we go for walks." Chloe blew out a breath. "You should have had Mom with you. Then you wouldn't have gotten hurt."

"True. When I knew your mom back when we were kids, she kept me out of trouble. She wants to make sure the people she cares about are safe."

She felt his gaze on her but refused to take her attention off the road. Still, the side of her face grew warm. When they were young, Pete often ignored her words of caution. He'd been fearless. While he jumped off a cliff into the lake, she sat on the shore hoping he'd swim out still in one piece. He'd been a bright flame that attracted her. Unfortunately, he still did. Only now she was older and wiser.

"We didn't have time to eat dinner," she said. "Do you mind if we stop somewhere to grab a bite?"

"Of course not. I'm starving and would appreciate having a chance to eat. Dinner is on me since you drove all the way over here to pick me up."

"Great. Do you need to stop at the pharmacy first? The one in Fern Hollow will be closed by the time we get back."

"Over-the-counter pain meds are good enough and I have a bottle at Jacob's house." He tapped his hand on his thigh to the beat of the music. The clothes he wore were the ones he'd had on to go hiking—twill pants, a white T-shirt and hiking boots. His baseball cap rested in his lap. A metal water bottle was placed securely down by his feet. Hot-pink socks stuck out from the tops of his boots. His fashion choices as a teen weren't so bold. Perhaps the rhinestone vest would have been a more suitable outfit for Pete than the traditional suit.

Sarah drove around until she found a place Chloe would like. It served burgers, hot dogs and fries and had an exterior window to order and outdoor seating. The warm weather invited her to enjoy the fresh air. "Is this okay?"

"Looks good to me. What do you say, Chloe?" Pete asked.

"Yum," she said from the back seat. "Can I get ice cream too?" She must have caught sight of the ice cream cone statue by the building.

"Only if you eat your dinner first." Wasn't that the standard mom phrase regarding dessert? Honestly, she didn't care if her daughter only ate ice cream but didn't want Pete to think she was a bad mom. Sarah's parents had been strict to the point of being suffocating. Rarely did she have a chance to indulge in sweets and only when her grandparents treated her. As a parent, she wanted Chloe to grow up healthy and strong but understood taking all the fun out of food left a kid feeling like they were missing out. So she didn't make Chloe eat all her peas like Sarah had to as a child. Chloe was allowed an afternoon cookie even if it was close to dinner.

"I will," Chloe promised. Once she was freed from her seat belt, she hopped out of the car and took Pete's right hand. "Do your fingers still work?"

He wiggled the fingers on his left hand. "They sure do. One of the bones in my wrist has a little break." He pointed to the area on his good hand. "When I fell, I put out my hand to catch myself. I landed hard and that hurt the bone. But it will heal. The body is wonderful that way. It gets hurt and then heals itself, with the proper care and rest."

"I cut my finger." Chloe held up her pointer finger to show Pete. "Mommy put on a Band-Aid because it was bleeding. Then when I took the Band-Aid off for bath time, it was better."

"That is amazing." Pete squeezed her hand. "Let's go pick out what we want to eat. I'm starving."

As Pete and Chloe walked to the menu board propped up by the ordering window, Sarah froze and pressed her hand over her heart. The sight of her daughter and Pete strolling hand in hand stole her breath. It should be Mike taking his daughter out for burgers and ice cream. He'd miss many wonderful moments like this. And Chloe hardly recalled her dad. Sometimes, Chloe spoke to a picture of Mike that Sarah had placed on Chloe's nightstand. Mike's death stole their family's future, and Sarah had to cope with raising Chloe alone. No, she wasn't doing it alone. Not when she had family and friends who all gave love and support. Which currently included Pete. She loved her daughter too deeply to push away someone who showed her a genuine connection. Guess she was stuck with Pete for the short term. As long as she made it clear to Chloe not to get overly fond of the man who wouldn't stick around long enough for Sarah to fall in love with him all over again.

THEY'D STAYED AT the small roadside eatery for almost two hours. Pete had soaked up every single second. His burger and fries tasted great. He'd convinced Sarah to let Chloe have a chocolate shake with her meal, and the three had split a large one. Sarah had dipped her fries into her chocolate shake just like she used to. Chloe told amusing stories about the horses and her friends from school. She reminded Pete of Sarah in all the best ways. All three of them enjoyed being outdoors, so they chose a picnic table under a tall oak tree.

Now, he rode in the passenger seat as Sarah drove back to Fern Hollow. He turned around and found Chloe asleep; her head rested against the rolled-up blanket that was butted up to the door.

“Is she sleeping?” Sarah asked.

“Yes.” He yawned. “I’m feeling a bit sleepy myself.”

“Go ahead and close your eyes.” Sarah glanced into the rearview mirror, then returned her gaze to the road. The two-lane road leading to Fern Hollow appeared quiet. A car would pass by every so often heading in the other direction. The sun was setting behind them, projecting light up onto the clouds above and turning the sky a brilliant orange, pink and purple.

“I’m not that tired.” He stifled another yawn. Today had not gone as planned. The fun hiking trip and night at the bar had turned into a hospital visit and dinner with Sarah and Chloe. Really, he liked this version better. Not that he’d admit it to Jacob.

“Does your wrist hurt?” she asked.

He shrugged and the motion jarred his wrist, causing a shock of pain. “Not much. I shouldn’t have climbed today. Especially wearing hiking boots.”

"You were always one to throw caution to the wind." She sighed. "You're lucky you didn't crack your head open."

He laughed. "Maybe a hard knock on the head would inject some sense in there."

"Doubtful if it hasn't happened already. Weren't you thrown from a horse on the ranch one summer while working with my grandad?"

Rubbing his head, he could almost feel the headache he'd suffered for a week after. "I hit my head good. Mr. C warned me not to try riding the mare until she had more time to settle. I figured I knew better since I'd been working with her for two weeks prior. That was the last time I didn't follow your grandad's instructions." Mr. Carmella had taken a skinny boy with too much attitude and taught him patience and empathy. Working with horses meant that Pete had to be still at times and wait for the horse to direct the course of action. While Pete's father had considered cleaning stalls and working with traumatized horses a waste of time, Pete wouldn't trade that period of his life for anything in the world.

"My grandad understood horses better than people. He's the reason I get up every day and try to make a difference. Even in the winter when the snow is deep and there's ice in the water buckets." Emotions threatened to overwhelm her as she reminisced about her grandad and how much she missed him. Tears welled in her eyes, and she quickly brushed them away. "I saw the new videos you posted and then looked through your page. You've got quite the following."

He shrugged and the motion jarred his wrist, causing a shock of pain. While building his platform over the past six years wasn't the most important work he'd accomplished, he did enjoy the creativity. "I wanted a way to document the places I've seen. It's fun to share my experiences with other people. And they loved the videos from the ranch. Animals capture people's attention every time."

"Well, thanks for sharing the rescue. I have some new followers due to you tagging our social media handle."

He was happy to help bring attention to her efforts. Glancing at her profile, he wished to capture this moment like a moonbeam in a bottle. An impossible fantasy but desired nonetheless. He'd missed her so much since he'd left Fern Hollow as a teenager on the brink of manhood.

"So tell me about what you've been up to." He needed a distraction from the ache in his wrist and the crushing pain of defeat in his chest. "Did you end up going to college? How did you and Mike meet? I'm sorry that you and Chloe had to go through losing him."

"Thanks. We've figured out a way to move forward without him." Her lips formed a sad smile. "Took a while. He was a great guy. I hired him to consult on a group of our apple trees that had a fungal infection. He gave us a successful treatment plan and asked me out before he left. I accepted after a few attempts. Anyway, he fell in love with the ranch and orchard. We fell in love with each other. I'm grateful to have Chloe to remember him."

His heart squeezed both with understanding of her pain and the knowledge she'd found love again. While he'd been engaged in an often dangerous and unpredictable career, Sarah had followed her calling within the security of her grandparents' ranch. "I wish I could have met him."

"He would have liked you, I'm sure." She adjusted the vent to blow directly on her face. "About college—I took a year off after graduation, then enrolled in the community college in the next town over. I finished in two years with an associate's degree in agriculture. Not exactly my parents' vision but better than nothing. After I lived with my grandparents for a while, Grandad asked me to work on the ranch and help manage the orchard at harvest time.

Of course I said yes and never left. Eventually, they grew older and it was nice to be there all the time and help out with daily chores around the house."

"Did they pass within a short time of one another?" He hated to continue bringing up unhappy memories but he really wanted to know everything about her.

"Grandad died about three months before Grandma. I don't think she wanted to carry on without him, and I couldn't fault her." After slowing, she put on the blinker and turned right onto another rural roadway. Headlight beams glowed against the pavement. The sky was growing darker by the minute with the setting of the sun. "My grandparents talked about you often."

"I should have kept in touch." Another wave of guilt crashed and dragged him under the water. Sarah's grandparents had been good to him. His actions, or lack thereof, gave testimony to his selfish nature.

"They understood. My parents, on the other hand, didn't mention you at all." She snorted a laugh that sounded devoid of humor. "I wish they would have stayed out of it and let me make my own decisions. Pete, I'm sorry I didn't take the time to talk with you before sending the annulment papers. That was awful of me and it wasn't right."

Moved by her words, he reached across and rested his hand on her arm. Touching her again brought a rush of emotions—love, sorrow, heartache. He'd never faulted her, only himself. Talking about what had happened between them had been top of mind since returning to Fern Hollow and now that the door was open, he struggled to step through. What if he said something that made things worse? "No one is to blame. Not even your parents." Though their harsh disapproval didn't help. "I wish things had turned out differently. Now, I only want you not to hate me." His throat tightened over the last part of the sentence.

She rested her hand over his. "I could never hate you, Pete. You were once my best friend."

A lump formed in his chest. He had feared she hated him but he'd never acknowledged the feeling. Not until this moment. Perhaps the path ahead for them wasn't as filled with danger as he'd imagined. With only a couple of days left in Fern Hollow, he'd make sure not to do anything to damage their friendship.

CHAPTER SIX

PETE RAN YESTERDAY'S call through his mind and then muttered under his breath. Four weeks. His new boss informed him that he'd have to wait at least four weeks before starting. Currently, he had no use of his left arm. If, in another month, he was able to lift at least twenty pounds, then he'd be cleared to start the onboarding period. He'd already completed his testing and initial training to join the department. But to fully perform his role, Pete would need a work release from the doctor. What to do now?

He stood on the front porch of Jacob's house and banged his right fist on the rail. Why did he climb that stupid rock? His impulsive act had delayed starting with his team. At least the Phoenix Police Department and SWAT team still wanted him. He'd have to tell his father. Eventually. Pete had ignored his father's calls and texts since arriving in Fern Hollow. In a few minutes, he'd drive with Jacob to the Carmella property for the wedding. As Pete was scheduled to leave tomorrow, he didn't have a lot of time to decide. Drive to Phoenix and rehab there? Sounded depressing. He'd only met a few people, all through his new job. They'd be busy—working. What about sticking around Fern Hollow? Was that wise given his complicated feelings for Sarah? She'd likely be relieved to see him go.

Jacob exited the house wearing a dark suit and a smile as big as the sky above. "It's time."

"Sure is." He patted his friend on the back. "You ready?"

"I was ready yesterday at rehearsal." Leaning against the rail, Jacob exhaled. "Is everything okay between you and Sarah? Last night, you both seemed uncomfortable around each other."

"We're fine," he reassured. "Only a little strange being together again. She was great bringing me home from the hospital. We had some time to talk and it's all good. I think we don't know now how to act given our history. I care about her but don't want to complicate her life. I'm sure her parents won't be thrilled to see me today."

"Tim and Emma will be polite. Don't worry. I'm happy you and Sarah had a chance to talk. It's been a long time coming." Jacob checked his watch. "We should get moving. I don't want to be late."

"I have one job and it's to get you to your bride on time." Pete clutched the car keys in his good hand. His other arm was supported in a sling with his wrist brace. Good thing he could drive with only one hand. "Let's go."

His stomach churned on the drive over. He wasn't nervous about standing up in the wedding or seeing Tim and Emma Carmella again. Being with Sarah on Thursday had been strained at first but the familiar comfort had returned. Today, he'd talk a little about his time in the army. Only the fun times. Where did they go next? Stay cordial and keep an emotional distance? Creep closer and hope not to get too close? His job might not have started as soon as he'd hoped but he was still leaving. Rebuilding their relationship long distance wouldn't work.

After a short drive, Pete pulled up next to the barn and dropped off the fidgety groom. "I'll park the truck. Go inside and don't peek at your bride. You'll see her soon enough." He found a spot on the gravel parking lot filled with other vehicles, then left the truck to head into the barn.

Sarah appeared out of a side door. She wore a long flowing dress the color of strawberries, and she looked just as fresh. Her red hair hung loose, and its wavy strands lifted with the breeze. The lipstick staining her lips was the same shade of red as her dress. "The suit fits. I'm not saying I doubted Jill…okay, I doubted Jill." She strolled over to meet him halfway. Her gaze assessed his formal wear. Or was she assessing him? Either way, she grinned. "The suit looks good. If I didn't know any better, I'd think it's new. The arm brace is a great accent piece."

Would she push him away if he leaned in to taste her delicious-looking lips? "I still liked the outfit at Blue Bar Outfitters better," he teased. "Though I'd steal the attention from the bride."

"We can't have that." She motioned for him to follow her to the wide double doors on the side of the barn. Both sides were slid open to provide a glimpse of the setup inside. Rows of white chairs filled the center space. Flowers and mossy green ribbon bows adorned the chairs and aisle space. Strands of white lights were swagged between ceiling beams, and candelabras on gold stands were filled with lit candles that provided a romantic atmosphere. Guests milled about, conversing in small groups. Their voices created a symphony.

At yesterday's rehearsal, the interior resembled its original purpose—a barn. Somehow, Sarah and her staff had transformed it into a magical place.

"You must have been busy late into the night. Everything looks great." He stepped inside and spun around to view the inside space in its entirety.

"I had a lot of help." Still, the expression on her face radiated satisfaction. "Helen, the event coordinator, takes care of most of the details."

"Don't sell yourself short. This is all you." He lowered his gaze and met her own, and his heart skipped a beat. The awareness in her eyes caught him off guard. She must have sensed how hard Pete was struggling to keep from kissing her in front of the wedding guests. Noticing Sarah's parents coming toward them, he cringed. Seeing them splashed cold water on any ideas of sweeping Sarah into his arms.

"There you are." Emma Carmella approached wearing a tight smile. "Will the ceremony start on time?"

"I expect it to." Sarah snuck Pete an apologetic frown. "Kay was dressed and ready the last time I checked. Jacob just arrived." As if on cue, the musicians played the first notes of a light instrumental melody. "Why don't you find a seat? We have about ten minutes until Kay walks down the aisle."

Tim held out his hand to Pete, and Pete accepted the handshake. "Good to see you again," Tim said. "Heard about your tumble."

"Nothing a little time won't fix." More time than what he'd prefer but he had to accept the reality that he'd be sidelined for at least a month.

"Tim, let's find a seat." Emma took hold of his arm and directed him toward an empty pair of chairs.

Sarah bit her lower lip. "They haven't changed. Well, my dad has mellowed out some but Mom is still as fiery as ever. They didn't approve of any of this." She waved her hand around the space. "Said I'd end up going bankrupt sticking so much money into an old rundown barn."

"You made the right call." Not that his opinion mattered but he'd share it regardless. "The community must appreciate having a place to gather and celebrate."

"You mean besides the old VFW Hall?"

"I'm sure it's still a contender." A woman wearing a headset waved at Sarah. "I'll let you get back to work." He watched her walk away with purpose in each step. Then he turned to see Emma Carmella watching him. He straightened, refusing to allow Sarah's mother to find another reason to disapprove. She had plenty already. A twinge of resentment pricked. Sarah's parents could have been more supportive of their daughter's choices. Then again, if Pete had a daughter and she'd run off with some boy to get married at the age of seventeen, he'd have felt the same anger—or even a wish to do the boy bodily harm. Guess Sarah's folks and his, for that matter, had been justifiably upset.

He went to find Jacob, who'd taken up pacing in a back room. Finally, they were notified the service was to begin. The groomsmen followed Jacob to the front, where they stood in line before a wide wisteria-covered arbor. Every seat was filled. When the music switched from classical to a tune more familiar to weddings, those in attendance stood. Three bridesmaids walked down the aisle, followed by an adorable flower girl and ring bearer. Kay appeared on the arm of her father. Pete glanced at Jacob, who was tearing up. The couple joined hands and the minister began.

During the recitation of vows, Pete's gaze wandered. He hadn't known he was searching for Sarah until he found her standing in the back. She appeared to be crying, with a tissue in hand dabbing at the corners of her eyes. Their gazes connected and for a moment, Pete was transported back in time. Instead of a barn he was in a cramped wedding chapel on the outskirts of Las Vegas. Neither had brought wedding clothes. Sarah wore a pink sundress and Pete a pair of nice jeans and a button-down shirt. He'd promised to love, honor and cherish Sarah until death.

For Jacob and Kay's reception, the event staff moved the chairs and arbor. Round tables filled the center area and a stage and dance floor took up the front of the barn. Since there was no head table per Kay's instructions, Pete found himself seated at what he dubbed the silver-hair table, placed between Mrs. Bryan, the baker of delicious chocolate doughnuts, and May Summers, who ran the town's outdoor movie theater.

"I found a projector that my late husband had stored in the attic." May continued on with the long-winded tale of how the movie theater came to be. "After I got permission, of course, I asked someone to slap white paint on one of the exterior sides of the school's gymnasium, found a used popcorn machine and old movie reels, and opened for business."

"Everyone loves going to movie night at May's Movies." Mrs. Bryan cut into her chicken breast. "It's the place to be in the summer. You should come sometime, Peter. Bring Sarah. She's such a busy girl and needs a break every now and then. May even has a few of the scary ones she loves."

Pete smiled at the memory of Sarah curled next to him on the sofa while *Frankenstein* or

Night of the Living Dead played. She couldn't get enough of the classic horror films.

May nodded her head in agreement. "She'll be even busier with the square dance coming up soon. I already picked out my outfit."

"Are you coming to the square dance?" Mrs. Bryan asked Pete. "It's always the Saturday after the Fourth of July. I have so much fun every year even though I don't dance like I used to."

"I wish I could but I'm leaving for Phoenix tomorrow." The look of dejection on both women's faces had him second-guessing his plans. He could stay. But staying came with problems. He'd already disrupted Sarah's life. And he'd made peace with her, which had been his goal in coming here.

"That's a shame." May tsk-tsked. "That means you'll miss the Splash and Dash Festival on the Fourth of July. Fern Hollow also has a Labor Day pie-eating contest, area church picnics, a giant maze made of hay bales in September, Lazy Days Apple Festival in early October, and Christmas Around the World Festival in December. Perhaps you could make one of those."

"Don't forget about the Daffodil Disco at the end of April and the Rhubarb 5k Race. That one we held only two weeks ago," May added. "There's stuff to do all year-round."

"They all sound like a lot of fun." He recalled a pamphlet left at the cabin his family had rented that listed every Fern Hollow festival and event. The list went on and on. "My new job is with a SWAT team in Phoenix. I don't know how much time I'll have to get away."

Mrs. Bryan set down her fork and knife with a clatter on her plate and patted Pete's hand. "Life is too short, dear, for that kind of attitude. You make time for the things you care about." She glanced at Sarah, who was inspecting the buffet line. "I know you care about her. It's written on your face."

"It's not that simple." He took a drink of ice water to cool the warmth building inside him. "Sarah's life is here. She has a great life. Mine is somewhere else."

"Why?" May asked. "Why can't it be here?"

Because it just can't. While he'd loved visiting Fern Hollow during summer vacations, Pete had never pictured his future here. A sleepy town tucked in a valley surrounded by mountains. It was in the middle of nowhere. The closest major city was a half day's drive. Another look at Sarah created a crack in his confidence. He caught a glimpse of a different future. One he dreamed about when alone at night, every once in a while.

NORMALLY, SARAH DIDN'T mix rescue and event work. During an event, she liked to keep her focus on providing the best service. But her animals didn't understand that she had something else going on, and their demands didn't run on a schedule. Thankfully, the event coordinator and staff had everything well in hand. Dinner was wrapping up and the band had taken the stage to set up for the dance. Milton had snuck in to report a foal had taken ill and he had a vet coming to check on it. After a quick glance at Mrs. Bryan, Milton slipped back out of the barn.

Earlier, she'd received an email about a gelding that had been found wandering alone in the countryside. No one knew how long he'd been out there, fending for himself. Likely abandoned, the horse was reported to be skinny and half wild. Of course, her immediate reaction was to reply that she'd take him in. Then her dad's words of caution rang in her head. If she wasn't careful, she'd lose the ranch.

Her gaze scanned the crowd until she found Pete. He'd moved from the table with Mrs. Bryan and Mrs. Summers to a group closer to his age. As Sarah watched the group of women surround Pete, a surge of possessiveness ran through her body, surprising her. Though she had no reason to be jealous. Pete was single, good-looking and successful. Of course women flocked to him. Certainly, he'd had relationships since her. She'd not only dated but married someone else. Still, witnessing the flirty banter left her with no appetite for a slice of the three-tiered wedding cake waiting to be cut.

She forced herself to move her view to Kay and Jacob, who couldn't look any happier or more in love than they did at that moment. Jacob had an arm wrapped around Kay's waist and squeezed her close. Sarah wished the best for them and that their story had a better ending than her own marriages. Every wedding she hosted in the Big Red Barn left her more set in her conviction not to marry again. Her wedding to Pete had been short and sweet, both the ceremony and length of the marriage. Mike had wanted a big affair. She'd wanted to keep it small. They'd said their vows on the outskirts of the apple orchard and then moved the party to open space by the barn for a cookout and dance—the first event she'd hosted at Carmella Ranch. It sparked the idea to renovate the barn and rent it out as an event space. Although everyone had told her the plan was reckless, Mike had believed in her. She wished he was here to see the results of their shared vision.

While her mind was distracted, her parents made an approach. They flanked her, Mom to her left and Dad on her right.

"Everything turned out well," her dad said. "Jacob's parents seem pleased."

"I'm happy if the newlyweds are happy." Sarah took a sip of water to wash down the panic she felt every time her parents tag-teamed her.

"The chicken could use a little more seasoning." Emma lifted her glass of wine as if to take a drink, then lowered it. "Pete's leaving tomorrow, right?"

"As far as I know." She hadn't heard otherwise. The reminder that tonight was the last time she'd see him dampened her mood. "Are you hoping he'll stick around?"

"Absolutely not." Emma shook her head. "The sooner he leaves, the better."

"You'll never forgive us for eloping, will you?" The question flew out before she could stop it. Anger loosened her tongue.

"We never blamed you." Her dad didn't meet Sarah's gaze. "Peter was a bad influence. You can't fault us for wanting to make sure he doesn't influence you again to make a poor decision."

"Oh, for crying out loud." How many times did she have to explain that the decision to elope was as much her idea as Pete's? "We ran away together—he didn't steal me at gunpoint. And we're both adults. Haven't you learned by now I am not easily influenced?"

"You're as stubborn as Giorgio was." Her mom huffed. "No wonder you bonded with that mule you have."

A laugh escaped. "Horace is a donkey, not a mule, and he bonded with Chloe, not me. So fair warning, your granddaughter may turn out even more stubborn than me."

"Great." Emma took a long drink of wine before waving down a friend. She must have had enough of Sarah for the moment.

"I didn't want to talk business at a wedding since it's bad manners," her dad said once her mom was out of earshot. "But I received an alert on the rescue nonprofit account that donations are coming in at a larger than average rate."

"Maybe someone asked for donations for a birthday or something?" Any extra funds were appreciated.

"Then they have many friends. We've received almost one hundred individual donations from people who visited the website. Most weren't large, only twenty-five or fifty dollars. A handful were larger. Did you do any advertising to drive up the website traffic?"

"Not recently." Every effort to promote the rescue only resulted in a splattering of donations. "Someone could have found the website and promoted it." Her breath caught in her chest. *Pete.* He'd shared videos of some of the ranch animals and tagged the rescue. He had a large following. Had people watched his videos, clicked on the link to the rescue, found their website and then been moved to donate? She didn't want to share her theory with her dad before she knew for sure. "How much?"

"As in money?" He appeared to do some mental calculations in his head. "Four thousand dollars, give or take. Whatever happened make sure it happens again." After patting her on the back, he walked away to join his wife over at a table of some of their friends.

Sarah stared at Pete. The influx of money was nice but wouldn't last. She'd have to thank him. Due to the donations, she had the funds to rescue the gelding.

After the cake cutting, the band started their first song, transitioning the gathering from dinner to dancing. Kay had found a band that specialized in old-school country music with a mix of seventies rock and roll tossed in every so often. Many of the guests took to the dance floor, including the bride and groom. Sarah stood to the side, tapping her foot on the floor to the beat of "Boot Scootin' Boogie."

Chloe twirled around in the crowd of dancers. She found Pete and pulled him in to join her. Pete did his best to keep up, but no adult could match the energy of a six-year-old. Finally, Chloe decided she needed a break and something to drink, leaving Pete to fend for himself.

He wove through the sea of dancing bodies until joining Sarah. "Why aren't you out there?" The voltage of his grin was stronger than the band's stage lights.

"It's my job to make sure everything goes smoothly. I can't do that if I'm dancing." She caught sight of Jacob spinning Kay in the center of the crowd.

"I don't think Jacob wants you to miss out on the fun." He laughed when five older ladies broke into a line dance. They tapped their heels and spun around like they were sixteen again.

"I'm not missing out." She studied him for a moment. "I'm glad you're having a good time."

"I don't attend many weddings but this has been great." Pete had shaved away most of his beard, leaving only dark stubble. Though he'd kept a mustache. His facial hair gave him the look of a cowboy too long on the trail. A hat, boots and dusty jeans would complete the look. "I'm happy I could be here for Jacob. I've enjoyed being able to see you again and talk."

Why did it feel like he was saying goodbye? Sadness wrapped around her, and she forced her face to show a happy expression. "I'm glad it worked out." While they'd talked about mostly superficial topics, the deeper hurts were left untouched. Too tender. For the best, really. She didn't want to revisit that dark and depressing time in her life.

"I wanted to thank you for the social media posts." A change of subject. The thought of Pete leaving was a mood killer and she didn't want to break into tears until after the wedding was over. "We've received a lot of donations. I really appreciate you featuring us for your followers. I received word of a gelding who was picked up wandering alone. He needs a place to get healthy again and recover. I didn't have the funds to cover the transport until these new donations."

"Great." His brown eyes crinkled in the corners with his grin. He'd aged well. "Some posts get more action than others. Your place is very interesting. You have a compelling story. And you do good work. A winning combination."

"I wish I had the time and talent to do what you do." She stepped to the side as the flower girl and ring bearer raced by on their way to the cake table.

"It took years to build the following I have now. I'm sure you can do the same with consistent content."

"I'd need to find someone to take the videos, edit and post them. Everyone is already busy the way it is." She sighed. "Maybe someday when life slows down."

"I doubt your life will slow down anytime soon." He stood quiet for a minute. The band switched to a slow song and many dancers left the floor, while couples replaced them. "Will you dance with me? I'm sure things won't fall apart if you enjoy one dance."

There were many reasons not to. Their history. The pain they'd caused one another. The strong feelings still lingering under the surface. The spicy scent of his cologne weakened her knees. Her parents were still here, watching. Yet, she found herself placing her hand in his and trailing along onto the dance floor. She'd enjoy the fleeting moment and then move on.

With his left arm in a sling, he wrapped his good arm around her waist, pressing the palm of his right hand against her side. "I've missed you, Sarah."

She rested her head on his chest and breathed him in. "I missed you too." Being close to Pete was like returning to a familiar place. He was sturdier than he'd been as a teenager. The prickly hair on his chin tickled the top of her head. Their bodies swayed with the gentle rhythm of the song.

"I found out I can't start in Phoenix until I'm released by a doctor, which won't be for at least another four weeks." He cleared his throat. "I could stay a little while longer and build more social media content. And help around the ranch as my bum arm allows. Only if you want me to. If you'd rather I didn't stick around, then I'll head south and hang out in the heat until I can start work."

Her head spun. Pete staying longer was her dream and nightmare combined. She already felt her heart slipping and he'd been here less than a week. What if she remembered all the reasons she'd loved him? In a month, he'd leave for a life she had no place in. The best thing for them both was that he left tomorrow. They could say goodbye tonight and be done.

Then she thought of the new donations Pete had helped bring in. And the gelding that needed rescue. And the many chores that needed doing every day—there were not enough hours in the day to see everything done. The apple trees would need to be sprayed soon. The square dance fundraiser was only a month away. Her daughter adored Pete.

Pete offered a lifeline. If she took it, she'd likely end up hurt. If she didn't, she was turning down the opportunity to gain attention for her rescue. Should she take advantage of the opportunity to keep Pete in her life a little longer? Sarah had survived a broken heart more than a time or two. Her animals' needs always came before her own.

Did she have any choice but to accept his offer?

CHAPTER SEVEN

"LET THE GELDING be someone else's problem." Her dad's booming voice bounced off the kitchen walls, which seemed to squeeze closer by the second. "Not every horse can be rescued."

Thanks for the support, Dad. Sarah lived with the guilt of the animals she hadn't been able to save. Some were too sick or broken by the time she arrived. Others slipped out of her hands due to people's disregard. But she always stepped in when she could. If she didn't have the money, she begged or borrowed. The gelding rescue was completely funded thanks to the recent donations.

"I'm leaving in a few hours to pick him up," she reminded him. "You're here to take Chloe with you overnight. It's not up for debate."

Tim stood at the counter by the sink and gazed out the window. "You're actually operating in the black for once and this uptick in donations will fizzle out. Take the new money and invest it. I have several stock market funds that are performing above average. You'll be further ahead in the long run than if you throw your money after every horse you come across."

Seated at the kitchen table, she opened up the Instagram app on her cell phone and checked Pete's page. Three more videos had uploaded since last night. He'd been busy. "I'm not interested in saving for the future. Not if it means I'm not fulfilling the mission of the ranch. The mission Grandad and Grandma started. Your parents. This is where you were born and raised, Dad. Doesn't that mean anything to you?"

"We never should have let you spend so much time with your grandparents," her mom piped in. Emma had been abnormally quiet since they'd arrived to pick up Chloe. Perhaps she figured their current battle was best fought by her accountant husband. "Instead of going to college and becoming a lawyer or businessperson, you spend your days with animals who show no gratitude."

"You're wrong. The animals show incredible appreciation. Not in the way humans do but in their own special way." Like a horse taking its muzzle and rubbing it against her cheek or one of her dogs rolling over for belly scratches. Sarah closed the app and set her phone on the table, breathing in and out in an extended rhythm. How many times had she discussed this same issue with her parents? At least a couple times a year since Mike died, they tried convincing her to sell the property and find a more stable career. Never going to happen.

"How much longer is Peter staying?" her mom asked.

Sarah braced for the final stop in her mom's train of thought. "I don't know." She refrained from shouting. "Pete isn't the monster you've made him out to be. Both of you have been unfair." She'd keep to herself what Pete was doing to help by getting the word out about the rescue. Her parents would only twist his efforts. Sarah opened her mouth to say more but Chloe entered the kitchen holding her duffel bag.

Her stuffed unicorn was tucked under her arm. "I'm ready. I have my swimsuit, pajamas, socks and underwear. Oh, and stuff to wear tomorrow."

"Good work, kid. You didn't even need me to help you pack." She took the duffel bag and performed a quick inspection just to make sure. "You even remembered to bring Grandpa's favorite game."

"Of course. We always play while Grandma makes dinner." Chloe zipped back up her bag and set it by the door. “I can’t wait to see the new horse tomorrow.”

“I’ll get home late tomorrow. Milton offered to be here to help me unload him into the paddock.” Going by the reports from the place the gelding was staying now, he wasn’t thrilled about being cooped up inside. He’d adjust. At one point, he’d lived on a farm or ranch. The recollection of regular meals and a soft bed would smooth the path back to domestication.

“If you get home too late tomorrow, let me know.” Her mom hooked the strap of her purse over her shoulder. “Chloe is more than welcome to stay another night.”

“Thanks.” Sarah walked them out. Her parents might be tough on her but they loved Chloe. Last summer, they’d put a fenced-in pool in their backyard for her to enjoy when staying. They watched her every time Sarah asked. Ultimately, it didn’t matter if they disapproved of Sarah’s choices, as long as they continued to love their granddaughter.

After Chloe was secure in the back seat of their car, Sarah knocked on the window. Her dad rolled it down so she could lean in and give Chloe one more kiss before they departed. Soon, the car was heading down the driveway, kicking up dust.

Time to get moving. She had an eight-hour

drive ahead. Tonight, she'd stay at a motel near the farm, then drive over to pick up the gelding first thing in the morning before making the return trip home.

A yapping sounded from the open barn door before a small brown dog darted out and made a mad dash for Sarah. "Hey, Snaggletooth." She bent over to pick up the Chihuahua, who wiggled in her grasp until the dog was able to freely lick Sarah's face. "Where's your dad?"

"Get over here, you rascal." Milton appeared running as fast as his bowlegs would carry him. Once he saw Sarah had hold of his dog, he halted. Panting, he leaned forward, resting his hands on his thighs. "Pete was taking some video of the dog sniffing around the barn and then Snaggle took off. Must have heard you nearby."

She kissed Snaggletooth on top of his furry head, then set him back down on all fours. The dog gazed up at her with his namesake bottom tooth sticking out past his mouth. Snaggletooth tilted his head and barked. "What's gotten in to you, mister?"

"He thinks he's a movie star now." Milton lifted the dog into the security of his arms. "I brought ol' Snaggy along 'cause I thought he'd add a certain charm to the videos."

"He most certainly does." She reached across

to give the small dog a scratch behind the ear. Milton often brought Snaggletooth to the ranch, not wanting to leave him home alone. The dog was older and spent most days snoozing on a hay bale. Today, he'd found a burst of energy.

"Is everything alright?" Pete strolled out of the barn, holding his cell phone. "Oh, hi," he greeted Sarah. "Just the person I need."

The sight of Pete still caught her by surprise, even though he'd been back in Fern Hollow for a week. Nothing like your teenage love to make you feel like you've stumbled into a time machine. "What do you need?" Hopefully there were no problems with his videos.

"I'd like to film some short clips of you telling the stories of a few of the horses. How they arrived and what you did to assist in their recovery." He gave her the same grin he had at sixteen when he'd convinced her to ditch her chores and go for a ride up into the mountain in his father's car.

She hadn't told him no back then. Surely she was made of stronger stuff now. "I'd rather not. I'm leaving soon to pick up a rescue gelding. Milton's back is still bothering him so I'm taking this one. It's an eight-hour drive there today and then back tomorrow."

"It's not that I can't, mind you." Milton shifted his weight back and forth between his legs. “Sarah likes a break from the ranch every once in a while. I won’t get in her way.”

“I’ll go with you, Sarah.” He accepted a wiggling Snaggletooth, who was attempting to move from Milton to Pete. “Shooting the videos won’t take long. We’ll do two horses, your pick. Then we can go.”

“You don’t even know where I’m going.” She huffed out a breath. No way would she spend sixteen hours alone in the truck with him. “And I’m staying overnight in a motel by the farm.”

“I’ll pay for my own room.” Pete set down the dog, who’d grown bored with their talk. The spry old Chihuahua sauntered back into the barn.

“It’s a good idea,” Milton interjected before following his dog.

“See.” Pete hooked his thumb over his shoulder in Milton’s direction. “The people who are coming to my social media page will grow bored and stop interacting if I don’t put up something fresh and compelling. You have the histories of every animal here, or at least how they came to you and their life since arriving. Plus, you are a pretty sight for the eyes.” He winked. “No offense to Milton.”

The nerve. Calling her pretty. His compliment did touch a neglected part of her that hadn’t heard that sort of thing from a man in a very long time. Her days on the ranch didn't require hairspray or makeup. She rarely dressed up in the anticipation of an event or church. Truth be told, it felt good to have someone notice her as something other than the horse lady. Even if that someone was Pete.

Her willpower slipped away drip by drip until there was nothing left. "We have thirty minutes. And if you're coming with me to pick up the horse, then you'll need to go back to Jacob's place to get a few things for the road. Are you sure you want to go? It's a long, boring trip."

"Not if I'm with you." His smile slipped as his gaze found her lips. Pete quickly recovered, clearing his throat. "With Jacob and Kay gone on their honeymoon, I'm in their house alone. I found a rental to use for the rest of the time I'm here but it's not open for another week."

So, he really planned on staying longer. There was a part of her that expected him to change his mind. She didn't know how to feel about Pete staying. Part of her wished he'd stick around forever despite the knowledge it would never happen. Mind switching to the present task, she considered what horses to feature. Of course, she had to start with her favorite girl. Sarah removed her ponytail holder and brushed her hair out with her fingers in an attempt to avoid looking like a crazy horse lady. "Black Beauty. I want to share her story."

THEY FOUND THE black Percheron mare out in one of the pastures next to the newly built stable. Black Beauty had to be twenty by now. Pete remembered when they'd brought her onto the ranch, close to death. There'd been no light in her eyes. When Sarah caught a glimpse of the unwell horse, she'd stopped everything and stayed with her morning and night for two weeks. At the age of fourteen, Sarah had nursed the horse back from the brink. It was witnessing Sarah's love and devotion to a helpless animal that had made him fall in love. He'd had feelings before that, but nothing like the certainty that he'd spend the rest of his life trying to make her happy.

Sarah walked through the field and then whistled. The tall black horse raised her head and then ran over to Sarah. Black Beauty was now a majestic animal. A queen among horses. When she reached Sarah, she neighed and bobbed her head.

"I'm happy to see you too, girl." She rubbed the side of the horse's large head. "How long should I talk for?"

After taking in the sight of the beautiful woman standing beside her horse, he almost forgot what he was doing out in the horse pasture. "Um…no more than three minutes. Introduce yourself and the horse, tell a short backstory of how she came into your care and maybe a fun fact about her."

"I can do that." She rested her palm on the side of the horse's face and squared her shoulders.

Pete made sure his phone was securely attached to the selfie stick. The little device came in extra handy now that he only had the use of one hand. After moving into the shot, he pressed Play and gave a quick introduction before stepping aside and giving Sarah the go-ahead.

As she spoke, he was taken back in time to when the mare had arrived at the ranch. Sarah had named her Black Beauty after one of her favorite not-scary movies. Pete would often find Sarah curled up in Beauty's stall, singing or speaking softly to her. Over the summer, the mare began to thrive, all thanks to Sarah's love. Pete had wanted to feel that same love directed at him. And so he'd vowed to win it from Sarah, even if it took him the entire next summer.

He recalled working with Giorgio during hot summer months, learning how to safely handle skittish horses. They had one chestnut mare that wouldn't allow anyone near her. Fern was her name. The farrier had insisted on a team of five to maintain control of her while he worked on her hooves. The vet made quick work on any shots or oral treatments. Pete had thought he could handle her alone, until she'd kicked him in the stomach. Fern taught him that patience was the best way of building trust and healing trauma. Some things couldn't be rushed. After a month of daily work, Fern had allowed him to stroke her mane. A small but significant triumph.

Mind back on the present, he focused on getting good videos. They got a usable recording after the first take. Not bad. "You have a future in front of the camera." Only if he was directing.

"I'll leave that to you." Sarah patted the horse's withers and released her to run back to a shady patch of field. "I have time for one more and then we need to get on the road."

"Sure. Who do you want to introduce to the world next?" He followed her into the barn to a long-legged foal, who huddled on a bed of straw at the back of a stall. The little fellow looked too small for the space.

"This is Sean." When the foal noticed Sarah approaching, it attempted to stand. She rushed over to sit beside him. "He was brought here after his mother passed away. He's being bottle-fed for now. We have an older mare with great mothering instincts. Milton has been keeping them together at night. Soon, Sean will join her in the pasture. If all goes well, he'll grow up under the protective care of his foster mom."

"He looks so little." Pete studied the foal, who appeared weak but bright-eyed.

Sarah leaned in to give the foal a kiss. "The vet believes he wasn't receiving adequate nutrition before coming here. His lack of appetite was likely due to depression." She had the look of understanding in her eyes. "He's eating well when the mare is nearby. I'm optimistic about his future."

Sarah had shared little about her sad spells. The fact he could do nothing to help her after they'd lost their baby had enraged him. His phone and computer times were limited. He'd relied on her parents, grandparents and Jacob to pass along information. His helplessness had led to frustration. Instead of sitting beside her, holding her hand, he'd been stuck on an army base. Why hadn't he come to her? His first opportunity arrived too late, the damage already done.

"Earth to Pete. Where did you go?" She snapped her fingers to get his attention.

He wouldn't admit how lost in the shadows of the past he often found himself since returning to Fern Hollow—and Sarah. "I was thinking of Sean's story. He's lucky to have found you."

"I'm lucky to have found him." Adjusting her legs so she sat crisscross-style, she continued caressing the foal. "My dad discourages me from taking on new rescues. He's concerned about finances. As the nonprofit's accountant, that's his job. Still, I don't want to be made to feel guilty about every rescue. If I stop taking in new horses, I don't fulfill our purpose."

He was not getting in the middle of a conflict between Sarah and her dad. Been there. Done that. "I'm sure you know what's best. Let's use the same format as we did with Black Beauty. Once we're done, then I'll head home to pack up a few things for the trip."

"Are you really sure you want to come along?"

No, he wasn't. At least his brain warned him to be cautious. Their relationship was in the past. He'd be content to be friends. They'd made the decision to move in separate directions many years ago. But his heart had a will of its own. His heart longed for a second chance. Sarah had been the *one*. Deep inside, he still believed that to be true.

AFTER DRIVING FOR the first two hours, Sarah switched spots with Pete. He'd insisted he could drive perfectly fine with only his right hand, and he still had the function of his left if needed.

While she had driven, he'd edited the videos he'd taken that morning and posted them. Currently, from her view in the passenger's seat, she judged that he managed the truck and trailer fine. And a break was appreciated. The last time she made a trip this long had been right after Mike's death. Word had come in of a horse that was about to be put down due to an injured leg. Sarah had found that unacceptable and left Chloe with her parents to drive ten hours to pick up the horse and then ten hours straight back. She'd used those long hours on the road to ponder the loss of Mike and what her and Chloe's future looked like without him. The journey had kick-started her healing. After returning, she'd thrown herself into working with the new rescue. Now, she recognized her manic drive as an escape mechanism. Back then, she'd only focused on surviving.

They stopped for lunch in a town not much larger than Fern Hollow. With its location next to the freeway, the town felt like more of a place to pass through than one to build a life in. After a quick bite to eat, they hit the road again. Pete offered to drive a while farther, and Sarah happily let him.

Pete shared more stories of his travels and some of the unclassified adventures he'd had. While he spoke, Sarah silently questioned what her life would have looked like if she hadn't lost the baby and they'd stayed together. Would they have lasted? How would she have handled her husband being sent away for months on end, deployed in dangerous areas, with limited communication? Probably not well. After consideration, she didn't regard herself as the type of wife who'd be content to carry on as normal without her husband home most of the time. Her marriage to Mike, who'd slept at home almost every night of their marriage, had helped her understand her need for stability. Traveling with Pete would have been fun for a while, until it wasn't. Sarah's place was in Fern Hollow at the Carmella Ranch and Orchard. She'd never leave and planned to be buried on the property in the small fenced-in plot that held her grandparents' graves.

Sarah took over driving for the last stretch of the trip, pulling into the parking lot of a small roadside motel in the early evening. She went into the office area with Pete and they paid for two rooms, one night each. Tomorrow, they'd be up early to make the thirty-minute drive to the farm and collect the gelding. Then they'd start on their journey back home.

"What do you want to do for dinner?" Sarah asked. They stood outside the doors to their rooms, and she glanced around at the nearby options. Not much. A greasy spoon diner was located on the other side of the parking lot. Her stomach rolled at the thought of eating anything prepared in there. She'd munched on too many salty and sweet snacks during the drive to have much of an appetite. What she needed was something healthy. A banana or an apple. *Good luck finding that around here.*

"I can take a walk and see if there's anything more down that way." Pete pointed toward the road that supposedly led into town.

"I'll come with you." Her legs could use a good stretching.

An hour later, she returned to the motel with Pete, more tired and hungry than when she'd left. Every business in town closed by six p.m., including the nearby diner. That was early even by Fern Hollow standards.

"I think I saw a vending machine around the corner," Pete said. He was clearly trying to stay optimistic.

Unlike Sarah, who'd grumbled more in the past thirty minutes than during her entire adult life. "Let's see what the vending machine has stocked. I wouldn't mind sitting outside and eating." The air was still pleasantly warm. A couple of round tables and chairs were set up around what had been the motel's in-ground pool at some point. Now, it sat as an empty hole filled with the memories of family vacations and laughing children.

From the vending machine, she selected a bottle of root beer, a bag of trail mix and a candy bar. She'd eat healthy tomorrow. Pete made his purchases—three bags of chips and a water. They selected the cleanest of the patio tables, then settled in.

She twisted off the top of her drink and took a long sip. The cold soda refreshed her dry mouth and throat. "Living the good life."

Holding up his bottle of water, he tipped it toward her in a toast. "I've learned to enjoy simple times like this. Eatable food, good company and fresh air."

"And no bombs or gunfire," she added.

"Always a plus." His grin disappeared. He tightened his jaw and closed his eyes for a brief moment. "Sarah, I've really enjoyed today and it's been great reconnecting. It's nice to know you still have a soft spot for old scary movies and junk food. There's something I need to get off my chest."

Discomfort pricked her gut. She sensed Pete was heading somewhere she didn't want to go. Taking another drink, she prepared herself. The impending conversation was like an approaching tornado. Sirens blared a warning to run and hide. Should she stop him here or brace for impact?

"I want to talk about what happened." He kept his gaze fixed on the side of the empty pool. Weeds had sprouted up through the cracks in the cement. Life always found a way to push through. "Our baby. The annulment. We never had a chance to make peace with everything that happened."

The tornado in the form of Pete hit hard. It picked her up and threw her into the air. Sharp pain poked the inside of her skull. She didn't want to talk about any of those things with him. She'd locked it all inside her and hid the key. "I've made peace with it."

"Well, I'm glad for you. I haven't." His voice held a hint of temper. "I lost a child, too. I never got to say goodbye."

Her stomach fell. The shadows that haunted her in the months following the loss of her baby waited on the edges with fangs bared. They crept closer and threatened to swallow her whole. "That wasn't my fault." Pete had been the one who didn't come back. He decided his military commitment was greater than her.

"I never said it was." He shoved a hand through his hair. "All I'm asking is to take some time while it's just the two of us to talk about the things in our past that really matter. So far, we've discussed my time in the Army, your work on the ranch, and Mike and Chloe."

"You asked about Mike." She straightened in the chair. Her defenses jumped into action. "He was a good husband to me." Mike had truly loved her. His leaving wasn't a choice.

"And I wasn't a good husband, right? You don't think I know that?"

"I'm not doing this." Her stomach rolled, and bile rose in her throat. The little food she had eaten threatened to heave. She stood to leave but Pete grasped her forearm.

"We *need* to do this. I don't want to go on acting like what happened between us wasn't a big deal. I was devastated when I found out about the baby. I tried to get back to you but my command wouldn't let me. They even locked me up for a few days until I settled down." He swiped his hand under his eyes. "Sarah, I didn't know what to do. What to say. You barely spoke during our phone calls. I felt you slipping away and there was nothing I could do. By the time I received the annulment papers, I'd lost my will to fight. That's something I regret every day. I should have fought."

She stood frozen, unsure if she should engage or run. The news he'd tried to come home felt unreal. Why hadn't he mentioned his efforts when her world had been falling apart? During that time, hadn't she made mistakes as well? Forgive and forget. "I'm not sure what you're hoping to accomplish by bringing up hurts of the past. It can't be changed. Talking isn't going to make me feel better about losing a child." *And losing you.* "What happened between us served a purpose." She made the mistake of gazing down at him, and her heart squeezed at the sight of his face and his body crumpled in obvious pain. *Stay strong.* She'd recovered from her relationship with Pete and she couldn't go back.

"I have a right to know what happened." Pete's voice cracked. "I never got to see my little boy."

Panic blinded her. Suddenly, she was back in the hospital with bright lights and nurses coming in and out of the room. Her mom trying to console her. Then she went home to a place that felt as if she was a stranger in a foreign country. She'd been surrounded by love but had felt alone. Because Pete wasn't there. He was thousands of miles away. And he never returned to her—until twelve years after the time that she'd needed him most. "I can't do this." She pulled her arm out of Pete's hold and ran back to her room. After slamming closed the door, she remembered her food and drink were still on the table. No matter. She'd lost her appetite. Her greatest fear since Pete's return had manifested into reality. Sarah tried blocking out Pete's pleading words from her head but they haunted her throughout her restless night.

CHAPTER EIGHT

PETE SHOULDN'T HAVE PUSHED. Instead of the meaningful conversation he'd wanted, Sarah had shut him out. He had apologized to Sarah when they'd left the motel that morning. The entire ride home from the farm, he'd beaten himself up. Why bring up Mike? Her late husband had nothing to do with his relationship with Sarah, yet Pete held some insecurities regarding him. Mike had had the loving marriage Pete dreamed of. Would Pete and Sarah be able to have a deep discussion of their past and find a way to be comfortable going forward? He wasn't hopeful.

She'd barely spoken to him. While at the farm, she'd conversed with the couple who'd temporarily taken in the horse. The gelding had been spotted on and off in the area for almost a year. Finally, someone had captured him and brought him to safety. Now, Sarah offered him a home.

It was five o'clock by the time they pulled onto the stretch of road that led to the driveway of Carmella Ranch. Rows of apple trees stood in lines with branches extended, as if welcoming him back. Sarah backed up the trailer to the entrance of an individual quarantine paddock where a small crew waited. There, the gelding could decompress and receive a good meal.

Milton came over to the side of the truck as Pete was getting out. "Y'all made good time."

"There were no issues on the drive home." Unless he counted Sarah icing him out. That was his problem alone. "Do you need a hand?" Anything to keep his mind off his failures.

"I have a couple guys here to help. Why don't you and Sarah take a break. Get something to eat and drink. I'll holler if I need you." Milton walked toward three others who hovered around the trailer, all peering in.

Two of them he recognized as teenage boys who worked part-time on the ranch, helping with the horses. The other man Pete had seen at Jacob's wedding but they hadn't been introduced. He approached the group and caught a glimpse of the horse inside, who snorted and swung his head.

"This should be fun," the man said. "Caleb Dearborn." He held out his hand.

"Peter O'Keefe. You were at Jacob's wedding, right?" Pete shook the man's hand.

"Yes. I've known Sarah and Jacob since preschool. I remember you from when you visited in the summers. A group of us kids would hang out at the park or ice cream shop."

Images flashed in Pete's mind. Caleb's face did look familiar. "Right. You played football. How do you spend your time now?"

"When I'm not helping Sarah and Milton out, I'm a county deputy." Caleb glanced to the side and pointed to a boy seated on top of a picnic table. His slouched appearance and glum face gave the impression he wanted to be anywhere but here. "I'm watching my nephew for a few weeks while his mom takes some time to straighten out her life. Or at least that's how she put it. He's staying with me for the time being. I thought he'd like coming to see the horses. I guess not." Caleb shrugged.

"I made that same face a lot growing up." Pete took another look at the horse before stepping away from the trailer. The pounding inside sounded like the horse was attempting to kick his way to freedom. "Your nephew will come around. Probably even before you leave the ranch tonight. It's good to see you again. I should see if Sarah needs anything." Likely not.

He went to her anyway, preparing to be told to leave and never come back.

"We can handle him," Milton told Sarah. "Everyone knows what they're doing and we'll take it slow."

"Make sure the fences are secure and the gate is shut once he's out. I don't want him trying to escape." Sarah blew out a breath. "Call me if you need me. I'll go inside the house and grab a drink." She caught sight of Pete and stiffened. "I need to talk with you before you go."

He followed her toward the back door of the house, then waited while she went inside to grab something. With keys in her hand, she headed to the garage.

"Sarah, I'm sorry." His entire body ached. Not with physical exhaustion but emotional fatigue. He couldn't lose her again. Not like this. "I hate you're upset."

An old golf cart sat in the garage. Sarah pointed to it and told him to get on.

He sat, then hung on to the side as she drove the cart down a narrow dirt path. Finally, an iron fence came into view.

She stopped before getting off. Motioning for him to join her by the gate, she waited, then grasped his hand. "You were right to push me to open up. I'm sorry for not taking your feelings into account. Can I explain?"

"Of course." His heart missed a few beats when he noticed a trio of headstones inside the fenced-in area. The thin branches of a weeping willow hung over the fence and touched the ground, creating a striking backdrop for the headstones. "But you don't have to apologize. I was out of line last night."

"Shhh." She pressed a finger to his lips. "Let me talk."

Pete nodded, anticipating and fearing what came next. He'd wanted to discuss their past but also dreaded the consequences.

"I'll be right back." She hurried to the golf cart, grabbed a blanket and then returned to where he stood. After opening the gate, she motioned for him to enter.

Placed inside was a bench surrounded by a flower garden. Toward the rear resided two larger headstones and a smaller one set to one side. A bouquet of daisies was assembled inside a glass vase. Sarah laid out the blanket on the ground, her gaze fixed on the small stone.

Pete studied the object, and his heart stopped. He'd often wondered. *Now I know.*

"I named him Tyler. Tyler Carmella O'Keefe." A sad smile lifted the corners of her mouth. "I'm sorry I didn't take you here earlier."

"I haven't exactly been around." He rested a hand over hers and absorbed the warmth of her skin. The contact grounded him when his emotions threatened to wash him away.

"No, you haven't. And that's mostly my fault. I shouldn't have shut you out. You didn't deserve the way I ended things."

"We both have regrets." He didn't hold anything against her. But now, sitting at the grave of his little baby, a new awareness overtook him. It had taken him over a decade for this moment—far too long.

"Last night, when you asked to talk about things deeper than where I went to college or my horses, I panicked. I worked so hard to block out the feelings that overwhelmed me back then. I was afraid if I revisited those memories with you, I'd regress into that eighteen-year-old girl whose life had just fallen apart."

"I never meant to hurt you." Tears burned his eyes, and his vision grew blurry. "But ignoring reality isn't healthy."

"I know." Seated on the blanket, she tipped back her head, gazing up into the sky. The clear blue of earlier had been replaced by a mass of clouds, some the fluffy white type and some gray that hinted of rain. "You're right. We do need to talk about it. Hiding won't solve anything. I know you're leaving soon and who knows if our paths will cross again but it's time to heal the damage done."

His chest expanded with affection and loyalty. He didn't want to think about leaving. The fall and subsequent fracture had been a gift. The frustration he'd felt over not being able to start his job in Phoenix had given way to gratitude for the extended time with Sarah.

"I know we were both excited when I found out I was pregnant. Then I was six months along when it happened, as you know," she said. "It was horrible. I was in so much pain. After I got home, I couldn't get out of bed. My body only wanted to sleep. My grandparents, bless them, did what I couldn't. Years before I was born, they'd fenced off this area and set it aside for when they passed. My grandma and grandad brought the baby to the land and placed him here with a little headstone. I didn't visit for almost a year. I couldn't bring myself to acknowledge what I'd lost. I was depressed and angry, and when my parents pushed for me to annul our marriage on the grounds that I wasn't of legal age, I didn't have the will to fight."

When Sarah had told him that she was pregnant, he'd been both scared and excited. They'd talked on the phone about what a future would look like as parents. They never made it that far. A gentle breeze blew strands of her auburn hair across her face, and Pete brushed them away, then ran his hand down her hair and stroked her back.

"I should have talked to you first but I was mad you weren't with me. I felt abandoned and that you picked the Army over me. I know it's not the truth but tell that to a young woman whose chest has been ripped out."

"I tried to get leave." He'd been in South Carolina at the time, preparing to travel to Germany and start more specialized training. "I didn't have the freedom to choose."

"I know that now." She rested her head on his shoulder. "But why didn't you fight the annulment?"

"I'm not sure," he replied honestly. "I was young and hurt." Just like Sarah had been. Not a combination that resulted in wise decisions. "I heard about the miscarriage from your grandma, and then every time I called you barely said two words. Now I understand you were depressed but back then I assumed you didn't love me anymore."

"I did love you." Sarah sniffled. "I loved you so much it broke me."

"Oh, honey." He kissed the top of her head. "I'm so sorry."

"No more apologies." She lifted her head and shook out her hair. "We could spend all night going back and forth, saying we're sorry for slights of the past."

True. Still, if she wanted him to apologize every day until he died, he'd do it.

"When I finally came to visit him—" she pointed to the small stone "—my grandparents came with me. They helped get me through seeing his little grave for the first time. I'd moved in with them since my relationship with my parents had grown toxic after everything that happened. My grandad, as you know, could be gentle but firm. He treated me with care, like one of his wounded horses. And finally, with enough prodding, I started working with the animals again and helping on the ranch. As the years went by I felt more stable and that my future was tied to the ranch. I stopped mourning for what could have been and began dreaming of the future and looking ahead to make the ranch better."

"You've done an amazing job." Pete knew in his heart that she had ended up exactly where she needed to be. Not as an army wife but a horse girl living her mission.

"I've had a lot of help." Her smile appeared full and free of grief. "When Mike came along, I had no interest in dating. He eventually wore me down. When we were married, I thought *this is it*. I know who I'm spending the rest of my life with. Mike was part of every aspect of my life for five years. And when he died, he took a piece of my heart with him." She pressed her hand over her heart as if needing reassurance the organ was still beating inside her chest.

He sat quietly, at a loss for words. No jealousy arose for the man who'd loved Sarah and won her heart. He'd wanted her to be happy. If that was with another man, so be it. But now close beside her and hearing the sorrow in her voice, he felt helpless to take it away. If only he could make her happy, like he had when they were young. Instead, Pete had nothing to offer other than the time he had left with her. Was that enough?

SARAH DRIED HER TEARS, willing herself to lock away her sadness. During the drive home today, she'd had a lot of time to think—about her past and how she often ran away from uncomfortable memories. Pete had been right to confront the issues between them instead of spinning around them like dancers doing a reel. The avoidance on her part had been for self-preservation. She'd been over the moon when she learned she was pregnant two months after Pete left. Her and Pete's little family would grow sooner than expected. Then tragedy struck. Remembering the miscarriage hurt like a knife stabbing into her chest. It had taken her years to put away the painful feelings and move on. Now having told Pete the complete story, she felt a weight lift off her shoulders.

She thought then of Mike and everything good he'd brought into her life. Her missing him would never go away but it had faded a little. His presence was still at the ranch, and she saw his smile each time Chloe grinned.

Turning her attention back to Pete, she studied his face. It was handsome and familiar. His mustache reminded her of the one her grandad sported for many years. While Grandad's had turned gray, Pete's facial hair remained dark. Someday, his hair would turn silver as well. Where would he be then? Who would he be with? At some point, would he settle down and make peace with a quiet life, or would his reckless streak always remain?

"Do you want some time alone?" She tipped her head at the tiny grave marker. Another gift she was thankful to her grandparents for.

"No." He held her hand and studied the stone. Engraved on its surface was the baby's name and a date.

Sarah came here once a week and placed flowers in the vase by the graves. The act was her way of honoring their memories.

"I should have come back." Pete exhaled.

"The next time I had leave, I should have come to you."

"That's water under the bridge. Pete, we were so young. Do you ever think about that?" she asked. "I look at some of the teenagers I have working at the ranch and I'm amazed at how young they are. And those boys do the craziest things. Not while working, but I hear some of the stories they tell one another. Driving too fast. Staying out too late. Breaking up with a girl only to ask someone different out the following day."

He laughed. "Sounds about right."

"I know. Think about all we went through when we were that age. The bad decisions we made. My parents pressured me to annul the marriage, and I didn't have the self-determination to go against them." While they'd approved of Mike, her mom and dad had never liked Pete, even before she and Pete had started dating. Running away with their only child to marry in Las Vegas didn't endear him to them. Quite the opposite.

"I don't blame you." He squeezed her hand. "By the time I had completed my last tour with the Army, I felt like the old man on the team. The guys joining up were babies, or at least that's how I thought of them."

"That was what we were. Children having to

make very adult decisions." Her gaze dipped to his lips, and she wondered if his mustache hairs would prick her lips if they kissed. She had to stop thinking about kissing him. Being with Pete at the burial plot overwhelmed her emotions.

"I have a deal for you." He scooted closer on the blanket. "Let's promise to only talk about the present and the future. No more rehashing the past. Let's leave it here. I don't want us to spend my remaining time in Fern Hollow reminding one another of the ways we hurt each other. We made some good memories together too—don't get me wrong. But I'd rather get to know who Sarah Carmella is now. What do you dream about? Where do you see yourself in twenty years? Are there any new movies you've seen?"

"That's easy. I'll still be at the ranch in twenty years. Hopefully it will have grown. And I don't like the movies made these days. The least old one I've seen recently is *The Princess Bride*." Pete would make a dashing Dread Pirate Roberts. "I'd like to get to know the current Pete O'Keefe. You can tell me about your new job and things you're looking forward to. Where do you see yourself in twenty years? Are you still good at Scrabble?"

"Deal. I'm great at Scrabble and challenge

you to a game before I leave." He leaned in, placing his face inches from hers. His breath smelled like mint. "The last time I watched *The Princess Bride* was when we crashed at Jacob's house for movie night."

Closing her eyes, she struggled to battle her willpower. He'd hurt her again if she let him in. She didn't want a romance with Pete or anyone else for that matter.

Decision made, she opened her eyes to find Pete staring at her with a look of uncertainty. Sarah inclined her head slightly, willing to meet him halfway.

He cupped his right hand behind her head and pressed his lips to hers in the sweetest kiss. For a second, she flashed back to the teenager who'd fallen in love with Pete the first time they'd kissed. They'd snuck away on horseback into the orchards for a picnic lunch. Their first kiss had been awkward and shy, but Sarah had felt certain her future would be filled with Pete.

As she leaned in closer to him now, her mind moved to the present. Her feet stayed firmly planted in reality. She was with a man changed from the boy she'd known. He was different yet still the same. His whiskers did prickle her upper lip like she'd expected. If she wasn't careful, the moment would sweep her away. She pulled back and stared into his eyes. Their kiss didn't change anything, yet she struggled not to question what came next.

"Your lips are as soft as I remember." He brushed the side of her face with his palm, its rough surface a contrast on her skin.

"I feel young again." Her grin hid a growing concern. She couldn't allow herself to make the same mistakes. Not with the responsibility of running the ranch and parenting her daughter. Sarah understood Pete wasn't long-term. She'd enjoy spending time with him while he was here. She'd take advantage of his social media savvy to help raise exposure and funds for the rescue. And then he'd say goodbye and she'd be fine. Or at least that was what she was trying to convince herself.

"Thank you for bringing me here and sharing what you went through." His gaze focused on the small grave marker. "I think about him a lot. Who he would have been. What he would have enjoyed doing. I have a sense of peace now, knowing where he is." Tears streamed down his cheeks.

Instantly, Sarah wrapped him in a hug. Although she'd cried at this spot many times, she joined Pete in their shared sorrow. The act was healing. It stitched up a wound that had been ripped open for a long time. The scar was still there but it ached less.

"I'm glad you pushed me back at the motel. I owed you more." More of herself and the emotions she'd learned to hide.

He stood, then pulled her up using his one good arm. "How do you think they're doing with the new horse?"

"Milton has it under control." She trusted only a few people with her horses and Milton was at the top of the list. "But I won't be surprised if someone didn't listen and got kicked."

Pete shuddered. "I remember not listening to your grandad and getting kicked many times. Once, an ornery gelding popped me on the knee, and I walked with a limp for weeks. I'd like to say I learned my lesson after that but unfortunately I'm hardheaded. If memory serves, it wasn't long after the knee injury that I was thrown off a horse that Giorgio told me to stay away from."

"Are you better now at listening to the wisdom of others?" she asked.

"If I wasn't, I wouldn't have survived combat." He took her hand and threaded his fingers through her own. Inclining his head, Pete brushed his lips across her cheek. "Can we enjoy the days ahead of us without becoming stuck in the past or worrying about the future?"

She could promise neither. Not worrying about the future and how her actions could impact others wasn't in her nature. Her impulsive act of running away with Pete had started a domino effect of negative consequences. It had taken her years to pick up all the pieces and put them away neatly in a box. Ever since, she played it safe. Nothing was done without deliberation. Before deciding to marry Mike, she'd weighed the pros and cons. She woke each day with a list of tasks. She operated with intention toward her goals. So she'd use the same mindset while Pete was in Fern Hollow. She'd appreciate him as an old friend but not grow attached. That way when he left, she'd move on without a bump in her carefully planned life.

"Sure. I'm game." She opened the gate and exited the fenced plot. When she closed and secured the latch, she did the same for her heart. Unfortunately, there was no padlock strong enough to completely withstand the charm of Peter O'Keefe.

CHAPTER NINE

EVERY DAY FOR the last week, Sarah watched the numbers in the rescue's account tick up like the jackpot in a lottery with no weekly winner. If only she'd take in millions of dollars like the lottery handed out. The increase was due to Pete's social media work. He not only posted on his own page with a link to the rescue but he'd logged in to the uninspiring Carmella Ranch and Orchard accounts and transformed them with engaging content. She was growing dependent on his skill, and she couldn't allow reliance on Pete—for anything.

In a little over two weeks, the new content would dry up due to his departure. Unless she found someone else to take over. The younger guys working for her had already expressed their disinterest. Most rarely used social media themselves. They preferred doing anything outdoors versus staring at a screen, which she respected as she felt the same.

Milton had a flip phone and no interest in furthering his technological skills. Basically, that left Sarah to carry on Pete's work or at least try her best. She'd observed how he took the video and added commentary. He sometimes appeared in them himself or had a ranch hand tell a story about the animal featured or even share something about themselves. Pete twisted Sarah's arm every other day for her to go in front of the camera. He insisted the public needed a better understanding of the person behind the mission, and he was right. She simply hated feeling the pressure of being watched by both Pete and the world.

The next video Pete asked to make featured a pony named Dandelion, who'd arrived three years ago and had quickly made friends with the larger horses and Horace. Chloe loved Dandelion, and Sarah had briefly considered allowing her daughter to be in the clip. Realizing she'd have no control over who saw Chloe's image, she decided to let her daughter talk in the background but not appear on-screen.

"Chloe," she yelled upstairs. "Time to go find Pete and Dandelion."

"Coming." The reply was loud and bright. Chloe was home during the day this week as her parents had taken a trip to Seattle for shopping and sightseeing. She bounded down the stairs and skidded to a halt in the kitchen.

"What have I told you about running down the stairs? You're going to fall if you don't listen." The reprimand reminded her of Pete, which brought a smile to her lips. "The stairs at home are not like the ones at Grandma and Grandpa's house."

"Sorry." She slipped on her rubber boots. Such a little horse girl already. Would Chloe want to take over the ranch someday? That remained to be seen, and the choice would be hers alone. With her boots on, Chloe flung open the screen door and burst outside like a sunbeam.

Sarah followed at a slower pace. When she started each day, she took the first few minutes outside to be grateful. Today, she was thankful for the rain overnight that watered the earth, the sound of her daughter's singing, the view of her pasture draped in morning fog, and Pete. He strode out of the barn, waving at Chloe. Never in a million years would she have believed Pete would blend into their life so effortlessly. That he'd even be here at the ranch for that matter. Yet, he arrived every morning and asked either Sarah or Milton what tasks needed doing. Even with the use of only one arm, he proved helpful. He'd learned from the best horseman, her grandad, who'd been able to train a horse with words and soft physical guidance. Grandad had a natural ability to understand the needs of each horse and not push it over its limits.

"There's the world's newest social media star." Pete met Sarah by the gate leading to a pasture. "You look very bright-eyed this morning. Sleep well?"

"I did but the two cups of coffee I drank are helping." She opened the gate for Chloe, who sprang inside and ran straight for Horace—the donkey was waiting for her with his big red ball.

"I still can't believe that donkey plays kickball with her." He shook his head. "Horace has been braying and pacing around since I got here."

"You don't have to come so early. I do have other ranch workers who feed and let the horses out to pasture."

"I know. It's a good routine." He closed the gate, then leaned against the railing with his forearms. "I need a routine. And I like staying active. Waking up early, grabbing a bite to eat, then heading over here is good for me." His rental home was only a five-minute drive from the ranch. Most days, if the weather was nice, he walked over.

"Well, I'm not complaining. The other workers are going to be sad to see you go." Her throat tightened after she spoke. While she knew he wasn't sticking around, thinking about the morning she'd come outside and he wouldn't be here left a touch of panic. She'd remain strong. She'd be fine. "Will your new job come with a strict schedule?"

"Sort of." He adjusted the brim of his cowboy hat. Pete made a good-looking cowboy. "I'll start off with the Phoenix Police Department to learn and understand their structure and rules. That will be a Monday through Friday schedule. Then I'll move to training directly with the SWAT team. It will be a process to find out where I fit in an existing team. SWAT teams are used to being called at all hours, any day of the week. The rhythm will be similar to when I was deployed in a war zone. You train all the time and so you're ready when the call comes in to activate."

"Sounds intense and dangerous." She nudged him with her elbow. "You know, you don't have to jump off the tops of buildings or bust through a door to make a difference."

He chuckled. "I know. My back is telling me the same thing. I can't get my father's voice out of my head, telling me to push harder and not take the easy road. He wasn't in favor of my leaving the army. The SWAT job is something he's learned to accept. 'You'll need to make a name for yourself all over again,' he said. It's hard not to compare myself to Chris, a navy fighter pilot who receives a hero's welcome everywhere he goes."

"Is your father's approval still that important?" Empathy toned down the judgment in her voice. Even as a teenager, Pete had borne the weight of his father's expectations. His older brother had blazed a path many couldn't compete with. Not even someone as amazing as Pete.

"I have no expectation of love. His approval is all he offers." He scratched at a spot on the back of his neck. In the distance, Chloe kicked the ball to Horace. The girl's giggle floated in the breeze. "Dad was always a tough nut, as you know. But when Mom died a while back, he lost any warmth that may have hidden inside."

"I'm sorry to hear about your mom." Sarah had liked Mrs. O'Keefe. She'd always welcomed Sarah into their vacation home and treated her kindly. "Her death must have been hard on you all."

"It was. I came home for the funeral and so did Chris. But my father." He snorted. "You would have thought it was just another day. He didn't deserve her, and I don't know why she stuck with him for so many years."

Sarah didn't know what to say. Yes, Mrs. O'Keefe could have left her husband and built her own life. But having children made the decision to leave more difficult. "She loved you and Chris. The fact she brought you to Fern Hollow every summer proved that. She wanted family time and to take you away from the city for a while. Spending that time together made her happy."

"She was very happy here." His smile appeared full of memories. "I think she would have lived here year-round if she could. She enjoyed visiting the ranch and feeding apples to the horses. I'm glad she's at peace now."

Sarah rested her hand on top of Pete's. They stood watching Chloe and Horace kick the ball back and forth.

Pete pulled out his cell phone and read something on the screen. He frowned while closing the texting app.

"Not good news?" she asked.

"Only my father is wondering when I'm leaving for Phoenix. His contract with the Department of Defense hasn't been renewed yet, which means he has free time on his hands. That's never a good thing."

"He's still consulting?" Pete's father was a military man in his blood. While his body could no longer perform the tasks needed of an officer, his mind was still sharp and filled with knowledge.

"He is. Still in California, working with the

Navy on their special operations training." He inhaled deeply. "I don't know what he'll do with himself if they don't renew his contract."

"Hopefully you won't find out." She checked the time. The person who sprayed the apple trees wasn't arriving until the afternoon. They used natural oils to prevent pests and disease. Still, she wanted to walk the aisles and inspect the overall health of the crop. Harvest time always filled the property with festive activity. Families came out to pick their own fruit, then the hired workers would collect the remaining crop. Some apples were sold. Some kept for the horses. Others she donated to a vendor to make apple cider for the Lazy Days Apple Festival held in the town square.

"I'll get Dandelion for the video. Where do you want to shoot it?"

Pete spun around and viewed the different options—an empty paddock where they worked with horses, the small fenced-off area right outside the barn or one of the large pastures that the horses enjoyed during the day. "How about you walk Dandelion and talk about her story? Did she come with the name?"

Sarah shook her head. "Her name was Shaggy. I wanted a special name for her, so I called her Dandelion."

"Like your favorite flower."

"You remember that?"

"How could I not?" he asked. "You're the only person I've met whose favorite flower is a dandelion."

Pete wasn't the only one who'd questioned her taste in flowers over the years. "People think of them as weeds and try to kill them. I see dandelions as resilient. They spread and thrive no matter what."

He chuckled. "My father curses them every spring while completing his system for the perfect lawn. I, on the other hand, have only fond thoughts when I see dandelions. They make me think of you." Pete gently tapped her on the nose.

While fighting the blush creeping up her face, she went to collect the chestnut pony. After slipping on and securing the halter, Sarah guided Dandelion outside. The pony grew excited when she caught sight of Chloe playing with Horace in the field. "Dandelion can't get enough of Chloe. She used to give rides to children. Dandy, not Chloe." She smiled down at the sweet pony. "She was very likely overworked given her lack of energy when she first arrived. But I think she remembers the children and maybe has good memories associated with them."

"Has Chloe ridden her?" Pete brushed his hand across Dandelion's mane.

"Chloe doesn't ride. I'm waiting until she's older."

"What?" Pete's dark eyebrows arched. "You were riding regular-sized horses at around four, right? That's what you told me."

She reluctantly nodded. "Yes, but I probably shouldn't have. It can be dangerous." Chloe was her little girl. Someone more precious to her than anything else in the world. Her main job was to protect her. She wouldn't risk her daughter's safety.

"Anything is dangerous. Even riding in a car. Chloe will be fine with the proper supervision."

Chloe had asked to ride recently. Almost every day as a matter of fact. Sarah knew someday soon she'd need to get over her fear and allow Chloe up on a horse. Maybe when she was sixteen. Unfortunately, that plan would never work. Chloe was too much her daughter to not want to ride as soon as possible. Did Pete have a point? "I don't know. She's so little."

"Dandelion is little too," Pete pointed out. The pony only came to his waist. "Chloe riding her may give Dandelion a purpose again. Obviously you'd make sure the experience was safe for both."

She chewed her bottom lip. Dandelion had been acting a little mopey lately. And she did gaze at Chloe with a light in her eyes. Could

Dandelion want to be useful again and experience the connection with a child riding on her back? Or would the feeling trigger bad memories? And what of Chloe? Once she introduced Chloe to riding, the child wouldn't be content with one experience.

"How about we give it a try? I'll record and if it goes well, I'll use it for a video."

"I don't want to show Chloe's face."

"I'll make sure any video I use doesn't show her face." He rested his good arm over her shoulder and squeezed. "If Dandelion or Chloe seems uncomfortable, then we abandon ship."

She considered all possibilities. What if Chloe fell? She'd wear a helmet and Sarah would be close by. What if Dandelion panicked? Then she'd take Chloe off immediately. What if both had a great time? Then she'd allow Chloe to ride Dandelion until Chloe outgrew the pony and subsequently moved on to a larger horse. Sarah's stomach churned. She hated risk. But she caught sight of Dandelion looking longingly at Chloe, and Sarah's heart melted. A pony with puppy-dog eyes begging to be included—how could she say no?

PETE UNDERSTOOD SARAH'S reluctance to place Chloe on a horse. Which made Dandelion the perfect gateway. The pony appeared docile and connected with the little girl. He was more concerned about Dandelion's reaction at having a saddle put on her back and a bit in her mouth. If he sensed even the slightest panic from her, he'd remove it. The last thing he wanted to do was trigger unpleasant memories. If having a happy child ride her for a short time brought a touch of joy, then Pete would call it a win.

Sarah called Chloe in from the field. Horace remained braying sadly before returning to graze on grass.

"Can I really ride Dandy?" Chloe asked with a squeak in her voice.

"We'll try and see if Dandelion is okay with you being on her." Sarah knelt to Chloe's eye level. "But Dandy may not like it and then you'll need to listen and get off. Understood?"

Chloe bobbed her head in agreement. "And I'll use both ears to listen."

Pete chuckled when Chloe wiggled her listening ears. "Are you always such a good listener?" He adjusted her helmet to rest snugly on her head.

"Yes," Chloe said at the same time that Sarah shook her head. "Grandma says I can't go out to their pool without a grown-up and I never do. And I do what my teacher says in school."

"What about what Mom says?" Sarah stood,

dusting off her knees, and grimaced. "I liked my knees better when they were younger."

Pete agreed and he'd add his shoulder, back, neck, ankles and most recently his wrist. He didn't remember bone fractures hurting this much for so long. Last night, the throbbing in his wrist had kept him awake for hours. He'd turned on the TV and found an episode of *The Twilight Zone* to watch until sleep found him. His dreams had been filled with strange aliens and an army of creepy dolls come to life.

"I sometimes listen to Mom, but I promise to listen extra good with Dandy. I've always wanted to ride a real horse." Chloe pressed a kiss on Dandelion's muzzle.

Sarah had secured the saddle on Dandy earlier. They were inside an enclosed field with no other animals. The dogs had been shooed out. Even a gentle pony could spook.

Pete lifted his cell phone and pressed Record. He stood behind the pony to only show Chloe's back.

"Are you ready?" Sarah asked.

He wasn't sure if she posed the question to Chloe or Dandelion. Or perhaps both.

"Yes." Chloe appeared to have no doubt about moving forward.

Pete recorded as Sarah lifted Chloe and placed her in the saddle with care. Sarah gripped the reins with her hand while Chloe set her feet in the stirrups. A nervous-looking smile pulled at Sarah's lips.

Pride swelled for Sarah. She loved her daughter and wanted to protect her. He understood she was naturally risk averse. Allowing Chloe to ride was a big step. The girl wouldn't be satisfied with riding on a pony while her mom held the reins forever. But Sarah's future issues with her child's love of horses were a problem for another day.

Dandelion held still under Chloe like she knew exactly what was expected of her. She didn't appear to flinch, and from what Pete could read from her body language, the pony appeared pleased with the responsibility. A touch of pride perhaps as Dandelion carried her head a little higher. Even animals needed to feel useful, similar to people. Did his work on her social media pages make him useful to Sarah? She'd mentioned the rescue account had brought in more income. More money meant she could do more good.

Still, Pete had felt untethered over the past two weeks. More precisely, since leaving the army. While in uniform, he'd had missions, a tight group of fellow soldiers whom he'd called friends and a common purpose. He'd traveled and met interesting people. Most days were filled with activity. His days after he left the army had been busy while he set up a life outside the military. His time in New York had been busy but unfulfilling. He'd traveled to Phoenix for interviews. Life would never be the same as when he was in the service. Which ultimately was a good thing. He'd been ready for a change. A change to what, though? He worried the next phase of his life wouldn't be enough to fulfill him. How long until he knew if he'd made the right decision?

A squeal captured his attention. He zoomed in to only show Chloe and the pony since Sarah had turned them around, making sure to crop Chloe at the shoulder level. The trio seemed pleased. Dandelion stepped with determination to provide a smooth ride. Chloe's grin could be seen from space. Sarah had relaxed her shoulders and gazed at her daughter with excitement glinting in her eyes. Could she envision a future in which she headed out on horseback rides with an older version of Chloe? For a moment, he pictured himself riding with them. Foolishness to believe he'd stay connected to them in a meaningful way after he left.

While recording, he spoke about what he'd learned about Dandelion's history from Sarah to be captured in the video. He'd ask Sarah to add more detail later. After about fifteen minutes, Sarah brought them to a stop. She lifted Chloe out of the saddle and placed her feet back onto the ground.

Pete ended the recording. Before slipping his phone back into his back pocket, he noticed several new texts from his father. He saw the text preview and inwardly groaned. More questions about his new job and the adjusted start day. He'd read the entire text later and reply. Would do the man some good to learn to wait.

"That was excellent riding, Chloe." He gave her a high five when she ran over. "How do you feel?"

"Great," Chloe shouted, then jumped in the air. "I want to ride every day."

"You can't ride every day. I don't ride every day, either." Stroking Dandelion's neck, Sarah leaned in. "You did good, girl. Thanks for helping Chloe learn."

The pony bobbed her head, flicked her ears and nickered.

When Chloe began running off, Sarah hollered for her to come back. "If you ride a horse, you need to take care of it afterward. You take Dandy's reins and guide her back into the stable. I'll show you how to take off the saddle and bridle, then you can give her a brushing."

Pete walked with them to the barn and assisted Chloe with her tasks. He took the small saddle from her and set it where Sarah indicated.

After Sarah gave Chloe a brush, the girl went to work, gently running the brush over Dandelion's coat.

"How does it feel?" Pete stepped toward Sarah, who was leaning back against the wall.

She'd moved out of the stall to give Chloe a sense of independence and trust to work. "Strange. I see myself in Chloe and it's kind of scary."

"How so?"

She shrugged. "I'm not exactly sure. Part of me wants her to love the ranch as much as I do and devote her life to running it with me and then by herself after I no longer can. But I also want her to know the world outside of Fern Hollow too. I'd dreamed of going other places, as you know, and I never did. I've gone on vacation a couple of times but it's hard to be away when you have animals that depend on you for everything. I don't want her to feel obligated or trapped."

"I think Chloe is strong-minded enough to make a decision when the time comes. Right now, she's your little girl and she'll be by your side. Obviously, she loves horses and all the animals here and will be a good rider. She may think of a path for her life you never considered."

"True. She could become an acrobat. Or learn how to be a trick rider for the rodeo. Oh, I hope not." Sarah's smile brightened the dim interior of the stable. "Thanks for encouraging me to loosen up and give both Chloe and Dandelion a chance. Dandelion seemed to enjoy having Chloe on her back. I'd never want her to carry someone for long and only a few times a week at most."

"I'm sure you'll do what's right for Dandelion." Temptation spun around him and whispered in his ear, telling him to kiss Sarah. Their kiss a week ago had sparked something inside him that he'd assumed was long dead. He wouldn't kiss her again with Chloe present. And he wasn't sure kissing her was a good idea even if they were alone. A deepening bond with Sarah would only make it harder. He had to keep some space between them. Firm boundaries were a good thing.

The phone in his pocket buzzed with an incoming call. He removed it and peered at the screen. His father had abandoned texting and moved on to calling. All his life, Pete had made decisions with the intention of pleasing his father. Of making him proud. His new job appeared to be a step in that direction after regressing in his father's eyes when he'd left the army. Pete would be in Phoenix soon enough. Then his father could move on to being disappointed at some other aspect of Pete's life. Like why Pete was thirty and still single. He had no hope of falling in love again. Not when he'd soon walk away from the only woman he'd ever loved.

He hit Accept and greeted his father in an effort to keep the peace.

CHAPTER TEN

SARAH WHISTLED A happy tune as she descended the stairs. She'd actually had a good night's sleep. No bad dreams. Actually, the opposite. Her most vivid dream involved Pete and a horseback ride. She'd make that a reality before he left. She'd pack a lunch and they could ride out to the creek that ran through the property.

After entering the kitchen, she poured a cup of coffee and set her mind on the more practical matters of the day. Since Chloe had stayed overnight at a friend's house, she didn't need to make the drive into town to drop her off at her parents' house. They'd pick her up at her friend's house sometime this morning and then bring her home before dinnertime. Someday, Chloe would be old enough to stay home during the days she wasn't in school and help out around the ranch. She assumed her parents understood that as well and were currently trying to make the most of their time with their young grandchild.

Milton mentioned yesterday he planned to come early today and check on the gelding, who'd been having a rough time readapting to domesticated life. The horse would soon figure out regular meals, companionship and shelter were a small price to pay in exchange for giving up the freedom of running wild all alone.

She peered out the window and noticed Milton's truck in its usual spot. Another worker's vehicle was parked next to the truck, likely Dylan's. The teenager had been working extra hard to make up for the few days he'd called in sick.

The sound of a vehicle coming up the driveway had her returning to the window. She didn't recognize the car as belonging to one of her employees. It wasn't Pete—plus he normally walked over. She was expecting a visit from a potential adopter for a few of the ranch rescue horses. But that wasn't until later in the afternoon. The family had recently moved to the area and purchased a house on twenty acres. They were looking to add horses and thought providing a home to two or three of Sarah's rescues felt like a good option. She had several horses in mind that had been with her for a while and recovered enough to make a good addition to the right family.

Had the family arrived early or did she write

down their appointment time wrong? She set her coffee mug on the counter and slipped on her boots. Thankfully, she'd taken a shower already and her hair was mostly dry. Ripping a Pop Tart out of the packet, she promised to start eating healthy soon. It was hard when her schedule left little time for meal prep. She went outside with coffee mug and Pop Tart in hand, and the wooden screen door banged closed behind her. The man she saw stepping out of the car sent a cold wave of unease through her body. What was Pete's dad doing here?

Sarah returned her Pop Tart and coffee to the kitchen, then went back out. She descended the stairs with care given her current state of shock. "Mr. O'Keefe. Welcome to Carmella Ranch."

"It's Retired Vice Admiral O'Keefe but let's skip the formalities. Call me Kenneth." His limp was pronounced as he moved to meet Sarah on the walkway. He extended his hand.

She felt very odd shaking hands with Pete's father as if they were old business acquaintances. *Should I salute him?*

Milton approached, and Sarah informed him of the identity of their visitor.

"Pete never mentioned his pa was coming for a visit," he said with a thickening of his southern drawl. Milton often reverted to a South Carolina boy when nervous. Pete's dad would make anyone nervous.

Kenneth O'Keefe stood an impressive six feet, approximately, and still had a thick head of hair though most strands had turned a distinguished silver. He had broad shoulders like Pete and a trim figure. His face was clean of facial hair, and silver-rim glasses framed his eyes.

"I didn't tell him ahead of time." Kenneth's smile was tight when he shook Milton's hand. The two men made brief introductions. "Peter never shared where he was living so I assumed I'd find him here. Is he around?" The tone he used when pronouncing *assumed* held a touch of irritation, like his son should be anywhere else.

"Not yet." Sarah grew more uncomfortable by the second. "He's not on a set schedule since he's a volunteer."

"I'm a volunteer and that doesn't stop you from telling me to arrive by eight o'clock." Milton rested his hands on his narrow hips. "I'd like to sit on my porch sipping my morning coffee instead of dealing with crabby horses who demand their breakfast the moment you walk into the stable."

Sarah rolled her eyes, then caught a glint of humor on Kenneth's face. Had Milton won over the hardened military man? Even if momentary, that was a huge accomplishment. She'd play along to buy time until Pete arrived. Hopefully he'd be here very soon. "Those horses remind me of you. And you aren't required to be here at eight. If your old body needs to sleep in, all you have to do is say so."

"It's not more sleep I need," Milton grumbled. "Just a little more appreciation would be nice every once in a while."

"I do appreciate you, Milton. Why don't you show the vice admiral around until Pete arrives?" Anything to get away from him. Whenever Pete's dad had come to stay at their rental house, Sarah had avoided it like it held a sinkhole to the pit of despair. Pete, on the other hand, had been trapped in the pit of his father's making all his life.

"I don't want to inconvenience anyone." Kenneth waved away Sarah's offer. "I'm sure you all have work to see to. Do you mind if I sit on one of the rockers on your front porch while I wait?"

"Be my guest." She'd forgotten his leg had been badly wounded many years ago, forcing him into an early retirement. A bomb blast, from what she recalled, during a meeting of high-ranking military officers in Iraq. "I can call Pete if you'd like."

"No, that's not necessary." Kenneth turned to Milton. "It was a pleasure to meet you. I hope we find time to talk again."

"Your son is a good fella." Milton nodded once. "I'll go see to the horses' breakfast then. I can hear them making a fuss from all the way over here."

Kenneth walked with a limp alongside Sarah as she escorted him to the front porch. She'd recently added containers of purple and pink petunias. A trio of potted ferns hung from the roof of the porch. A row of four rocking chairs ran along one side and a swinging bench resided on the other. Some of Sarah's favorite memories took place on this porch. She'd sit and rock with her grandparents, sipping sweet tea and munching on her grandma's shortbread cookies.

Once Pete's dad was seated, Sarah hesitated. It felt wrong to just leave. He was still a guest even if he intimidated her. With a deep breath for courage, she took the rocker next to him. "Pete will be surprised to see you."

He released a sound similar to a laugh. "I suppose he will be. I found myself with some downtime recently and decided to take a trip. He can use some encouragement. He always enjoyed coming here with his mother and Chris during the summer. He'd pout for a month after we left for home."

Sarah had hated when Pete left. She'd count down the days until he planned to return. "His trip is lasting a little longer than expected. But his wrist seems to be healing well. He should be as good as new soon." And then vanish from her life. Poof, like a carnival magician's trick.

"If he was smart, he would have gone to Phoenix regardless of the injury and started building relationships with those on his team. It's never too early to impress your commanders." Kenneth glanced at her and exhaled through his nose. "Peter was never wise in regards to you, was he?"

Her throat closed around any rebuttal that came to mind. She was better off not saying anything instead of the snappy retort on the tip of her tongue.

"I trust neither of you will make the same mistakes you did when you were younger," he said. "You have this beautiful ranch to maintain and a daughter, if I remember correctly. I didn't agree with Pete's decision to leave the army but he's still young and can continue building his career."

She pushed to her feet, unable to sit still any longer. Her mind begged her to run away. A crushing feeling overtook her chest. Yet, she normally didn't flee from a bully. And that was what Kenneth O'Keefe was—a bully. She'd sensed it whenever she was around him during her younger years. He couldn't veil his tyrant nature even though his politeness never slipped.

"I'm sure Pete knows what's best for his future. He deserves to be happy." She dug her fingernails into the palm of her hand in an effort to not say more.

"Happiness," he said with a snort. "An O'Keefe doesn't go chasing after feelings. There is no honor in that. I raised my sons with a sense of duty. That always comes before fulfilling one's own needs."

She caught sight of Pete coming over the horizon in the distance. He strolled down the side of the road, not a care in the world. *Enjoy it while it lasts.* Because with Kenneth O'Keefe's arrival, Pete's peaceful morning wouldn't last much longer.

PETE KNEW THE time had come to face the man he'd so far avoided since returning stateside. Concerned to see the look of distress on Sarah's face, he quickened his pace. She didn't deserve to be stuck with his father when it was Pete he came to see.

"Hello, sir." He stepped onto the porch and shook his father's hand. No warm hug or tight embrace between this father and son. Not even when they hadn't seen one another in almost two years. The handshake was firm and released quickly. "Did I miss your message that you were coming?"

"No. I wanted it to be a surprise." Kenneth turned to Sarah. "I appreciate your company until Peter arrived." A polite dismissal.

And Sarah accepted it with a gracious smile. "You're welcome anytime. Milton would be happy to show you around sometime if you'd like. He loves nothing more than to talk." She glanced at Pete with a hint of panic in her eyes, then disappeared inside the house.

Pete would love to follow her but he stayed to face the man who pushed Pete to be the superhero Kenneth could no longer be. If his father hadn't suffered a career-ending injury, would the weight of expectations have been lighter? He'd never know. Pete had a hundred questions but decided to let his father start the conversation. His father would soon make clear his intentions. Kenneth O'Keefe wasn't one to dance around an issue. He attacked first and fast, getting straight to the point.

His father sat back in the rocking chair with a grimace. He rubbed the spot on his thigh that had been badly wounded many years ago, forcing him to retire. "You really are hurt." His gaze flicked to Pete's wrist brace.

"The fracture is healing. I see the doctor in another week for an X-ray." He flexed his fingers. The healing bone, which had been feeling better recently, started to ache again. Must be the proximity to negative energy. "I can start working with the Phoenix Police Department as soon as I'm cleared to use my left arm."

"Remind me how you fractured it."

How his father managed to make Pete go from feeling like a man who had his life together to a boy fearful of disappointing his father remained a mystery for the ages. "Rock climbing." He shrugged. "It was fun until I fell."

"You should practice more common sense." The motion of Kenneth's rocker over the old wooden porch floor produced a rhythmic creaking.

"Yes, sir." What more could Pete say? It was true he often acted on impulse. But he didn't do so with complete abandon, and he always put the safety of others first.

"As you know, the leaders at the DOD are reviewing my contract renewal. Someone decided to slow the process by adding extra levels of approval, and I had no work to keep me occupied. Since you haven't come to San Diego to visit me, I flew up here to touch base with my son."

"I appreciate the effort." Sweat beaded on his forehead. "How long do you plan on staying?" Hopefully only a day or two.

"I didn't make reservations for a return flight yet." Kenneth pushed back to rock in the chair and smiled up at Pete, though the smile didn't reach his eyes. It never did. "I need an idea of where your head is these days, son. Fern Hollow is not a place that will do anything for your future. I know you are already aware of that."

Oh, he was aware. His father had told him many times during their summers here about the trap of small-town living. Especially a small town far away from any military centers. What could he, a future soldier, gain from a town like Fern Hollow? To Kenneth, nothing could be done without attaining something. Life wasn't a zero-sum game.

"I'm using my time to help Sarah and the ranch." He wouldn't go into too much detail. His father didn't care. "Plus, I'm finding being close to nature is helping heal some of my emotional battle scars." That *was* something his father could understand. While Pete hadn't experienced serious emotional trauma, he still suffered the aftereffects of serving in war zones and witnessing some fairly horrible things. Caring for the horses served as therapy.

His father continued rocking and gazing across the front yard. The pasture across the street was grassy and flat. In the distance, the elevation rose to meet the rising sun. "Chris will be in San Diego at the end of August for training followed by a short leave. Ashley and the kids will be there too. I'd like you to come for a few days, if you can work it into your schedule."

"It would be good to see them again." He hadn't seen his brother for almost three years. They spoke on the phone and emailed, but that wasn't the same as talking face to face. Chris was usually on a ship in the middle of the ocean and couldn't say much about what he was doing. While Chris had made an active military career work with a solid marriage and family, Pete had yet to figure out the magic. It probably helped that Ashley was independent and accepted Chris being gone for nine months to a year at a time. She enjoyed moving to different parts of the country and even the world. Pete had thought Sarah wanted that as well. Likely, neither of them had fully thought through the realities of such a life.

His father stood and jiggled his bad leg. "I'll need you to guide me to where you're staying. I want to get settled and have some paperwork to see to."

Of course he assumed he'd stay with Pete—show up unannounced and expect Pete to drop whatever he was doing to offer a warm welcome and comfortable accommodations. Luckily, or unluckily, Pete's rental house had a spare bedroom. If Pete could convince his father he had no intention of staying in Fern Hollow any longer than his healing time, Kenneth would be on a plane back to Southern California within a day. Kenneth hadn't particularly liked staying in Fern Hollow when his sons were young. He wasn't a fan of animals, especially big ones like horses. His father's only mission was to put a wedge in between Pete and Sarah to ensure Pete didn't stumble on the road to success like he'd done at the age of eighteen.

"Let me tell Sarah I'm leaving with you," Pete said. "I'll meet you by your car." He left the front porch before his father could add another comment. Finding Sarah feeding the dogs, he took a moment to watch her.

She bent over a metal bin and scooped up dry kibble before depositing the food into two bowls. With that task completed, she carried the bowls to the pen where the dogs spent their time when indoors. They were housed with the trio of goats the rescue had somehow acquired. He'd have to ask Sarah about the background of the goats and the dogs. A beam of sunlight made her hair shimmer. It always appeared redder under natural light.

"Beaker. Gonzo." She called and rattled the bowls. "Time to eat." When they approached with tails wagging, she set down the bowls. Sarah turned and noticed Pete standing in the aisle. "Hey. Any hope your dad is heading home?"

"No hope." He'd considered denying his father's request for room and board while here, then quickly dismissed the idea. His lifetime of obedience was a testament to his father's iron grip on Pete's entire existence. "He's staying with me while he's in Fern Hollow. I think once he's satisfied I'm not going rogue on my new job, he'll leave for home."

Her gaze dropped to the dogs, who now stood devouring their breakfast. "I'll tell Milton that he'll have to do without you for a few days. I'm sure he'll survive."

"I'll come back once I drop him off and give him the lay of the land." Pete sensed her posture deflate slightly. He shouldn't have mentioned his job, which meant leaving. "I committed to helping you out while I'm here, with the animals, for what it's worth, and social media."

"You don't owe me anything, Pete." She looked up at him with sadness surfacing in her eyes like a child watching a balloon drift away in the sky. "You didn't even mean to stay this long to begin with."

I owe you everything. The admission would bare his soul, and with their time together coming to an end in two weeks, he needed to keep some pieces of himself protected. "Actually, I'm glad I climbed that rock and broke my wrist if it meant reconnecting with you."

"Then what?" she asked, then waved away the question. "Never mind. We promised to enjoy the present. I'm not good at living in the moment. My mind is usually five steps ahead. It's a hard habit to break."

What happened after he left? Pete would move to Phoenix and become immersed in his new responsibilities. Sarah's work kept her busy. They'd become two ends of an elastic string, stretching until the tension broke the thread. He didn't want to lose her again. But how could he keep her in his life without giving her his complete heart and soul?

That was a problem for another day. Currently, his father waited. Kenneth had plans for his younger son, that was for sure. Pete's goal was to survive the stay with only minimal damage to his other relationships. And stay true to himself—a difficult task, judging from history.

CHAPTER ELEVEN

SARAH'S MOM ENTERED through the front door and dropped Chloe's duffel bag on the table. "She's barely spoken since I picked her up from Abby's house," Emma said with a huff. "She's probably overtired. Who knows if she got any sleep last night."

Sarah stopped stirring the pot of spaghetti sauce on the stove and peeked outside. "Where is Chloe?" Going without talking was rare for Chloe but she did get ornery when tired. "Supper is almost ready."

"She took off running toward the barn." Emma set Chloe's water bottle on the kitchen counter. "Didn't say goodbye. I hollered out that I loved her but she didn't turn back. Just kept on running."

"I'll find her and remind her ignoring people is rude." She turned off the burner, then wiped her hands on the kitchen towel. The noodles had finished cooking and sat inside a covered bowl.

She'd put in the garlic bread after she returned with her wayward daughter.

"Text me later to ease my mind that everything is alright with her." Emma set her hands on her low spine and arched her back. "Chloe reminds me so much of you it's scary sometimes."

"Thanks." Sarah snorted a laugh. "I think. Is your back bothering you again?"

"The pain goes away and then I carry too much or sleep in the wrong position and poof, it returns. Don't get old. Something always hurts."

"I'm already there." Sarah slipped on her shoes, then tied the laces. "Working on the ranch doesn't give my body much of a rest."

"I suppose not. That's your choice." Emma picked up her purse from the counter. "You wanted to spend your days cleaning horse stalls."

Her job entailed more than mucking stalls but she'd save that argument. "We're hosting another wedding this week. The barn space is booking fast."

"Good to hear. I'll talk to you later. Let me know if Chloe's coming over tomorrow or if she needs a day home to rest." Her mom left the house and soon the sound of her car engine faded.

Sarah strode to the barn and walked inside.

"Chloe," she yelled. A dove cooed in reply. Most of the horses were still in the pasture. She checked each horse stall, the pen where the goats and dogs bedded in for the night and the office area. No Chloe.

Stepping out the rear door, she shouted Chloe's name again. Her voice echoed across the field.

"You looking for Chloe?" Milton rounded the corner of the barn, shovel in hand. "Didn't she go into the house with your ma?"

"No. My mom said Chloe ran off to the barn." Sarah rested her fists on her hips and turned her head to gaze around. Chloe was nowhere in sight.

"I haven't seen her." Milton rested the shovel on the side of the barn. "You already checked the barn?"

"I did but wouldn't mind you checking again." A touch of panic rose in her chest. Chloe hadn't gone far. She never would.

As Milton entered the barn, Pete appeared. His face was streaked with dirt, and his shirt was sweaty. He'd been working hard. "What's going on?"

"I can't find Chloe." Her voice broke. She wouldn't cry. *Don't overreact.* "Did you see her after my mom dropped her off?"

He shook his head and removed his work

gloves. "I was moving the manure pile with Milton. Sorry."

Taking in a sniff, she scrunched up her nose, thankful she had other people to assist with that task. "I'll go check the fields. Maybe she went to find Horace."

"That's very likely. I'll look around too. Do you have your cell on you? Call me if you find her."

She patted the phone in her back pocket. "Thanks."

"We'll find her. It's a large property and she's comfortable here. She didn't go far." Pete strode away toward the left.

Kenneth's car pulled into the property, and Sarah's gut clenched another notch tighter. She didn't have time to be a polite hostess right now.

She headed to the right and the pasture Horace usually resided in. When she located Horace but no Chloe, her heart rate increased. She checked her phone and her pulse kicked up at the sight of no messages or calls. Pete would have reached out if either he or Milton had found Chloe.

"Chloe." Her throat grew scratchy. "Chloe." She continued walking up over a hill and down into a narrow valley, which housed a small pond used to provide drinking water for the livestock. Had she fallen in? Running at breakneck speed, she nearly tripped over a branch. *Please don't be in the water.* She reached the bank and choked out a sob when she didn't find her daughter. What would she do if she lost Chloe? *No, don't go there. Trust Chloe is fine.*

Where to look next? She continued walking the pasture, looking around every section of brush and tree. There was about four hours until sunset. They'd find her by then.

She moved along the fence line back to the gate. Rubbing away tears, she found Milton.

"No sign of her," Milton said. "I crawled up in the loft, checked the Big Red Barn, even went down the road a way. I'll keep looking."

"Thank you." She patted him on the shoulder as he seemed as distressed as she felt. "Have you heard from Pete?"

"Not since he went over to check the apple orchard. Pete's pa is here. He said he'd stay by the house in case Chloe comes back. I gave him your phone number to use if he sees her." Milton left to continue the search.

Sarah checked her phone again. Nothing. Should she call the sheriff's department and ask for help? The ping from a text made her jump.

Found her

She exhaled a huge sigh of relief.

Where are you?

Under an apple tree. She was waiting for a unicorn to come eat the magic grass that grows under the tree.

Despite her swirling emotions, she barked out a laugh.

I can't believe she remembers that story. Mike read it to her when she was a baby.

Sarah had read the story as well after Mike's death in fond remembrance.

Do you mind if I stay out here with her for a little while? She's upset and I'd like to try and talk with her.

Sarah's first instinct was to ask Pete to bring her back immediately. If Chloe was upset, then she should be with her. Rational thought made a path through her brain. Pete had always been the best listener and gave pretty good advice whenever she had a problem. I'll be waiting on the back steps. Don't take too long.

She went to find Milton to call off the search. Then she found Kenneth and reported that Pete had found Chloe and that he'd be back shortly.

What had upset her daughter? Did something happen at her parents' house? Guess she'd have to wait to find out.

PETE DIDN'T KNOW exactly what to do. He sat next to Chloe, keeping a foot of distance between them. When he'd asked Sarah to give him a chance to talk with Chloe, he hadn't fully considered he'd never dealt with a six-year-old girl before. His brother's kids were older and both boys. He took a steadying breath. While serving in foreign countries, he'd had to communicate with people who didn't share his language. He'd had to defuse tense situations with facial expressions and tone of voice. *Pretend you're dealing with a very short, redheaded, upset village leader and everything will be fine.*

"Chloe, your mom was worried about you." He'd start with the obvious issue that came to mind. "I let her know I found you."

She sniffled. Her forehead was resting on her tucked-up knees, proving the young possessed a flexibility Pete's older body did not.

"Can you tell me why you came to the apple orchard after your grandma dropped you off?"

A quiet grumble was her only response.

This was harder than he'd expected. Chloe was usually so bubbly and talkative.

"Okay, we can sit out here for a little while

longer." He stretched out his legs and set the palm of his good hand on the ground behind him to lean back. "Do you know this was your mom's favorite tree to sit under? I found her right in this very spot when she was mad at her mom for not letting her go to the movies with me and a few other friends. We all ended up going over to your grandma's house and piling into the living room to watch a movie on the TV. It was a fun time." Although he didn't believe Emma Carmella had felt the same way the next morning when she'd had to tidy up the living room and kitchen. That night, they'd watched *Friday the 13th* and his love of older horror movies had been born. An addiction shared by Sarah.

"I've only gone to the movie theater once. It's small and smells funny."

Pete chuckled. He was surprised the movie theater building was still standing and hadn't been condemned. When he drove past the other day, the sign featured a movie that had originally played there fifty years ago. They likely stuck with the classics to keep down costs. Or the rest of the town had similar tastes in movies to Sarah: the older the better.

"Televisions these days can stream almost any movie you want right at home. Back in my day, we had to go to the store to rent a movie.

No one could ever agree on what movie to rent so we each picked one and then watched them all." He was making himself sound a hundred years old.

Chloe raised her head and wiped her eyes with her small hands. "I'm never going to Abby's house ever again."

Now we're getting somewhere. "Why not?"

A sob escaped followed by more tears. "Abby said Mom adopted me like she did the horses. No one wanted me so she brought me home."

Unsure whether to put his hand on her shoulder or maintain his distance, he scooted in a tad closer but kept his hands on his lap.

"Abby isn't right. You weren't adopted." He considered his next words carefully. "But even if you were, that isn't a bad thing. The horses your mom brings home are very glad to be with both of you. They are loved and cared for."

"Horace was adopted by my dad. I don't remember because I was just a baby." She rubbed her nose on the sleeve of her shirt. "Abby also said I don't have a dad. All the other girls have a dad."

His heart fractured, a pain deeper than the break in his wrist. "Oh, honey. Abby shouldn't have said that to you. That wasn't nice at all."

"I told her it wasn't nice. She made me promise not to tell her mom or I won't get to play with her at recess at school."

"Do you want to play with her after the mean things she said?" Pete asked, genuinely curious.

"I don't know." She shrugged. "Abby plays on the swings, and I like to play on the swings too. She's still my friend."

Such a simple rationalization. If only adults considered problems in the same manner. There'd be less war, that's for sure. "Kids have all sorts of different families. Some live with both a mom and a dad. Some only with a mom or a dad. Some kids live with their grandparents or an aunt or uncle or even another family that cares for them. As long as the people in your family love you, that's all that counts."

"I get to stay with my grandma and grandpa and Abby's live far away." She crossed her arms and lifted her chin. "Are you sure I'm not adopted like Horace?"

"Your mom would have told you if you were." He ruffled her red hair, which was a slightly lighter shade than Sarah's. "Plus, there is nothing wrong with being adopted. My brother Chris was adopted." And he fit into the O'Keefe family better than Pete ever had.

"Really?" Chloe gazed up at him in wide-eyed wonder. "Where did your mom and dad find him?"

Pete grinned. "Adopting a baby is different from adopting a horse or a donkey. Chris's mom couldn't take care of him so she gave him to my parents to raise as their son. He is my brother even though he had a different mom and dad in the beginning." He hoped he was explaining it in a way Chloe could understand, not having had much experience communicating complicated family issues with a child.

"I'd like a brother or sister," she declared.

"I liked having an older brother. But he teased me a lot." Recollections surfaced of the times he didn't like his older brother as much as he did now. Pete looked back on those days with fondness. Chris hadn't been too mean to his little brother. At least not as mean as he could have been.

His parents had been told they wouldn't be able to have a child naturally. After his mom pressed for adoption, his father eventually relented. They welcomed Chris into their home, and he became their pride and joy. He did everything right, from walking early to learning his numbers and letters before starting school. Then his mom discovered the doctor had been wrong, and she was pregnant when Chris turned three. Surprise!

From the stories shared, Chris had enjoyed having a little brother for the first few months.

The boys hadn't really bonded until Chris entered high school and Pete grew old enough not to be annoying. When Chris left for the Naval Academy, Pete had been devastated over losing his best friend—and his biggest ally in standing up to the demands of their father.

Of course, Chris excelled. He'd followed their father's path by completing his college degree, joining the navy and quickly rising in rank. Pete never stood a chance of living up to his brother's standard, which he'd accepted a long time ago. Still, he did his best.

"I wish for a sister. I'd be nice to her and brush her hair." She smiled dreamily. "If Dad didn't die, then I'd have a sister."

What could he say to that? How did one explain death to a child? He'd ask Sarah once he brought Chloe home.

"How about we go back to your mom? I'm sure she'd be happy to see you're okay."

"Not yet." She held up the stuffed pink unicorn she'd shown him when he first arrived. "Lilac hasn't had a chance to eat yet." Chloe tipped the head of the stuffed animal until it touched the grass. "Dad told me only unicorns can eat the magic grass. I want to see a real unicorn."

The story must have special meaning. "I imagine real unicorns are shy and only come out to eat the special grass when there is no one around."

She released a long exhale. "That's what Mom says. I know I'll see one if I keep looking." Her stuffed unicorn continued with its head lowered to the grass while Chloe made munching sounds.

"Never stop looking." He reached out to softly squeeze her small hand and breathed a sigh of gratitude he'd thought to quickly wash his hands before going off in search of Chloe. His clothes were another story. "Promise that you won't come here again without telling your mom."

"Promise." Chloe stood and gathered her stuffed unicorn to her chest. "I'm hungry."

Oh, to be young again. Nothing was a problem for long. He'd love to shake off his worries about his new job as easily. Would he make a good impression or would his superiors view him as another former soldier looking to prove his worth? Pete did have something to prove still. Only he wasn't exactly sure what it was or to whom. Himself? His father?

"Will you hold my hand walking back?" he asked, not wanting to risk losing her again. After she put her hand in his, they started the trek home. Pete shortened his stride to accommodate her much shorter legs.

Chloe began singing a happy song about a

group of little monkeys jumping on the bed, and Pete's chest warmed. Was this what it felt like to be a father? A real father likely held similar emotions but experienced them more intensely. The desire to protect and nurture had to be amplified the day one's child was born. Pete considered his own father. Had his father's love always come with strings attached? Would the sentiment his father felt toward his sons even be classified as love? Pete suspected Kenneth loved him in his own way. He had a cold and distant approach to parenthood, unlike Pete's mom, who'd been kind and affectionate. His mom's sage wisdom would really come in handy right now.

He and Chloe exited the row of apple trees, and the house, barns and pastures came into view. Chloe finished the monkey song and moved on to a tune featuring Horace. The girl might become a singer/songwriter someday.

He was struck with the reminder that to Chloe, Pete was only a friend of her mom staying for a short visit. The reality of the situation created a sharp pain inside him. He wasn't a father figure to her. He may have kissed Sarah, but they had no plans for the future. His shoulders sank. For a moment, he'd pictured a future on the ranch with Sarah and Chloe. And the knowledge that future wouldn't be a reality disheartened him.

As THEY APPROACHED the house, Sarah stood from her position on the back stoop. She watched Pete and Chloe walk toward her hand in hand. When they reached the edge of the back yard, Pete let go and Chloe ran to her.

Sarah was so relieved, she wanted to kiss Pete. Though she wouldn't make that same mistake again. Kissing him hadn't been wise. The feelings she carried for him had escaped in full force and she struggled to push them back down.

Kenneth stood beside the house, watching Pete and Chloe. What was going through his head, she couldn't be sure. Likely nothing positive.

"I'm sorry, Mama." Chloe wrapped her arms around Sarah's legs. "Lilac was hungry for the special grass under the apple trees."

Sarah placed a hand under Chloe's chin and tilted her face up to meet her gaze. "I was very worried about you. Please always tell someone where you are going. Actually, get permission first."

"I will. Promise."

All was forgiven. But Sarah's heart rate hadn't returned to a normal speed. "Go inside and wash up. I'll finish dinner so we can eat."

Chloe darted into the house. The screen door banged behind her.

"Thank you." She moved to where Pete stood. "Did she tell you anything more than that Lilac was hungry?"

"Her friend Abby made some not very nice comments, but we talked about it and I think Chloe feels better." He gave Sarah a quick run-down of their conversation.

"That's horrible. I'm calling Abby's mom tonight." Outrage made her body hot. How dare anyone tell Chloe she was brought home like one of her rescue horses. She believed adoption was a beautiful thing but to tell a child she was adopted simply to cause hurt wasn't right.

"Check with Chloe before doing that. There will be fallout with her friend if she knows that Chloe told."

"I don't want Chloe to be friends with her anyways." She considered what Pete had said. "You're right. I should let Chloe decide what to do next."

"She's a good kid. I'm sure she'll be alright."

"I didn't know Chris was adopted," she said. When Pete had mentioned that fact during his accounting of what he'd said to Chloe, she'd been surprised.

"Chris never felt anything other than a brother. My parents never treated us any differently. I sometimes forget he was adopted, actually."

"That's fair. He's lucky to have you for a brother." She should get inside and restart dinner. Something about Pete always made her want to stay with him a little longer.

"I'm the lucky one. He saved me from getting in serious trouble more times than I can count."

"Yes, just imagine all the trouble you would have gotten in if not for an older brother." Her smile was filled with the memories of some of the trouble she'd gotten in alongside him—sneaking into the movie theater through the back door when they didn't have money for tickets, borrowing her dad's computer without his knowledge to set up email accounts in order to keep in touch and skipping the church picnic to have their own, just the two of them, on the shores of the Columbia River.

Pete rocked back on his heels. "I'll let you get inside to Chloe. Milton invited Dad and I over for dinner. He claims he caught a few trout and plans to cook them special for us."

"You're in for a treat. Milton is a good cook. Ask for a jar of his applesauce. He makes it like my grandma did and cans close to fifty jars every year."

Kenneth walked closer, as if sensing Pete and Sarah's conversation was coming to a close. "I'm looking forward to dining on freshly caught trout," he said, rubbing his hands together. "I have a fondness for seafood, as a navy man. I'm here to give Pete a ride home. How is your little girl?"

"She'll be fine. Pete found her and they had a nice talk. Your son is really good with kids." She watched for any change of expression on Kenneth's face. Nothing. Not even an eyelid twitch. The man was good.

"His nephews enjoy the rare times they get to spend with their uncle." Kenneth sent a fleeting glance in Pete's direction. "I suppose there are some benefits to you leaving the army. Perhaps you'll make more time for family now that you're living in one spot."

What he meant exactly by making more time for family, she wasn't sure. Have a family of his own? Get together more with his brother's family? Both? There was no analyzing the vice admiral. He could be sculpted out of granite for his complete lack of transparency.

"Have a good night and say bye to Chloe for me." Pete leaned in and kissed her on the cheek. "I should get home and change."

"You'll shower as well." Kenneth's gaze took in Pete's dirty clothing and sweat-dried hair.

"Of course, sir."

"Drop the *sir*," Kenneth said with the air of a military command. "We're both no longer bound by protocol."

Pete turned to her, eyebrows raised with the hint of a grin.

The spot on her cheek where Pete's lips had touched tingled. "Enjoy dinner." She waited for Pete and his father to drive away before going into the house through the back door.

Reheating the spaghetti, she wished she were about to enjoy Milton's culinary creation instead. Her mind drifted ahead. After dinner, she and Chloe would make sure all the horses were tucked into their stalls, had food and fresh water. They'd bring in the goats and the dogs and the ducks. Then once Chloe was put to bed, she'd run over the agenda for this weekend's wedding and reception at the Big Red Barn. Maybe review the business and nonprofit finances if she could stay awake long enough.

She sighed with the longing for a partner. She missed Mike and his loving companionship. He'd helped carry some of the burden of running Carmella Ranch and Orchard. She could have used him today with Chloe. A father sometimes had more success at getting through to a willful child. At the end of the day, the ranch and Chloe were fully entrusted to Sarah. Her grandparents had believed she'd carry on their mission. She'd promised Mike to raise their daughter with their shared values. Sarah vowed to spend every day for the rest of her life seeing the ranch was secure to hand off to the next generation. Even while doing it alone.

CHAPTER TWELVE

ALTHOUGH MILTON, PETE and several other ranch helpers had come in very early to help get the morning chores done so Sarah could attend the Splash and Dash Festival in town, she still felt reluctant to go. The gelding she and Pete had brought back still hadn't settled down. He was constantly trying to escape. Sarah wouldn't leave him in the pasture unattended for fear he'd jump the fence and be gone.

"Take Chloe," she insisted to Pete. "You can find my parents and they'll watch her. I have too much to do." She loved Fern Hollow's annual Splash and Dash Festival. It was the kick-off to the Fourth of July celebrations. But this year the weight of her to-do list felt heavier. The square dance fundraiser was a week away. The Big Red Barn still needed a deep cleaning and reset after the last event.

"You deserve to have fun. You've been working hard." He took her hand and pulled her closer. “Everything is taken care of that needs seeing to this morning. We’ll all come back later and help with evening chores.”

“Yeah, come on, Mom.” Chloe’s tone was full of exasperation. “You promised we’d go together and get hot dogs from the cart.”

“I know.” She had promised. Not only to eat her fill of hot dogs but to participate in the competition. Ever since morphing into an adult, she’d elected to sit on the sidelines and cheer on those not afraid to get soaked.

“Remember the summer I met you in the town square for the festival and we had a contest to see who could eat the most ice cream?” Pete asked.

“It was no contest. I tried keeping up without success. I went home that night with a very sick stomach.” There’d been no overdoing it with ice cream since. Especially without Pete egging her on.

“Can we have an ice cream eating contest?” Chloe peered up with hope gleaming in her eyes.

“No. One hot dog and one dish of ice cream.”

“And a big pretzel.” Chloe was persistent.

“Maybe.” Sarah thought of all the reasons she should stay home and work. Once Pete left, his social media posts would end, and the donations would dry up. The fundraiser had to be a success. She couldn't be distracted by Pete's ruggedly handsome face. Still, she'd disappoint her daughter if she didn't go. And the festival was a lot of fun. "Okay, you two twisted my arm. I'll go but only on one condition."

"What?" Pete and Chloe asked in unison.

"You go to bed tonight with no arguments."

Pete groaned and stomped his foot. "I hate going to bed."

"Mom meant me." Chloe giggled. "I will, Mommy."

"Then let's get cleaned up to go." She patted the top of Chloe's head, then sent her inside to wash her face and hands. "Don't forget to change your clothes," she called after her. "You can wear your swimsuit underneath."

"I'll head back to my place and check on my father." Pete rubbed at his chin. He was still sporting a full mustache, which gave him a sort of outlaw appearance. "He'll probably want to stay back and read. That's all he's been doing since he arrived. I didn't know there were that many books on World War II."

"Do you still avoid reading?" she asked. On days she'd brought a book on their picnics, Pete had been content to stare up at the sky and identify shapes in the clouds. Was he still a daydreamer or had life worn away the idealist in him?

"I read on occasion. It has to be a book about something I'm really interested in." He shrugged. "I get antsy if I'm bored and sit for too long."

That hadn't changed. Though back when they were seventeen, sitting still while kissing her never seemed to be a problem.

"Any idea when your father's leaving?" Thankfully, she hadn't seen much more of the retired vice admiral. Kenneth had come along with Pete one afternoon for a brief tour. His time wandering the ranch property lasted less than an hour. Milton, who gave a good tour, had been more than happy to accompany Kenneth, his new friend.

"Not a clue. He's being vague on purpose. Wants to keep me on my toes."

Sarah knew exactly why. Pete's father wouldn't leave until he was confident his son wasn't falling under her spell again, but that magic had fizzled out a long time ago. The last thing she needed was another complication in her life. And attempting any type of meaningful relationship with Pete would definitely be complicated.

"Did your father ever come along to the Splash and Dash Festival during the summers you were here with your family?"

"No. He stayed back at the house." Pete dusted

off dirt from the front of his jeans. “Small-town fairs were beneath him. So is coming home dirty and smelling like horses. Lucky for you I’m not such a snob.”

She laughed. “Lucky for me. I’m amazed at what you can do with one arm.”

“It’s a very powerful arm.” He flexed the muscles of his right arm, and she tried not to swoon. “I’ll see you in town. Don’t forget to wear your swimsuit.” After wiggling his eyebrows at her, he hustled away to his truck.

Sarah did not put on her swimsuit but instead tossed it into her bag at the last minute. While getting into her car, she hesitated and scanned the area for anything she’d forgotten. All appeared calm and peaceful. One of the ranch workers planned to stop by around noon to check in. Helen would arrive in another hour to start cleaning the barn after last night’s wedding festivities. Sarah had been running things here for so long mostly on her own, it seemed strange to let others carry some of the load. She was grateful. Still, it had taken time after Mike’s death to release her hold on every aspect of the ranch and orchard, and trust others.

Same could be said for Pete. When he first offered to help, she’d scoffed. But now, she had a hard time imagining the place without him. He’d be missed by everyone here.

The ride into town was uneventful. Chloe's excitement was contagious and soon Sarah was eager to arrive. She found a place to park on a side street and walked with Chloe the few blocks to the town square. Sounds of laughter and screaming greeted them. When they turned the corner, the sight of people dripping wet while carrying large water pistols made her chuckle. Leave it up to Fern Hollow to host an annual festival around water pistol fights.

The normally quiet town square had been turned into a makeshift battlefield. The area sat in the center of the business district, which took up a city block, and offered a large open grassy area with benches for the townspeople to gather. A white gazebo resided in the center. Built in the shape of a hexagon, it boasted ornate gingerbread trim and a two-tiered roof. Currently, the gazebo was draped in red, white and blue banners in celebration of the Fourth of July.

Sarah approached the area with caution. She found a safe and dry place to leave their bags and towels, then sent Chloe off to play with her friends with a promise to meet back at their spot. After spreading out a blanket on the grass, she observed the action through her sunglasses. Each year, a few of the men from town rigged up an action field with barricades set up for tactical cover. Players would split up into teams and try to tag the other group with the dyed water in special water pistols. No one kept score, and the water combat from people's personal water pistols often spilled out of the contained field. Anyone attending the festival should expect to be hit by a water balloon or stream of water at any time. No one was safe. Especially the town's mayor, who declared he was exempt from getting wet but instead became the kids' number one target.

"Hello." Her mom approached wearing a bright floral sundress and wide brimmed hat. "I wasn't sure you were coming."

"I had help this morning. With the morning chores completed, Chloe convinced me to come." She dabbed at the sweat beading on her forehead with a hand towel. The day was growing warmer by the minute. She'd picked a spot in the sun to sit in case she got wet and needed to dry off. Maybe later she'd move into the shade. "Did Dad come with you?"

"He's over there talking with some of the men from church. They're planning a golf outing." Emma's gaze flicked from her husband back to Sarah. "He told me about all the donations the nonprofit has been receiving lately. What have you been doing differently?"

"It's from social media content. Pete's work

actually." She watched her mom arch one perfect eyebrow in surprise. "You should check it out if you haven't already. He's really talented at creating content that captures people's attention."

"I have looked at your Instagram. Pete appeared on some of the videos so I assumed he was involved." Emma ever so slightly lifted her chin. "He's leaving soon, right?"

Here we go. The inevitable question. "Yes. He plans to leave the morning of the square dance." A bitter reminder. Her mom believed Pete couldn't be gone soon enough. And Sarah should agree. But she'd grown fond of him once again. He was a good man and had been fantastic with Chloe. It was no shame to admit to herself that part of her wished he'd stay.

"Good. Don't get me wrong, I'm grateful for the help he's given and the funds he's helped raise. But I don't want to see you hurt again. He's simply not the man for you."

"Well, don't worry yourself over it. All will be back to normal soon." A depressing thought. She liked the excitement Pete had brought to her boring, safe life.

A group of giggling kids ran by shooting water in every direction. Emma scoffed and wiped a few drops of water off the side of her face. "I'm finding somewhere safer. Really, I ask myself every year why I come only to spend the entire time avoiding these little miscreants and their water pistols. Where are their parents?"

"Getting wet is what makes the festival fun." While her mom went to find a spot farther from the center of the action, Sarah sat on her blanket, happy to be squirted every once in a while. The cold water helped counteract the scorching sun, which gleamed down and heated her skin.

"You came," Pete's voice announced.

She tipped her head and shielded her eyes with her hand to see Pete's face backlit by the sun. "Of course. Have a seat." She patted the blanket beside her.

Pete hooked his thumb over his shoulder. "Brought my dad. He ran into Milton."

"Wonderful." She watched as Milton spoke animatedly with the stiff-backed military man. "Does he know what he's getting into?"

"With Milton or the Splash and Dash Festival?" Pete asked.

"Both." She turned her head to a trio of kids chasing another with water pistols going full blast. "Do you remember teaming up against Jacob and Caleb? They were both in my class."

"I don't remember exactly a specific water battle. I do know we had a lot of fun. My mom made sure to stay in the dry zone." He pointed to a cluster of lawn chairs set on the sidewalk in front of the shops on Main Street. The adults, mostly women, had cordoned off the area as a water-free zone. To date, no one had been brave enough to squirt anyone in that area. Or if they had, they hadn't lived to tell the tale.

"Thanks." He sat on the blanket beside her. "I think my father is going to be occupied for a while."

She rolled her eyes. "Milton has many talents but storytelling is his finest."

"Sure is. Did you know he joined the circus for a year during his teens?"

"No," she exclaimed. "He probably told you a tall tale."

"I don't think so." Pete sat and then reclined, resting back on his elbows. "He trained the trick ponies. Said he dated the bearded lady for a few months before she left him for one of the clowns. I guess the clown was better looking without his wig and makeup."

"He's pulling your leg." Glancing back at the old guy, Sarah wondered. Really, Milton working with a circus wasn't that farfetched given his colorful life. "He and my grandad would have competitions to see who could tell the most unbelievable story." Her heart squeezed with the reminder of her grandad. Would he be proud of what Sarah had done to carry on his legacy? She hoped so.

"Hey, hey." Lauren came walking up holding a very tall chocolate ice cream cone. "What a great day to get soaking wet." She took a long lick of ice cream, leaving a dab on the corner of her mouth, which she wiped away with the napkin she'd been smart enough to take with her cone.

"I need to touch base about the square dance." The big fundraiser was coming up fast, and she wanted every aspect to be perfect. Well, as perfect as it could be without Pete there.

"Now's as good a time as any," Lauren said. "Although, I promised Mrs. Bryan I'd watch her bake sale table for an hour around lunchtime."

"Is she planning to borrow a water pistol and step into the arena?" Pete questioned.

"I don't think so." Lauren chuckled. "She wants to check on her cat, Indy, who leads a better life than I do, by the way."

"Indy has a better life than anyone in Fern Hollow." Sarah sighed, imagining spending her days curled up on the back of the sofa, basking in the sun and then dining on the finest kitty foods. Indy even enjoyed being the main taste tester for all of Mrs. Bryan's baking.

Chloe ran up to the blanket, water dripping

off of her soaked hair. "Pete, you have to be on my team. We're getting creamed."

All three adults burst out laughing.

"Creamed, huh. We can't have that." Pete stood and studied the action field about fifty yards away. Currently, three teenagers were hiding behind a short wall, using it for cover as three women crept toward them. They had nowhere to go. The teens could either fight or flee. After getting off a few sprays of water that landed far from their opponents, they ran for the other side of the playing field. Laughter filled the air.

"Please help." Chloe grabbed his hand and pulled him forward, off the blanket. "I have to get Parker Johnson. He's the meanest boy in my class and makes fun of my red hair."

Pete saluted Chloe. "I'm at your service. He's going down. Where do I get a water pistol?"

Sarah pointed to the booth that rented them out for the colored water battles. Most townsfolk had their own water pistols for the fights outside the arena and were proud to show off what they could do. Some were even modified for greater shooting distance. "The lady who rents them will hunt you down if you don't return it after you're done. And her weapon of choice is not a water pistol."

“Ten-four.” He removed his wrist brace. The sling had gone unused for the past week.

“Shouldn’t you wear that all the time?” Sarah didn’t want him reinjuring his wrist during a silly water fight. But then he might stay longer. Would that be a good or bad thing? Good for the rescue’s bottom line. Not great for her heart.

“It’s feeling fine. I won’t do anything stupid. Promise.”

“Yeah, right.” She scoffed. “Have fun. Chloe, make sure Pete stays out of trouble.”

“Ten-four,” she hollered before leading Pete to his potential doom.

Lauren took Pete’s spot on the blanket and sighed. “How are you doing having to see Mr. Handsome every day?”

“Luckily, I don’t see him every day.” Almost, though. While his father had been visiting, Pete maintained his volunteer schedule only leaving early once in a while. He likely wanted to get out of his house during the day. Kenneth held high expectations for Pete—for both his sons. But with Pete, Sarah had witnessed the way the pressure affected him. Pete was a grown man now. Had served with honor in the army. He was more than capable of making his own decisions about his future. Hopefully his father had come to the same conclusion.

"You didn't answer my question." Lauren nudged Sarah with her knee.

"I'm doing okay. Busy, so that helps." She smiled at the sight of Pete walking alongside Chloe, both holding water pistols. Chloe's pistol was almost as big as she was. "I've come to terms, we both have, that the past is what it was. There's no changing what happened. We believed we could make a marriage work at eighteen and seventeen years old. Of course things didn't work out." They were too young and too different to make a lifelong fit.

"You're not young now. No offense." Lauren patted her on the shoulder. "Neither am I. Why not try again?"

Sarah shook her head adamantly, showing that the option was not on the table. "Pete isn't staying. He has a new job in Phoenix and he'd never be content living here. And most importantly, I am not open to a romantic relationship. Especially a long-distance one with no hope of that ever changing. I was blessed with a good marriage to Mike. I already had my Prince Charming. Now that he's gone, I'm content staying single and devoting myself to the ranch and Chloe. I don't need anything more." No more heartbreak, that was for sure. Nothing could have prepared her for Mike's death. If she offered herself to Pete only for him to leave her, she might never recover.

"Fair enough. Mike was one of the good ones."

"He was one of the best." Her throat tightened with sadness but also gratitude. Mike had healed her in so many ways. He'd offered his love with no strings attached. He'd given her Chloe, her most precious gift. He'd shown her that she didn't have to compromise to be truly loved. She'd never go back to believing she had to follow a man around the world to be worthy of his love as she had with Pete.

"Anyway, let's talk about the dance next Saturday." Lauren must have sensed Sarah's mood shift and offered a change in topic. "We've sold over two hundred tickets."

Her jaw dropped. "How is that possible? The highest attendance we've had before was one hundred and twenty."

"The page that was set up for the square dance has received a lot of views. Almost one hundred people have purchased tickets using the internet option. That's unheard of for Fern Hollow. I was under the assumption most people here didn't believe the internet was real."

With Pete's help, Sarah had added a link to the square dance fundraiser page from the rescue's website. The social media exposure he'd created drove people to the website, which in turn led them to the square dance page. Pete had also added posts specifically advertising the square dance to create excitement. "What are we going to do? We didn't plan for that many. And there will be those who show up and want to buy tickets at the door." A wave of panic fizzed inside. The event was only a week away.

"I spoke to those supplying food and they are planning on doubling our initial order." Lauren jolted as a stream of water landed on her lap. Two young boys each holding water pistols went back to shooting at one another. She brushed the water from her bare legs. "That actually felt good."

"I'll put out a request for those bringing baked goods to fire up their ovens. I'm sure Mrs. Bryan will be happy to supply us with tables full of treats. And we have the pie auction to boost dessert offerings."

Lauren rubbed her hands together. "I'll bring extra brownies. It's going to be great. The more people, the more money the rescue brings in."

Yes, and all due to Pete and his social media work. If she could find a way to keep up the momentum Pete had started, Sarah might be able to expand her rescue. She'd buy more land, bring in more help and rescue more horses. The dream made her smile. Her grandparents would approve.

Her aspirations these days tended to involve creatures with four feet instead of two. But when those two feet were wearing cowboy boots and belonged to Pete O'Keefe, she struggled not to include him. Despite her knowing in her heart how dangerous counting on him would be.

CHAPTER THIRTEEN

No spot on Pete remained dry after engaging in a water battle with Chloe and her friend. The three had waited their turn to enter the arena. Once inside, the cute little girls turned into ruthless soldiers. They shouted orders to him like an Army captain, giving him flashbacks of boot camp. Their group had been set against Jacob, Kay and a teenage girl. After they spent the first minute hiding behind a barricade constructed out of plastic storage totes, they decided to move forward as a unit, with Pete charged with watching their backs.

First up was a battle with Chloe's nemesis, Parker Johnson. The boy was tagged out by Pete in the first minutes.

The next game didn't come so easy. Pete had done his job admirably but had fallen victim to a surprise attack by Kay, who'd jumped out from behind a flower planter to shoot Pete square in the chest. The water used had been dyed.

His team's color was purple while the opposing team was green. He glanced down at the green spot on his formerly white T-shirt. After he'd been tagged out, Chloe and her friend went on to squirt Kay and the teenage girl. With Jacob up against the two little girls, he didn't stand a chance. They cornered him against one of the plywood walls that made up the sides of the battlefield and the rest, as they say, was history. It would forever be remembered as the famous last stand of Jacob Woods.

"Great work." Pete high-fived the girls as they exited. Each had their water pistol slung over their back.

"You did okay for your first time." Chloe grabbed her towel and dried off her face.

He had done this before as a teenager, but he'd keep that to himself. His embarrassment over being tagged out before the girls was still fresh. He shook Jacob's hand before the newlywed was dragged away by his wife for a flavored ice. "Thanks. Where are you off to next?"

"I'm getting hungry. Mom promised me hot dogs and ice cream." She pointed down the street to where the food trucks were set up, far away from the unruly water pistol enthusiasts.

Pete reached for his wallet, then stilled his hand. His first instinct was to give Chloe money for food. Or take her over and buy her anything she wanted. But he wasn't her father. Not family. Not even her mom's boyfriend. He'd almost overstepped. "Looks like your mom is sitting under that tree."

Sarah met his gaze and waved to them. She looked so beautiful it took his breath away.

He recalled the first time he'd seen Sarah at ten years old. Back then, he hadn't appreciated her red hair, freckles and long skinny legs. She'd been friendly enough and Pete liked being at the ranch with the horses, so he tolerated her hanging around whenever he visited the Carmella Ranch. By the time he'd grown old enough to be hired by Giorgio as a part-time stable hand, Pete had found Sarah's red hair and freckles more pleasing. And her long skinny legs sticking out from her jean shorts started to intrigue him. It was her smile that had captured his heart first, though. After that, he'd been helpless to keep from falling, like a rock tumbling down the side of a hill, picking up speed. Now, he found other elements of Sarah attractive, besides still loving her looks. He liked the way she didn't give up on a horse, even after others told her to. She attacked each day with purpose and drive. She was an attentive mother and placed Chloe's needs first. Sarah had lived a full life in the twelve years since he'd left, and he saw how she'd bloomed despite some very dark times. That showed resilience, which he deeply respected.

Chloe went off to talk her mom into lunch.

He hesitated about where to go next. Should he join Sarah? He didn't want to interrupt the conversation she was having with Lauren, even though Chloe had burst right in and sat on the blanket between them. His father and Milton had found a comfortable spot on a bench in the shade and appeared content chatting with one another. Standing by himself served as a reminder he was an outsider. While he'd spent summers in Fern Hollow, he was never a local. He'd never fully embraced what it was like to live in Fern Hollow with its small-town flavor and quirky festivals, like the one going on now. The charm was growing on him instead of repelling him like it had when he was a teenager. Strange. He could almost see himself as a part of this unfamiliar landscape. Must have taken too many water shots to the head.

"Hey." Caleb Dearborn approached, appearing slightly drier than Pete. "I wasn't sure you were still around."

"I'm leaving next Saturday, bright and early. I'll take two days to drive down to Arizona." The idea of stepping into that desert heat made him grateful for the eighty-degree weather currently visiting Washington state.

"Do you want to have a seat and dry off?" Caleb gestured to two lawn chairs not far away. "These are mine. I don't know where my nephew ran off to so you can use his."

"Sure. Thanks." He cupped his left wrist and got seated. It had started aching after getting jostled around. *You should have listened to Sarah and worn your brace.* Women tended to be right about ninety-nine percent of the time, so why had he declined her suggestion? Male stubbornness was the most probable culprit.

"How's the wrist?" Glancing at Pete's wrist, Caleb flexed both of his hands.

"Healing. I go to the doctor on Thursday. They'll take X-rays to make sure everything is where it should be. If so, then I'll get the all-clear to start work." He hoped so. His new employer might not be accommodating for long. Although they had offered desk duty to get him started when he'd first reported the injury. Which he'd declined. If his father ever found out, he'd be livid. That was why Pete would never mention it. He hadn't wanted to start his time with the police department stuck at a desk. Not when a more tempting option sat at his doorstep.

"I'm sure your experience in the military will make you a great asset for the Phoenix police. I went into the police academy straight out of community college and then into the sheriff's department. I enjoy looking out for the community. Then again, we all look out for one another, whether we're in law enforcement or not."

"That's the benefit of a place like Fern Hollow and the surrounding region. People know one another." Why was he talking up Fern Hollow? Next, he'd offer to do social media content for a tourism initiative, if they ever agreed to one. Those who came to the area for vacation stumbled upon it naturally, like his mom had after hearing from a friend about a cabin for rent in the Columbia River area of Washington state. Once his mom viewed the mountains, river and landscape that rolled on for miles unobstructed, she'd insisted on returning every summer. Their last visit had been the year Pete and Sarah had run away. He hated the thought his actions had spoiled something precious for his mom. Would she have traveled here in the summers in the years to come, even alone? Perhaps. His mom had been very independent.

"People do know one another, which is both good and bad. Take me, for instance. Everyone knows I'm a thirty-year-old single man and therefore attempt to set me up with any single female they know. Having my nephew living with me helps keep away most of those offers.

It's hard to find time to date when I'm chasing around a preteen boy with a mind of his own."

"I bet. How long is he staying with you?" Pete remembered what he was like at the age of twelve and shuddered at the thought of being responsible for someone like himself.

"My sister is out of rehab and asked for a week or so at home alone before Danny comes back." Caleb rubbed at his eye. "I really hope she gets it right this time."

He didn't want to pry but imagined Caleb's sister struggled with substance abuse. He'd seen soldiers succumb to the temptation of a quick fix to deal with a physical or mental ailment, or sometimes both. "Danny is lucky to have you."

"Try telling him that. This morning he told me I'm ruining his life by making him come along to the festival. And now amazingly he's having a great time. He's even made a few friends."

"Boys that age are rebellious for the sake of being rebellious."

"Don't I know it," Caleb said. "You couldn't tell me anything from ten until I turned twenty. Even now I have a tough time listening to good advice."

"We seem to have turned out alright. There's hope for your nephew." Pete rubbed at the sore area of his left wrist again. "If I ever have a son, I'll encourage him not to be a daredevil like me." No wonder his mom had gone gray early. Pete had always had an adventurous nature, seeking new and exciting things. It wasn't until he joined the army that he felt real danger and the exhilaration of putting his life on the line for a purpose greater than himself. And when things grew slow and monotonous, he sought out ways to spike the adrenaline.

"Jacob mentioned you fell while rock climbing. I wish I was crazy enough to find a rock wall and scale up."

"Don't wish to be that crazy. I'm not sure what came over me. I normally don't go around climbing without the proper gear." He really hadn't made a smart choice when he'd gone up the rock wall during the hike with Jacob and his groomsmen. What had gotten into him to throw out his normal safety precautions? Pete enjoyed a thrill but he generally wasn't stupid.

"Breaking my wrist has led to some good things," Pete said. "I've helped build the rescue's social media presence. Sarah deserves the added attention."

"Are you and Sarah back together? Don't answer that. Sorry I asked." Caleb waved away the question.

"It's fine." His gaze sought out Sarah, causing his chest to squeeze. She was perfect. They were not perfect together. "No. There was too much damage done in the past. We agreed to focus on rebuilding a friendship but nothing more. We want very different things for our lives."

Caleb nodded. "I get it. She's a great girl and has been a good friend since our school days. She loves the ranch and her animals, and I don't think anything or anyone could convince her to give them up."

"No one ever should." Sarah's roots were firmly planted where she belonged. Too deep to be pulled up, especially by the likes of him.

"Uncle Caleb." The boy Pete had seen slouching on the picnic table at the ranch two weeks earlier jogged up to where they sat. He looked strikingly like Caleb. His hair dripped water and the colors on his T-shirt gave evidence of multiple engagements in water pistol fights. "Can I get some money for a hot dog? Marcus and Liam and I want to eat and then skateboard over at the park." Danny held out his hand in anticipation.

Caleb reached into his wallet and pulled out a five-dollar bill. He slapped it into Danny's open and waiting palm. "When you're done at the park, come back to the town square and find me. And don't get into any trouble."

"Yeah," Danny mumbled before running off to join his friends.

"How well do you know Marcus and Liam?" Pete asked.

"They're good kids but anyone has the ability to find trouble at that age." Caleb returned his wallet to the back pocket of his shorts.

"Ain't that the truth." Pete stood and stretched. "We've both dried off nicely. How about we team up and head into battle? I could use some redemption after being tagged out first when I was teamed up with Chloe and her friend."

"I'd be honored to serve alongside you." Caleb pushed to his feet. "I heard that no one's been brave enough to squirt the mayor this year."

Pete's gazed focused on the town's mayor seated comfortably in his chair inside the gazebo. "That sounds like a mission for a couple of real men. A couple of heroes."

Reaching out, Caleb shook Pete's hand. "It's been a pleasure getting to know you again—in case one of us doesn't make it out."

Pete tipped back his head and barked out a loud laugh. "Come on, soldier. If we survive, then I'll buy you a beer."

"It's a deal."

YAWNING, SARAH STOOD and checked the time. She should be heading back. There were always more chores to do and not enough time in the day. But Chloe was having fun, and she didn't want to drag her daughter away early. She'd stay for another hour, letting Chloe continue to enjoy the festival. After visually searching the crowd, she found her girl tucked in with a small group of girls her age. They were seated in a circle on a blanket spread out on the grass. Chloe leaned over and appeared to whisper into another girl's ear.

Sarah remembered similar long summer days spent with friends. Her problems then seemed small now in comparison. Instead of worrying about getting the pair of sparkly sandals the other girls had, she currently lost sleep over the price of feed, hay and veterinary care.

"Fern Hollow knows how to run a festival." Pete's father appeared beside her. His khaki slacks and crisp blue polo shirt looked untouched by the rampant spraying water. Proof that no one messed with the retired vice admiral. Not even the wild boys running around the town square. The mayor likely wished he was so fortunate.

She'd witnessed Pete and Caleb leading the charge to drench the mayor. The wild boys in that case were men, who should know better than to antagonize the town's mayor.

"We do." She smiled at Kenneth, trying to remember he was Pete's family and as such she should treat him courteously. "Are you having fun?"

"Surprisingly, yes." He leaned with his right hand on his cane. "Milton is a character. I've come across my fair share of men like him while in the service. Good men with a few rough edges. Then again, don't we all have parts that need smoothing?"

"Agreed. That's Milton." Her heart warmed that Milton had won over Kenneth, a man whose tough shell seemed hard to crack. "He's my most trusted helper and a miracle worker with the horses. Most are terrified and traumatized when they arrive. Milton has a way of reassuring them that they are safe."

"Peter was like that when he worked with your grandfather, if memory serves," Kenneth said. "I was against him working there at first. Then I went to see him one day. I stood off at a distance and watched your grandfather instruct Peter on how to handle a skittish horse. By the end of the lesson, Peter had calmed the horse enough for him to touch it. I recognized the benefit of the responsibility. He was not only learning how to handle a horse—he was learning leadership."

Her eyes widened at his unexpected words. "You're absolutely right. Leading a horse is very similar to leading people. Although a person usually doesn't kick or nip at you when they don't get their way."

Kenneth laughed. "Navy men, not so much. I can't speak for members of the other branches."

"How is Chris? I hear he's a fighter pilot."

"Chris is well. He loves what he does and is a very talented pilot." Kenneth's eyes lost some of their focus, as if he was picturing his son on a faraway warship. "He's coming home soon on leave. The whole family is coming to San Diego for a long visit. I haven't seen them in almost a year."

"That's really great you're all getting together." Engaging in casual conversation with Pete's father made her feel like she was having an out-of-body experience. Was this really happening? Kenneth was acting so…normal.

"I suppose it's no surprise I came to visit Peter because I was concerned." He cleared his throat. "He's in a transition time, from a military career to civilian. It's tough. I struggled after retiring from the navy. For a long time, my identity was in my rank. After that is gone, one is left to forge a new course."

"You're still Retired Vice Admiral O'Keefe." As she was reminded when he'd first arrived.

"Ah, yes." Kenneth adjusted his stance and his grip on his cane. "That's mostly when I move in military circles. I was fortunate to find a new calling performing consultant work for the Department of Defense. In some respects, my new course wasn't far from my original."

"Pete will be working in law enforcement. How do you feel about that?" Sarah asked.

"His role with the Phoenix Police Department is a start. I assume he'll excel and take on a leadership role within the year. That is if he gets through the final stages of onboarding and start working with the SWAT team. The fracture to his wrist unfortunately set him back."

"I know he initially planned to start in June, but he's been such a help to me. His work with our social media has brought in increased donations. I'm hoping we can continue what he's started." One more item to add to her chore list.

Kenneth's brown eyes studied her for several seconds. "I was furious with Peter when he told Patty and me that he'd run away with you to get married. Such a foolish thing to do right before leaving for basic training. Patty was beside herself. She always liked you, Sarah, and was sad to have missed her son's wedding."

"I understand. We hurt a lot of people." Including her own parents and grandparents. Guilt stung anew. The feeling was different now. Sharper and wider. She'd been aware Pete's parents had been unhappy with their actions.

Hearing it directly from Pete's father made their disappointment more real.

"Young people do unwise things. I won't bore you with some of my exploits from my younger years." One corner of his mouth lifted. "Patty and I never told you how sorry we were when we heard about the baby. We should have reached out afterward. Patty wanted to. I felt it was best to leave the situation alone."

Sarah had received a sweet card from Patty about two months after the miscarriage, though she wouldn't share that with Kenneth. The communication appeared to have been sent without his agreement or knowledge. "You were protecting your son."

"I've always wanted the best for both my sons. Peter worried me more than Chris. I sensed a restlessness and indecision in him, and that his choices were made more to please me than because it was what he really wanted." Kenneth paused and glanced around. The festival was still going strong, and a bluegrass band had started playing on a small stage. The cheerful music floated in the breeze along with a chorus of chatter and laughter. "You may not believe me, but I've always wanted Pete to live according to his purpose, not the life I expected him to lead."

Then why did you never tell him that? She

shook her head, too afraid to say that she didn't believe him. As far as Sarah knew, Pete's father had been nothing more than a strict commander who set the rules and expected obedience.

"I don't blame you," Kenneth said as if reading Sarah's mind. More likely, her true feelings were showing on her face. "Peter wouldn't believe me either. I'm leaving in three days. If Peter decides to make his future here with you, I won't be an obstacle."

Had she heard him correctly? She looked at Kenneth, stunned. "You came here to make sure he didn't stay."

"True. I won't pretend otherwise. That day when your daughter ran off and Peter brought her back, I realized I'd been wrong to steer him away. He loves your ranch and cares for your little girl. I do want to see him settle down and have a family. I'm not telling him what to do, mind you. Those days are over. I wanted you to know." Kenneth grimaced and gripped his thigh. "I need to sit down for a stretch. Find Peter for me and let him know I'd like to go."

"Of course." She walked with Kenneth to a nearby bench and made sure he got seated without issue. "I'll send Pete over as soon as I find him."

With her head spinning, she wove her way through the crowd in search of her tall ex-husband. Had she misjudged Kenneth O'Keefe all these years? Or perhaps he'd reached an age where retrospection came easier. The real question—did less pressure from his father to pursue a bigger and braver career mean Pete would be willing to stick around Fern Hollow?

Was a future together possible? Her heart soared. *Don't get ahead of yourself, Carmella.* Did she even want to pursue a romantic relationship? And with Pete a second time around? Her resolution to stay single cracked a tiny bit. If the man she surrendered her heart to was Pete, then maybe.

She spotted him standing in the shade of the Timeless Treasures awning. He stood tall with straight posture, at least a head taller than everyone else around him. Sarah stepped onto the sidewalk and halted at the sound of her mom's voice.

"You complicated things for her," Emma said in her distinctive tone of disapproval. "I know you mean well but I'm only looking out for Sarah."

Her first instinct was to rush forward and stop any further comments from her mom. Instead, she slipped beside a tree trunk to stay out of her mom's view.

Pete had his back to her. "I understand. Sarah is special and it's natural you want to protect her. The last thing I want to do is hurt her or make her life more difficult."

Complicated—yes. Make more difficult—absolutely not. The exact opposite, actually. And she'd tell them both if she convinced her feet that eavesdropping never led to anything good.

"You will hurt her, Pete. Unless you plan on building a life here in Fern Hollow, your leaving again will hurt her. Not as deeply as last time, mind you, but Sarah has suffered more heartache since then and she's more fragile."

"I am not," Sarah muttered to herself. A group of moms from Chloe's school passed by and she gave them a friendly wave, hoping to appear normal.

"I stayed because I thought I could help the ranch," Pete said. "Your in-laws did so much for me when I came for summer visits. Giorgio taught me about more than horses. My time at the ranch is as much about honoring their memory as it is about finding a way to rebuild a friendship with Sarah."

"That's all it is, then?" Emma pressed. "A friendship? No big plans to run away together and get married."

"Of course not." The back of Pete's neck reddened. "What we did back then was a mistake. We're both old enough to understand. I want Sarah to be happy, and she's happy on the ranch.

I'm not the type of person to enjoy the quiet life she loves. I need more."

Her heart sank. Her dreams evaporated. For a few minutes, Sarah had envisioned the possibility of waking up every day to see Pete in the barn or eating breakfast in her kitchen. How ridiculous. *You know better.* They weren't meant to be after high school and they weren't meant to be now.

Not willing to hear anything more, she stepped away from the tree and toward where Pete stood. "Pete," she said with a crack in her voice. "Your father asked me to find you. He's ready to leave."

He swung around wearing an expression she couldn't read. Guilt, perhaps, at telling her mom the truth? "He's lasted longer than I expected. It was nice speaking with you, Emma."

Her mom nodded once. "If I don't see you before you leave, have a safe drive and good luck."

"Thank you, ma'am." Pete turned to Sarah. "I'll see you tomorrow?"

She wanted to tell him to leave for Phoenix now. That spending more time together would only make his departure hurt more. But she couldn't do that to him. He hadn't done anything wrong. He'd never lied. He didn't want to live in a small, rural town. Pete had made the same declarations when they were teenagers.

Nothing had changed. Why had she expected him to?

"I need to find Chloe and make sure she's eating something other than ice cream. I'll talk to you later, Mom. See you tomorrow, Pete." With tears stinging her eyes, she rushed off, not wanting Pete to see her cry.

She could survive his presence for one more week. With so much to do between now and the square dance, she'd be too busy to focus on her fractured dreams. She'd put him to work. Then he'd be gone.

And she'd find a way to carry on while missing him—until losing him faded like it had the last time.

CHAPTER FOURTEEN

"I CHANGED MY MIND." Sarah shut the refrigerator door and turned to see Chloe and Lauren staring back. "My back hurts."

"That's ridiculous." Lauren folded her arms over her chest, and Chloe mirrored the pose. "What's changed from when you asked me to come over and hang out with Chloe?"

A lot. Sarah had planned to take Pete riding before he left. They hadn't had a chance to go out on horseback in the weeks he'd been at the ranch. At the Splash and Dash Festival, she'd asked Lauren to come over and have dinner with Chloe. That was before she'd overheard Pete tell her mom he'd never settle for the quiet life Fern Hollow offered. Of course she'd already known his boots were too big for a small town. But for a brief moment she'd hoped he would change his mind. And then his words had slapped her back to reality.

"I was going to tell you not to come. I forgot.

I'm sorry you drove all this way." She pulled out a frozen pizza from the freezer. "You can still stay for dinner."

"Mom, you need to leave. I want a pizza and movie night with Lauren." Chloe tugged on the hem of Sarah's shirt. "It's not special when you're here."

"Thanks," she said with a hint of sarcasm. "Obviously I am not wanted."

"Don't be offended." Lauren smiled and looked down at Chloe. "We both want you to enjoy a nice ride with Pete."

"Lauren puts M&M'S in the popcorn and brought sour gummy worms." Chloe smacked her hand over her mouth. "I forgot Mom isn't supposed to know."

Sarah blew out a breath. Those little affections were so easily bought. "Fine. I'll see if Pete is still here." Perhaps she'd get lucky and he'd have left early, forgetting about their ride. "Have fun, you two troublemakers." She exited the house to the sound of giggles. While she grumbled that she'd lost her excuse not to go riding with Pete, she was grateful for a good friend who snuck sour gummy worms and M&M'S into her daughter's popcorn during movie night.

"There you are." Pete appeared from behind one of the storage sheds like a country music fantasy come to life. If only he wasn't so handsome. He removed his cowboy hat and wiped his brow with a red bandana. "I've been looking forward to tonight. What horses should we take out?"

Butterflies fluttered inside her belly. She never should have mentioned horseback riding. Too late to back out now. Not when everyone else seemed to be pushing her to spend one last night with Pete. He was leaving in three days, and she'd yet to come to terms with his departure. When they said goodbye, she wanted to hug him with a smile on her face and best wishes on her tongue. Would it be another twelve years before she saw him again? *He may get married and start a family.* The idea depressed her.

"I thought we could take Brownie and Elf. They haven't been out on the trail in a while." She walked with Pete to the stable. He went to work tacking up Elf. Sarah did the same with Brownie. She took a few minutes to stroke the mare's velvety soft coat. Once the horses were ready, they mounted and steered them to the trailhead by the west pasture.

The weather today was a touch cooler than it had been recently. Along with jeans and boots, Sarah had put on a long-sleeved flannel shirt. She wore her grandma's straw cowboy hat. The hatband, made of multi-colored glass beads set in a repetitive diamond pattern, had been handcrafted by her grandma many years ago. The gentle rhythm of the horse underneath her soon calmed her nerves. Gonzo, deciding to accompany them, raced alongside Sarah, then darted off ahead.

Pete was dressed similarly to her, only he wore a black T-shirt. He always did run hot. “Do you get to ride often?” He patted Elf’s neck. The horse nickered with seeming appreciation.

“Not as often as I used to. I should make the time though.” Most of her riding involved training. A horse with little experience wearing a saddle with a rider or a horse that carried a negative association with those things needed conditioning. Bearing a rider could be a pleasant experience for a horse with the right preparation.

They crested a hill and paused. Sarah never took this view for granted. For miles, the landscape rolled on until encountering the Columbia River. Then it continued until the foothills and mountains. How could Pete not want this? Not want her? *You’re not a teenager anymore.* She reminded herself she’d disavowed relationships. Regrettably, Pete made her forget all her strongly held beliefs when it came to romance.

She gently nudged Brownie with her feet, and

the horse responded by resuming her unhurried trot. The trail she'd selected was a gravel path wide enough for both horses to travel side by side. When the path ended, instead of looping back, she guided the horse to the right. A pond waited about another mile across the pasture. A cluster of small black birds coasted by, only a few feet above the tall grass. Their chatter sounded similar to Chloe and her friends.

"My father left this morning. I dropped him off at the airport. He's taking a puddle jumper to Seattle and then catching a flight to San Diego." He turned his head to gaze at Sarah. "The man has softened with age. I didn't think I'd ever say that."

Sarah had kept to herself what Kenneth had shared. It didn't matter if his father no longer pressured him to leave Fern Hollow. Not when Pete wanted to go without the extra encouragement. "Did you have a nice visit?"

"It was unexpected." He moved the reins to his other hand. "He's never been one for showing emotion. He drilled it into Chris and I to always think with our heads. Use logic and clear judgment. Not make rash decisions based on feelings."

"Like eloping with your girlfriend weeks before starting basic training?" She smiled at his laughter.

"Exactly. He almost disowned me after that." His face turned serious. "He actually said he likes seeing me happy. I almost fell out of my chair."

"I bet." She'd been equally shocked at his change of heart. People changed. It had taken awhile for her parents to accept her choice to take over the ranch. They'd loved Mike and now doted on Chloe. What had started as disappointment had turned into respect. Pete's father may have taken longer to conclude that children didn't always turn out as a perfect mold of their parents but that didn't make them any less valuable or deserving of joy.

"Chris and family are coming to San Diego and staying with my father for a few weeks at the end of August. I'd like to be there for part of that time. Not sure how long I'll be able to get off."

"I'm sure you'll make it work. Spending time together as a family is important." She breathed in a lungful of air through her nose. The familiar scents of the land comforted her. Up ahead in the grass, two brown rabbits hopped away from the approaching horses, their white tails bouncing until they disappeared from view.

"That's why Mom insisted we come here every summer. Even if Dad couldn't join us for the entire time, she wanted us away from the busy life at home. At the cabin, we disconnected from school and sports and reconnected to nature and one another."

"Watch out or the mayor will make you the face of a Fern Hollow tourism campaign." Always a tourist. Never a resident. Pete loved to visit—had too many big plans to stay.

"No chance of that after Caleb and I soaked the mayor at the festival." He adjusted his cowboy hat.

They continued riding until they reached the pond. The sun still had a way to go before it touched the horizon. Frog songs filled the air. The amphibians resided inside the reedy area along the edge of the pond. Her grandad had dug the pond to make a watering hole for the horses. Sarah had never been brave enough to step in and take a swim. She'd leave it for the four-legged creatures.

A grander body of water was located about a twenty-minute drive from town. The beach area was often crowded in the summer months. Homes dotted the shoreline surrounding the lake. She'd only taken Chloe there a few times for a picnic and swim. There was still time yet this summer to plan a trip. She promised herself she would take a day off after the square dance and spend time with her daughter at the lake.

Sarah dismounted and dropped the reins.

Brownie and Elf were calm horses and had been at the ranch for at least five years. They wouldn't run off unless spooked. Brownie stepped toward the edge of the pond, then lowered her large head for a drink.

Once Pete had dismounted, Elf followed Brownie to the pond. The humans stood in silence until the horses had their fill of water. Then the horses strolled over to a patch of taller grasses near a cluster of trees and started munching.

She wasn't sure what to say now. What was in her heart? Sarah couldn't ask Pete to stay. She had no right. Not when he'd made it clear his life was taking him in a different direction. Their deal had been simple—heal from the past and focus on the present. Not the future. Her future didn't include Pete. Which meant she'd only think about the present for now and the man who would help her move on by letting go.

PETE SPREAD OUT the blanket Sarah had brought. He sat and then lay back. Gonzo the dog crawled in beside him and sniffed Pete's shirt and pants. When Sarah lowered herself down, Pete presented her with the pink wildflower he'd just picked in the nearby grass. He tucked it behind her ear, then brushed a finger down her cheek. Her skin was as smooth as he remembered. *Careful. Don't get carried away.*

"You're visiting at the best time of year. I love all the seasons, but summer is my favorite." She touched the flower resting on her ear. Her hair was pulled back in a ponytail, and her hat shaded her face.

Gonzo moved over to Sarah, sprawled out beside her, and rested his head on her lap.

"I'd like to visit in the fall for apple harvest." He imagined the scents during that time of year—sweet and earthy—mixed in with the sound of children's laughter as they picked plump, red apples off full branches. Each time he ate an apple, he thought of Sarah.

"Maybe someday." She removed her hat and set it on the other side of Gonzo. "It's nice to see your vision expand beyond what you wanted to accomplish in the military."

"The world has a lot more to offer this vagabond." While his statement was true, his desire for exploring had dimmed. Pete's years in the army had taken him many places. Part of him did wish for consistency. Waking up in the same bed. Seeing the same people. Loving the same woman. He shook his head. All this fresh country air must be messing with his mind.

"I'd like to travel to Europe someday." She stroked Gonzo's white fur. "Eat a croissant in

Paris. Travel the Rhine River. Drink wine at a vineyard in Spain. It's silly, I know, for me to imagine leaving the ranch for a long period of time. Hopefully someday when Chloe is older."

"You'll make it happen. Growing older has us looking at the bigger picture instead of what is directly before us," he said.

"Growing older does tend to change your perspective. I'm more of a realist than I used to be. I used to hate getting up early, but now I'm up most days before my alarm and the sun." She tipped her face up to the remaining warmth of sunshine. "During high school, my grandma used to have to drag me out of bed when I stayed with them."

"Same." He chuckled. "Though I'm still not a fan of mornings. Coffee makes it bearable."

"Isn't it funny how we've changed but yet are the same deep down in our core." She bit her lower lip. "Take you, for instance. You're more patient than I remember. When you were younger, you seemed distracted by the next thing. When you were mucking stalls, you'd want to ride. And when you were riding, you were thinking about going into town for a meal. Now, I watch you with a horse and even with Chloe, and I don't see your mind working as hard on what's next. I think it's still there but you are able to focus longer on what is in front of you."

"All true. The military taught me patience. Lying on a ridge for a day while waiting for our target to move past drilled into me a tolerance for the mundane. I learned to appreciate the quiet times as well, away from the action. Sitting in bed with a crossword puzzle took on a whole new meaning after a day trudging through the desert." Pete sniffed and caught the scent of ozone and rain. A thunderstorm would visit later tonight. Growing excited for thunder and lightning, he acknowledged he was getting old.

"Have you noticed any changes in me?" Sarah asked, cocking one eyebrow. "I mean besides the wrinkles at the corners of my eyes."

"You don't look a day over seventeen." He winked, though he wasn't teasing. She'd held on to a youthful air. Perhaps a gift from the universe in repayment for all the good she'd done in the world. "I sense you're more settled than you were back in high school. You know exactly what you want and have a drive that I doubt anyone could dampen. I'm truly in awe of you, Sarah Carmella."

Her cheeks grew pink, and she glanced away. Their horses remained nearby, grazing on crisp grass. "I can be a bulldozer."

"A very pretty one." A flutter started in his chest.

Her smile faded, and her happy expression turned sorrowful.

"What's wrong?" Had he said something wrong? They'd been having an easy, breezy time until now. Although he did sense her mood had been tense while getting the horses tacked up to ride.

She didn't answer right away. Her hands closed into fists and then released. "I overheard what you told my mom at the festival on Saturday."

Pete racked his mind for that conversation. Emma had expressed concern over Pete's involvement in Sarah's life. No surprise. Otherwise, he didn't remember anything that would have upset Sarah. "I don't understand."

"I should know better." She stood and stared at the pond, arms folded. His space disrupted, the dog sauntered off to check on the horses.

Concern exploded through Pete. He got to his feet and rested a hand on her arm. His heart stopped at the sight of a tear rolling down her cheek. "Honey, what did I do?"

"Nothing." She sniffled. "You did nothing. You've been honest with me from the start. It's all on me. I shouldn't have believed anything was different."

"Different how?"

"I talked with your father at the festival, before I came to find you. He told me that he thought you were happy here. He said he hopes you'll settle down someday and have a family. Did he say that to you?"

Pete nodded. "Something like that."

She swiped the back of her hand under her eyes. "For a minute, I wondered if once the pressure from your father eased, you'd consider…"

"Consider what?" Stroking her arm, he fought the urge to gather her up and hold her tight. Something inside him cautioned now was not the time for physical overtures.

"Staying." She jerked forward and out of his reach. Then she spun to face him, and the sadness he'd seen a second earlier had been replaced by anger. "But you'd never stay, would you? Not in a quiet small town in the middle of nowhere."

What he'd expressed to Emma suddenly rushed back. His stomach sank. "I didn't mean it as a slight to Fern Hollow or your ranch."

"I know." She huffed. "It doesn't matter if your father is pushing you or not, you'd never stay."

Sure, he'd said he wasn't suited for a small town because he couldn't admit, especially to himself, that his beliefs all these years might be wrong. "I'm sorry." He'd keep the truth to himself because he wouldn't plant hope where there was no rain. He wasn't staying. Not with the commitments he'd made. Maybe in a few years he'd return and things could be different.

"Don't be." Her breath shuddered. "Like I said, it's my own fault. After Mike died, I promised myself that I'd stay romantically unattached and focus on Chloe and the ranch. I don't want the complications that come with dating. I'm not looking for anything from you. The last thing I want for either of us is to go through another breakup."

Ouch. Their past mistakes didn't define their future. Still, if they tried for a long-distance relationship and failed—again—they'd never be able to salvage a friendship like they'd done now.

"You should want something from me. Don't shut me out of your life." Like she had before.

"I couldn't shut you out, even if I tried. I appreciate all your help and don't want to lose your friendship because I'm being an emotional wreck."

His control slipping, he wrapped his arms around her and held her close. Pete rested his chin on the top of her head. Her hair was soft and smelled like herbal shampoo. He leaned back slightly and lowered his head. The kiss he planted on her lips was soft. His devotion to her would never cease, no matter how many miles lay between them.

He ended the kiss, then gazed deep into her gray eyes. “How about you get out that bottle of wine and the checkers board you brought along? Beating me at a board game could always put a smile on your face.” He longed to see her smile and hated that the words he carelessly spoke to Emma had caused her pain.

“You know me so well.” She nudged him with her elbow. “A glass of wine and beating you at checkers is exactly what I need right now.”

His past remained tangled up with hers. His future spread out like a lonely desert highway. Could he survive without her by his side?

CHAPTER FIFTEEN

"WHERE ARE THEY AGAIN?" Sarah asked for the hundredth time. While she'd agreed to take over the regular posting of social media content, her tech skills were lacking. So was her motivation. And who had the time to properly edit all those videos?

"Under the drafts." Pete pointed to a tiny icon on her phone screen. "I've saved almost twenty. Post one a day until they're used up. Either you or someone else will need to create more. Don't forget, viewers like positive stories and they've really connected with you. Include the tough days and real life but always spin it to something happy at the end."

"I'll do my best." Pete had done such an amazing job that Sarah doubted anyone, including herself, could emulate his success. Social media engagement had exploded. Website traffic was up. And most importantly, so were donations. People had pledged to give monthly.

Income she could count on helped with budgeting, which pleased her dad. He still pleaded with her to take on more boarding and training horses and fewer rescues. He likely always would. The small amount the rescue received in adoption fees paled in comparison to the fees charged to an owner paying her for food and board.

"You'll do great. Horace is a crowd favorite. Include him in a video at least once a week." As if he heard his name, the donkey brayed loudly somewhere in the pasture. Pete clicked through a few more icons on her phone, then held it in front of them. "Let's take a selfie. Something to remember me by."

She'd have no trouble recalling the soft hair on his face or the way he smelled when he came over in the morning—like coffee and the doughnut he'd eaten during his walk to the ranch. Despite her hurting heart, she pressed her face next to his and smiled brightly.

He took a few pictures before giving her back her phone. "Hope there's one you like. I tend to look cross-eyed in selfies."

Laughing, she glanced through the photos he'd taken. They looked like a happy couple, not a man and a woman planning to go their separate ways tomorrow morning. "You look great. No crossed eyes."

He swiped his hand across his forehead. "*Phew*. Oh, and I left my selfie stick in the office inside the stable. Thought you could use it."

"Thanks. Are you going to keep up with your own posting? I'm sure there'll be plenty of exciting things to share in Phoenix." Like cactus and desert animals, and perhaps someday a romantic partner to take hikes with into the mountains. She'd grown used to knowing what Pete was up to most days over the last five weeks. After tomorrow, she'd have no idea what he was doing or who he was with—if he went out on a date or stayed home for the night. He could be out on a dangerous mission and she'd have no idea. A worrying thought.

"I'm sure I'll find something to share." He shrugged. "We'll see how I feel and how much free time I have."

Milton, who stood outside the stable, called for Pete.

"I'd better make myself useful on my last day. I'll see you later." He kissed her quickly on the cheek, like a good friend would do, and ran over to see what Milton needed.

Sighing, she brushed her fingertips over the spot his lips had touched. Getting over him wouldn't be easy. But she'd managed to do it once before. She'd do it again.

Sarah found Helen and Lauren inside the Big

Red Barn, flitting around tables and adjusting centerpieces. While she'd seen the space set up for several different types of events, the decorations for the square dance had transformed the barn into someplace magical. Fresh peonies and daisies filled mason jars. Every table had multiple floral arrangements. Straw covered the floor. A stage had been set up for the band, and a large area had been sectioned off for dancing. Square dancing took a lot of space. With the size of the crowd they were expecting tomorrow, every inch of the dance floor would be put to good use.

"I love the photo booth." She headed over to the area and reviewed the setup. The donkey statue had found a good home here. It stood wearing a bright sombrero and a big toothy smile.

"Thanks," Helen said. "Everything we used was stuff found in the storage room and donations from Timeless Treasures."

"You both did an amazing job." Still taken aback, she spun around to take it all in. "I'm sorry I wasn't more help."

"You've been busy." Lauren patted Sarah's shoulder in an unspoken acknowledgment of the emotions running through Sarah. "Do you think we overdid it on the twinkle lights?"

Sarah looked up, and her mouth opened.

"How many are up there?" Strings of white lights swung from beam to beam, crisscrossing the ceiling. There seemed to be no rhythm or plan to their layout. But the chaotic nature of the lights was a good match for the high energy and joyous event that would be taking place underneath.

"We lost count," Helen said. "I bought out every store in an eighty-mile radius."

"It's fantastic. Everything is." Tears welled in her eyes. "The Hollow Hoedown is going to be the best square dance fundraiser yet."

"Are we married to that name?" Lauren asked.

"It's on every flyer and ticket, so yes. You should have said something sooner."

"I'm kidding. Kind of." Lauren spun around to take in all the work she'd done. "You should see my outfit. I found these vintage cowgirl boots and silver belt."

"Mine looks like I got it off one of the dancers in a square dance video." Helen laughed. "Promise not to make fun of me."

Both Sarah and Lauren reassured Helen. The dance was supposed to be fun and quirky. Clothing was to reflect history—of Fern Hollow and the rural community as a whole.

Sarah hadn't had much time to shop but did find a long skirt and an off-the-shoulder blouse for the dance. She had boots that were well broken in and wouldn't leave blisters on her feet by the end of the night. Excitement bubbled up to replace some of the despair she felt over Pete's departure. Fortunately, the dance tomorrow night would help take her mind off of Pete. At least that was what she was counting on.

PETE STOOD NEXT to the fence and watched as Nate, one of the young men who worked at the ranch, attempted to calm Hayes, the gelding he and Sarah had brought back several weeks ago. The horse remained in quarantine since he had no health history they could refer to. So far, he'd passed every health test. Hayes had retained his wild streak and acted untrusting of everyone who'd attempted to engage. Milton had managed to slip on a halter but after that, the horse had refused to cooperate.

Hayes reared up on his hind legs and whinnied loudly. After landing back on all fours, he turned on Nate, who tried to regain his grip on the lead, and snorted. The horse nipped a few times without making contact. Nate dropped the rope, and Hayes galloped off to the opposite side of the paddock.

"I give up," Nate shouted. He removed his gloves and brushed them off on his jeans. "That horse won't be happy until I'm dead."

The younger generation could be melodramatic. Pete waited for Nate to climb over the fence, then patted him on the back. “Hayes needs some time and patience.” Didn’t they all, even the humans. Hayes kicked up his rear legs while galloping around the paddock. A good reminder that working with horses could be as dangerous as rushing in with a team of soldiers to clear a building.

Get in there if you need a life-endangering activity to make you feel alive. Since spending so much time at the ranch, he’d felt the need to take risks diminish. Today, he wore his brace per the doctor’s orders. He’d keep it on for another two weeks for support and protection. Since he’d been faithful with his home exercises, his range of motion in the wrist was good. Pete would follow up with an orthopedic specialist down in Phoenix and hopefully be fully released soon. Until then, he’d work on paperwork and build connection with his new team.

At the other side of the paddock, Hayes snorted and observed the group of men with wide eyes. Poor creature. He had no idea what had happened to him or if any of the people around him were a threat. Up until now, Pete had left the training to Sarah and Milton. He hadn’t worked with a troubled horse in a very long time, and the idea made him slightly nervous. If Pete used some of the techniques Giorgio had taught him, there might be a chance of gaining Hayes's trust, showing him that humans weren't bad.

Pete entered the paddock and then stood still.

Hayes shook his head and neighed. The horse tried to move back, but with his hindquarters pressed against the fence, he couldn't retreat far.

"It's alright." He spoke in a soft, gentle voice. "I know you're scared." He slid one foot forward and moved up slightly. Keeping his hands at his sides and his gaze focused more on the ground than the horse, he inched his way forward. "It's alright, buddy. Let's stay cool and work through some issues together."

Hayes stomped his front hooves on the packed dirt ground when Pete stood within ten feet.

Despite the bluster, Pete continued his slow progress. While maintaining awareness of the horse's actions, he continued looking down at the lead rope resting on the ground. Once close enough, he made quick work of picking up the end of the rope. He held it loosely in his right hand.

Blowing hot breath out of his nose, Hayes appeared to be calculating his next move. The muscles in his shoulders and thighs twitched with tension. "I'm not going to hurt you, my friend. We want to take care of you. Running wild isn't a good way to live. Not for a good horse such as yourself. With Sarah, you'll have cover from bad weather and regular food and friendship. That doesn't sound so bad, does it?" Part of his brain prodded him to follow his own advice.

While avoiding eye contact, Pete leisurely lifted his hand. He hovered it in front of Hayes's nose and allowed the horse to catch Pete's scent. Giorgio had told Pete that touch triggered either a stress response or a release of good hormones. The goal was to make the contact a positive experience so the horse associated touch with pleasure.

He allowed his fingertips to brush the soft portion above the nose. His other hand hid a sugar cube that he'd pulled from his pocket. He offered it to the horse on an open palm. After several seconds of contemplation, Hayes scooped up the sugar cube with his floppy lips.

Hayes stiffened before relaxing. His snorts held less intensity.

"That's it, my friend. That's it." Pete increased the contact, stroking the side of the horse's smooth face and then moving to the neck. Every movement was slow and controlled. Pete's own body held no tension despite his mind warning him to run at the first sign of aggression. He wouldn't run away like Nate had, which only reinforced the horse's dominant and unruly behavior. "How about you come with me?" Pete lightly pulled on the lead to test if Hayes would follow.

Shockingly, Hayes took a few cautious steps away from the safety of the fence.

"Attaboy." Pete kept his voice even. "If you trust me, I promise not to let you down." But he would. He personally would no longer be around to continue working with Hayes. Milton would take over and keep building trust. But knowing that didn't ease Pete's conscience.

Pete glanced down at Hayes's hooves, which needed trimming. Sarah's farrier had come to inspect the horse's hooves but left without getting near him. Hayes had to calm down a bit more before being worked on. Sarah had mentioned this farrier had asked her out numerous times. Yet, she'd always declined due to her commitment to stay single. Pete didn't like the idea of another man asking Sarah out. In truth, he had no right to any information about her love life.

The horse tossed his head, and Pete's mind returned to the job at hand. Pete continued guiding Hayes into the center of the paddock. On one side, a generous lean-to offered everything a horse could desire, with fresh straw spread on the ground, hay stuffed into a feeder, a tub filled with water and a delivery of a grain-based feed mix three times a day. Hayes was probably lonely in the quarantine paddock by himself, though. That would change in a few more days as long as his tests continued coming back clear. The isolation was for the good of the entire herd. One sick horse led to many sick horses and huge vet bills.

Hayes stomped while Pete led him in a circle. Simple work—that was the foundation of any good training relationship. Over the next five minutes, Hayes loosened up. His steps grew lighter. He held his head high in apparent pride.

Pete slowed and then came to a halt. "Excellent job." He stroked the horse's mane. "You are a handsome man. Sarah will fall head over heels for you if she hasn't already."

The horse leaned into Pete's hand ever so slightly, but the sign of affection brought a smile to Pete's lips.

Dcciding not to push it any further, Pete unhooked the buckle on the halter and slipped it off in one smooth motion. He patted the horse's side to set him free. Hayes strolled over to the lean-to for a well-deserved drink.

"Nice work." Milton lowered the foot that had been resting on the lower rail of the fence. He met Pete at the gate and then shut it behind him. "Earning a horse's trust is a true measure of a man. They aren't impressed with money or status. They don't care what your last name is or what you've accomplished in the past. And a horse like that one, who's seen abandonment and fear—it's even harder to earn his confidence."

"That felt really good," Pete admitted. "When I worked with Giorgio, I didn't like taking the slow approach. I wanted the horse to like me and cooperate because I said so."

"How did that work out for you?" Milton asked with a chuckle.

"I was thrown more than once." He shook his head in remembrance of all the stupid things he did in his youth. "Bit at least a dozen times. I think I still have some teeth mark scars on my arms."

"Kicked?"

"Of course." Pete removed his cowboy hat and set it on the fence post. The breeze cooled his face and head. "Giorgio was always patient with me. He allowed me to make mistakes. Ones that didn't risk my life too much. I wouldn't be the person I am today if not for him."

Milton's eyes grew misty. "The world grew dimmer with his passing. I see a lot of Giorgio in Sarah. She's got his fighting spirit and also his loving nature. She gives everything to the ranch and the animals she rescues. Partially, I think, because she doesn't want to disappoint her grandparents. Things are different these days than they were back when Giorgio inherited the property with an apple orchard. Taxes have gone up. Food and medical care for the animals are more expensive every day. I worry she'll burn out because she will never give up."

"Do you think it will come to that?" If Sarah lost the ranch, she'd lose part of herself. He'd give her every cent of his own money to ensure that didn't happen.

"She's a clever girl." He hooked his thumb to point at the large barn to their left. "No one believed she could remodel that old falling-down barn into a place people would pay to rent. The fundraiser tomorrow will help fill the coffers some. I heard the videos you put on that social media have brought in extra donations. I think Sarah will find a way to survive, no matter what."

Pete had always considered himself a survivor—of the loss of the woman he loved and their unborn child, of years in combat, of the expectations that came with his family. But Sarah. He exhaled. She'd been through worse and still bloomed. A desert flower. The dissolution of their marriage had harmed her too. The baby they'd lost had been from her body. She'd fallen in love again and had another child, only to lose her husband. His chest hurt thinking about her heartache.

"Don't you want more for her than to simply survive?" Pete asked.

Milton cocked his head, resembling a horse that was considering whether to cooperate or kick. "Of course I want to see Sarah smiling from ear to ear every day. She's the closest thing I have to family, you know. I promised Giorgio and Lucille I'd care for her after they were gone."

"I didn't mean to suggest otherwise." With him leaving tomorrow morning, this conversation should best not go any further. He needed to pack yet. And he didn't want any more thoughts about staying placed in his head. Judging by the glint in Milton's eyes, that was exactly the argument he planned on making. Pete took a few steps backward. Not fast enough.

"If you're so worried about her, then why don't you stick around and be of some help," Milton challenged. "You believe you're brave. I see someone acting fearless to mask a real fear deep in his heart. Both you and Sarah spent so much time running away from each other, I don't think it's ever occurred to either one of you to come back together. Or if you have, you're too scared to try."

Ouch. Milton knew how to land a good verbal blow. It had occurred to Pete to try again. Many times. He'd had dreams of spending a long day mucking out horse stalls, then cleaning up and joining Sarah and Chloe for dinner. Not exactly the high-intensity work he was used to. He wouldn't need to use a gun or a flashbang or wear bulletproof gear. But would he be happy despite the absence of danger? A smile pulled at his lips at the sight of Hayes prancing around his paddock. Trying for a second chance with Sarah involved a completely different kind of danger.

"Fire!" The shout came from the direction of the Big Red Barn. Three people exited the barn, all covering their mouths with their arms.

Pete raced over and skidded to a halt. Black smoke billowed out of the open door. "Sarah!"

"I'm here." She stumbled out and coughed. "The fire department is on its way."

"What happened?" Pete asked.

"Electrical fire, I think. The wall started to smoke and then there were flames. I ordered everyone out."

He moved closer to get a look inside. The smoke-filled space was packed with decorations and set up for the square dance. "Can I move anything outside?"

"There's too much." Her shoulders slumped. "The square dance will need to be canceled."

CHAPTER SIXTEEN

"THANK YOU." SARAH HUNG her head as the last of the firefighters returned to their engines and trucks. She'd have to cancel the square dance. Refund all the tickets purchased. She closed her eyes, imagining all those dollars departing the rescue's account. Her stomach sank.

Stepping inside the barn, she felt tears burn her eyes. The spot on the wall where the fire started was scorched black, marking a four-foot section. The foam fire suppressant used on the wall had been cleaned up. Thankfully, the wooden structure had been spared. Sparks had landed on the straw spread across the floor. But between Sarah and those who ran in to help, they stepped on any hot spots and snuffed out the fire. The firefighters used water to put out any fire not located near the guilty wiring. A few sparks had started a fire, and now the annual dance would miss a year.

She ran her hand across the top of a table

and grimaced. Everything was soaking wet, including all the linens that had been placed over each table. The floral arrangements drooped. Water droplets dripped from besieged petals. The straw under her boots squished with each step. There was no way the space could be set back to rights in less than twenty-four hours.

"Wow," Helen said when she came to stand beside Sarah.

"Yeah, wow." Sarah wiped away her tears.

"Insurance will cover the damage, right?"

"I assume so. It won't help save the dance, though." She flipped through the upcoming rental schedule in her mind. A wedding was set to be held here next Friday. She'd call her insurance agent today and get the ball rolling. The last thing she needed was to lose the income.

"What if we move the dance to another location?" Helen offered. "Somewhere in town maybe?"

"I don't know who would have the room. Not the VFW Hall. We have over two hundred tickets sold with others expected to buy when they arrive." No one building could accommodate a group that large. Not unless they found a large event space in another town. One that wasn't already rented. "I should start sending emails to ticket holders tonight and post an announcement on the website and social media."

"Hold off." Pete came striding in like he was ready to clean up the place all by himself. "Isn't there something we can do to salvage this? We can take everything outside to dry."

"I think it's supposed to rain overnight," Helen said. "It's a good idea though."

"There is no way we can have people in here." Sarah sniffed the air and wrinkled her nose. "Everyone would come out smelling like smoke."

"What if we set up in the town square?" Pete glanced around with a frown.

"I don't think so. The grass area isn't very large. People would need to dance in the street. Plus, I'd need a permit from the town council." Dejection overtook her, which brought on acceptance. They'd try again next year. People would come back. Hopefully.

"We'll make it work." Pete rubbed her back. "What can I do to help?"

"Didn't you say earlier you had to pack tonight?" She'd already raised her emotional fortress and reinforced her defenses. Pete wouldn't be around tomorrow. His capacity to be of much help was handicapped by his eagerness to get out of Fern Hollow.

She had planned to ask him to stay for dinner. A casserole sat in the refrigerator, a chocolate cake on the counter. She'd pictured Pete, Chloe and herself eating a good meal while coming to peace with the fact that Pete was leaving their lives, maybe for good. With all the work that now needed to start as soon as possible, a nice quiet dinner wouldn't happen.

"It can wait." He gazed down at her, then tucked a strand of hair behind her ear. "Hey. I can throw my stuff into suitcases tomorrow morning. I'll stick around as late as you need."

"You're driving to Arizona tomorrow. You need sleep."

"I'm not driving the entire way in one day. Don't worry about me. Tell me what you need."

To not abandon me. To stay like you didn't before and be there when I need you. To want me more than a new job chasing danger. Of course, she didn't say any of the pleadings in her head. Instead, she locked away her true feelings in her heart. She wouldn't let Pete hurt her again. She didn't need a man in her life to be fulfilled.

"There's nothing to do now. The fire chief recommended I leave the doors open to help with the smell." She walked out of the barn, back into the daylight. The brightness temporarily affected her vision. She blinked a few times to adjust her eyes. When she caught sight of six horses grazing in the pasture, her blood pressure instantly lowered. She couldn't lose track of the reason for everything she did. Her horses didn't care about a square dance or refunding money for tickets. They currently had everything they needed. Sarah would find a way to make up what she'd lose by cancelling the dance.

Helen went back inside the barn to grab her purse and car keys.

"I need to go in the house and make phone calls." Sarah worked to clear the lump in her throat. "Is this goodbye then?"

His eyes widened. "You don't want me to stay?"

"There's nothing to do. I'll need to schedule a restoration company to evaluate the damage and then work with the insurance company to get started on repairs." *Be strong.* "Maybe we can have the square dance some other time. I can reschedule during harvest and make it an autumn festival."

"I don't like that you're giving up. You aren't even attempting to make the dance happen tomorrow." He crossed his arms, and the muscles in his forearms flexed.

"Didn't you see the inside of the barn?" Her voice had rose to an octave bordering on frantic. "There's nowhere else close that is big enough to fit all the people coming. It's done. I'll live to fight another day."

"I have no doubt about that." He reached out

and pulled her in tight to his chest. "This isn't goodbye."

Her heart skipped a beat. The pressure of his hands on her back grounded her.

"I'll stop by tomorrow on my way out of town."

Her heart dropped into her stomach. She pulled away. "Text me when you're heading over. I'm sure Chloe will want to say goodbye."

After Pete drove away, Sarah sat on her front porch and stared off into the distance. She should be inside making calls. Her heart wasn't in it. Maybe there was another place to host the event. She'd cook dinner, eat with Chloe, call her insurance agent and then go to bed early. An idea could come to her in her sleep. It was a long shot, but she couldn't make herself cancel the event tonight. If no solution came by tomorrow morning, she'd send out the emails and refunds, and pray the hit to her bottom line wouldn't cut too deep.

THE NEXT MORNING, the sound of car horns jolted Sarah awake. She rubbed her eyes. It was six o'clock. The dim light in her room let her know the sun had risen. Tossing a pillow over her head, she attempted to get a few extra minutes of sleep. More honking and the barking of dogs forced her out of bed.

"Mommy." Chloe peeked in from behind Sarah's bedroom door. "What's that noise?" She pointed to the window.

"I don't know. I'll see what's going on. Get back into bed." She put on a pair of jeans and a shirt that she'd thrown on the floor the night before. Whoever was making a ruckus better quiet down. She had no interest in dealing with a crabby child all day because someone drove onto her property and decided to disturb the peace.

On her way through the kitchen, she hit the Start button on her coffee maker. The grounds and water had been readied the night before. At least she'd be caffeinated if she had to be up this early on a Saturday morning. After slipping on her shoes, Sarah marched outside to give the offender a piece of her mind. What she saw stopped her in her tracks.

A line of trucks ran up the driveway, leading to the Big Red Barn. Each pulled a trailer. The trailers were loaded with tables, chairs and other miscellaneous items. "What's going on?"

The damp earth gave off a familiar, comforting scent—clean and fresh like a new beginning. A few small puddles lingered on the gravel drive. The cloudless sky promised a warm day ahead.

"Fern Hollow Rental crew at your service."

Pete appeared from the other side of a truck. One that Milton was driving. "We've come to make sure your fundraiser goes on as scheduled."

"How?" She stared open-mouthed at the scene. "The barn is unusable." Looking down at the row of vehicles, she noticed Jacob leaning out the window of his truck, waving. A huge grin lit up his face.

"We don't need the barn. You have all the room needed outside." He gestured toward the grassy area beside the barn. "Milton is going to get on the riding lawnmower and trim down the grass. The rest of us will set up."

Sarah approached a trailer and examined its contents. "Are these the tables from the patio outside Hussy's Bar?" Each table had to be close to ten feet long and came with benches.

"Hussy donated them for the day." Pete grinned. "Twelve of us spent the night going all over Fern Hollow, collecting tables, chairs and anything we thought you'd need for the party. We even got a dance floor."

She went to the open driver's side window of Milton's truck. "Is that true?"

"We didn't steal anything, if that's what you're wondering." Milton tapped his hand on the steering wheel. "It was Pete's idea. I helped call around town to ask what people would loan out. Everyone was real eager to help."

"I don't believe it." A bang sounded behind her.

Max Lane, the owner of a property down the road, had lowered the gate of a trailer and began pulling out one end of a table. Leo Mayer came over to help.

"Believe it." Pete put an arm around her shoulders. "The Hollow Hoedown is back on."

Laughter worked its way up from her heart and burst out of her mouth. The dance wouldn't be cancelled. They'd even found a dance floor. From where? She didn't care. "Thank you. Let's get to work."

About two hours later, the area around the barn looked nothing like it had before. Enough tables and chairs had been set up to accommodate the expected crowd. A section had been set aside for the band, with power cords running across the grass for their amplifiers. Buffet tables were lined up by the exterior wall of the barn. Someone had brought serving trays with butane heaters to keep the food warm without electricity. Those bringing the food would arrive around noon to start setting up. Her mom planned to bring the desserts the volunteer bakers had made. Lauren had talked to every resident with a garden. She'd spent the night collecting flowers and then added them to what flowers could be salvaged from inside the barn. Each table had a beautiful centerpiece. Someone had strung up white lights to swag in the air above the event space. They'd create a romantic atmosphere once the sky darkened tonight.

She pressed her hand over a heart filled with love and appreciation. "Was this really all your idea?" she asked Pete, who sat in a chair only a foot away.

"I brought it up to Milton and he agreed to help. He called in some favors." Pete rubbed the back of his neck and yawned. "The town didn't want to see the dance cancelled. They all know how important the money is for the rescue. They believe in the good you do here."

"I'm speechless. Truly speechless."

Pete yawned again.

"I have coffee inside the house. Let's get you a cup. Or do you want to take a nap?"

"Coffee would be nice." He glanced at his watch. "I have about an hour before I should hit the road."

Reality returned with icy fingers, gripping inside her chest. They squeezed until she couldn't breathe. Pete didn't plan on staying longer. He wasn't staying for the dance. He wasn't staying forever.

She could ask him to. Beg him to give their

relationship another chance. But she wouldn't put him in that situation. He'd apologize and remind her that he'd never be happy in a small town. He needed travel and excitement, neither of which Sarah could offer.

TIME TO GO. All Pete had to do was stand up, set his coffee cup in the kitchen sink, say goodbye and get in his truck. Easier said than done. After Chloe had come out to join the team setting up, he realized he'd be leaving her as well as Sarah. He'd need the right words for them both. Unfortunately, nothing profound came to mind. How could he justify his departure when it felt close to abandonment?

"I'm still hungry." Chloe let her head fall on her arms, which rested on the table.

"You had enough pancakes for four children." Sarah took Chloe's plate and rinsed its sticky surface. "Plus, Pete is getting ready to leave. How about you wash your face and then we can see him off?"

"I don't want him to leave. Don't go." Chloe raised her head and pulled at his shirt sleeve, leaving syrup marks. He didn't mind. They'd remind him of her during the drive. Or at least until he washed off his shirt. "You'll miss the dancing."

"I know. I'm sorry to miss the fun." More

than sorry. Devastated was closer to it. He'd been raised to not make decisions based on emotions. To use logic and then stick to the plan. The one time he'd deviated from his father's teachings, he'd ended up with a broken heart.

"Fine." Chloe pushed off the table to move back her chair and then hopped down. She darted off to the bathroom.

Using all his willpower, Pete stood and finished the remaining coffee in his mug.

"I'll take that." Sarah reached out her hand while avoiding eye contact. "How far do you think you'll drive today?"

"I'm hoping to make it to somewhere around the Oregon and Idaho border. I might be overly ambitious, but we'll see how I feel. If I get tired, then I'll stop early for the night and start out fresh tomorrow." The long drive, which had excited him before, stretched before him like a twenty-mile hike in the mountains lugging a full rucksack—slow and boring.

Chloe returned to the kitchen with a clean face, carrying her stuffed unicorn.

"Do you mind if I talk with Chloe outside, just the two of us?" he asked Sarah.

"Of course not. Holler when I can come out." She kissed Chloe on the top of the head before her daughter slipped her little hand in Pete's.

He walked with her toward the fence that

enclosed Horace's favorite field. The donkey greeted them with a loud bray before returning to eating grass.

How does one explain to a child why he had to leave? The thing was, he didn't have to. He did have obligations in Phoenix. His new job did still rouse his interest. He'd been anticipating living in the large, desert city and exploring a new section of the country. Chloe wouldn't understand any of his reasons.

"I'll call your mom and ask to talk with you. We can video chat if you'd like."

"You won't be here." Her arms hugged her body tight.

"I know." He blew out a breath. This was harder than he imagined. "Promise you'll be good for your mom." His gaze dropped to the stuffed unicorn in her arms. "And no more running away. Even if you're upset."

"Lilac likes eating the special grass by the apple trees." She picked at her stuffed unicorn's plastic eyes. "I won't go there without Mom. Promise."

"Good." He rested a hand on her slight shoulder. "Did your friend Abby tell you she was sorry for teasing you?"

Chloe nodded. "She said she's sorry. I think her mommy made her."

He tried to hide his smile.

"I'll go get your mom and say goodbye. I'll miss you, Chloe-bear." *Hold it together.* He'd have almost twenty hours to sulk.

"Miss you too." She hugged his legs and squeezed. "Don't get hurt again. No climbing. Mom caught me climbing a tree and yelled at me to get down."

"Your mom is smart. If you climb too high, you can fall." He touched his wrist brace. Standing with Chloe in the peaceful environment of the ranch, danger was the last thing on his mind. He understood partially how soldiers who had children felt when on a mission. Their main priority was to stay safe and make it home to their loved ones. Since Pete had no one waiting for him at home, his focus often had stayed fixed on making sure his fellow soldiers made it back. And when those carrying emotional battle scars returned, did they find calm and healing in a place like this? And if so, did the sounds of gunfire and bomb blasts slowly drift from their memories? He hoped so.

The sun was now high in the sky, signaling his imminent departure. He'd miss this little girl, who had the same strong character as her mother. Pete thought about the son he and Sarah had lost and wondered once again what could have been.

CHAPTER SEVENTEEN

PETE STRODE WITH Chloe back to the house, and then she went inside to get Sarah.

Sarah came out alone and put her hands into the back pockets of her jeans. “Chloe wants to color you a picture quick. Sorry. I know you’re eager to leave.”

“It’s fine. I don’t mind waiting for a Chloe original.” He reached for her arm and pulled her close. Without overthinking, he brushed his lips against hers. A mistake for sure. But this might be the last kiss he’d get to enjoy with her. She tasted sweet, like syrup.

“We shouldn’t.” She put some distance between them.

He wanted to argue with her but stilled his tongue. She had a right to protect her heart from a man like him, who refused to settle down and give her the stable partner she needed.

“I’ll call when I get to Phoenix.”

She nodded. “I hope you have a good trip.

But Pete, I think it's best we don't try to keep this going."

"What do you mean?" He scratched at the scruff on his jawline to give his hand something to do. He'd rather touch Sarah while he could because soon she'd be out of reach.

"I'm glad we had a chance to reconnect and heal from what happened in the past," Sarah said. "I need to close that chapter of my life. And I can't do that if I'm waiting for a call or text from you, or hoping someday you'll come back for a visit. You'll be busy. I'm busy. It's always been either all or nothing where you're concerned. If I can't have it all, then we should walk away with no regrets."

"I understand." Although he struggled to come to terms with the finality of the moment, she was right. Only getting a part of Sarah would never be enough.

The back door burst open and Chloe ran out holding a sheet of paper. "Here." She handed it to Pete. "I colored a picture from my fairy princess coloring book. That was the only one I found."

He accepted the gift and gave it an appreciative look. She'd used every color in her box of crayons. "Thank you, honey. It's beautiful. Clover is my favorite fairy princess." That comment produced a large smile on Chloe's face.

"You know the names of the fairy princesses?" Chloe asked.

"Doesn't everyone?" Pete winked at Sarah. The fairy's name, Clover, was typed at the bottom of the coloring page.

The three stood in silence for a moment before Chloe stepped forward. "Bye, Pete. I'll miss you."

He knelt down and gave her a hug. "I'll miss you too." After Chloe returned to stand by her mom, Pete studied the little girl's face, trying to memorize her innocence and light.

"Goodbye, Pete." Sarah hugged him.

He clung to her like he'd clung to the rocks he'd been descending before he fell and broke his wrist. This impending fall would hurt a hundred times more.

"Don't forget to continue posting on social media." He kissed her cheek. "Keep showing your true self and the realities of running a horse rescue. You're the reason people enjoy watching the video clips."

"I'm not sure about that." She pushed hair out of her face. "I'll try to keep what you started going. Thanks for that. The money brought in is really making a difference."

"Happy to help." The voices urging him to cancel his plans and stay grew loud in his head.

It was time to quiet them. "Well, I should get on the road."

Sarah and Chloe walked him to his car. He got in and started the engine. It sounded like the dissolution of all the hopes and dreams that had occupied his mind since coming to Fern Hollow.

Heading down the driveway, he gave one final wave out of the open window. He turned onto the road and began the journey south.

He'd made it about thirty miles when the accusations started ringing in his head. *You're running away. Don't be a coward.* They sounded an awful lot like Milton's voice. He wasn't running away. He was moving toward something new and exciting. And he wasn't a coward. Not when he felt the urge to fly up into the bright blue sky and jump out of a plane—with a parachute strapped to his back, of course. He recalled the thumping sound of the rotary blades of an army Black Hawk. He pictured the view of the ground as it moved underneath. He craved the rush of adrenaline he got during the initial descent.

Why was he thinking about parachuting now? His mind should be on what was waiting for him in Phoenix—new job, new home, new people. A realization struck him like a lightning bolt hitting a mountaintop. Since making peace with Sarah, he hadn't felt the need to chase danger. But the moment he left and the feeling of missing her returned, he wanted to jump out of a plane.

Milton was right. *I am running away. Have been all this time.* He wanted to slap himself on the forehead. He'd been running away since their annulment. Every dangerous mission he eagerly accepted. He never complained during high-adrenaline training. Barely felt fear. Because those feelings replaced the tougher emotions he'd buried after losing Sarah and their baby. *You really are dull.*

Had his father seen the truth during his visit? Was that why he'd eased off on the career expectations and encouraged Pete to decide what direction was best for him?

Pete pulled off onto the shoulder and sat in contemplation. No wonder he'd had the impulse to rock climb during his hike with Jacob when their conversation turned to Sarah.

After five minutes of weighing his options, he made a choice. He made a quick call to Jacob. Then turning the car around, he experienced a stillness in his heart. He knew what waited for him was the best adventure yet. That was, if she'd have him. First, though, he had a stop to make.

EVERYTHING WAS GOING WONDERFULLY. All due to Pete and his heroic efforts. With the blessing of good weather, the square dance festivities fit even better outside than in the barn. Dusk was approaching, and the white lights hanging above provided the event with a festive air. Chloe was on the dance floor, following Milton's lead while the band played the "Tennessee Bird Walk." The square dance caller had been performing splendidly, and all appeared to be having a good time. Even those who elected not to take to the dance floor had plenty to entertain them. The buffet tables were filled with delicious smoked brisket, mac and cheese, rolls, cornbread, baked beans and assorted fresh vegetables. The busiest spot was the dessert tables, which were loaded with so many items Sarah was worried the table legs would give out. Mrs. Bryan had outdone herself, along with the others who'd donated items. The pie auction started soon. All would have been perfect if not for the absence of the man who'd made it possible.

Pete was long gone—likely in Oregon by now. He was making his way to Idaho. The distance shouldn't bother her. She'd lived for twelve years with him residing mostly outside the country. During his stay, things had changed. They'd grown close again, and Sarah remembered all the parts of him that had made her fall in love. He was a gentle man who demonstrated patience and understanding. His care of the horses and Chloe, and herself, proved he'd grown up during their time apart. Pete had all the qualities she wanted in a man—with one exception.

"What a marvelous job you did, dear." Mrs. Bryan approached wearing a white-and-yellow dress trimmed in yards of ruffles. A straw bonnet was fixed on her head with a yellow ribbon, which tied underneath her chin in a neat bow. "This may be the best yet."

"I never could have pulled it off without Pete, Milton and the others from town who helped and donated items." Each table, chair, decoration and forkful of food had been due to someone's generosity. "The fire really threw me off. I was ready to cancel."

"I'm glad you didn't. Can you believe the crowd?" Mrs. Bryan waved her hand around at the vast space filled with people—dancing, eating and socializing.

"We're at just over three hundred attendees." Half of whom wouldn't have heard about her rescue or the Hollow Hoedown if not for Pete. Not long ago, she'd cracked open the door to a possible future together, despite the warnings in her head. When he remained steadfast that country life wasn't for him, she slammed it closed and locked the door. Sarah would be fine moving on. Since Mike's death, she'd accepted that Chloe was the only family she needed, besides her parents, of course. She didn't need a romantic partner to be happy. But Pete had shaken her convictions. He was the type of man a woman didn't easily forget. She'd never fully gotten over him to begin with and probably never would.

"Good thing I baked extra pies." Mrs. Bryan turned her attention to the pies for the auction spread over the table and huffed out a breath. "Milton Monroe, you are strictly forbidden to bid on one of my pies." She marched off to deal with poor Milton, who hadn't been quick enough to slip away unnoticed.

Sarah planned on doing something to repair the relationship between Mrs. Bryan and Milton. What exactly, she wasn't sure. They were too old to be acting like children. If she could trick them into spending time together and actually talking, perhaps the hurts of the past would mend. Kind of like Sarah and Pete.

"Yeehaw!" Chloe shouted along with the square dance caller as she rushed toward Sarah. "Mom, come dance. It's so much fun." Her giggles sounded like the wind chimes hanging on their front porch.

"Yes, I see that." She steered her daughter to a chair and asked her to sit for a few minutes in order to catch her breath. "You're doing a good job following along."

"I watch Milton and he shows me what to do." Chloe's face glistened with sweat. "Come on, Mom." She hopped to her feet and tugged at Sarah's hand.

"Okay. I'll join for one song." As she walked to the dance floor, her long skirt fluttered around her legs. She'd gone with an ivory skirt with lace trim. She wore an off-the-shoulder blouse in light pink. The toes of her boots peeked out from underneath her skirt with each step. Her hair had been left down, though as the afternoon progressed into early evening, she considered getting a tie to pull it up.

As she stepped on the wooden dance floor at the start of a new song, her body grew lighter. When the caller instructed to *do-si-do*, she and Chloe circled around each other. Their laughter blended into the sweetest sound. Finally, the song ended, and all dancers meandered off the dance floor. Some went to get a drink, others something to eat. A few wandered over to the pasture fence to visit with the horses that were still out.

"We did it!" Lauren squealed and gave Sarah a quick hug. "The weather is perfect. Everything is so charming."

"It really is." Sarah gazed up and found the

first star of the night. She'd make a wish if there was any hope of her wish coming true. "Even the teenagers are having fun."

"Amazing."

Sarah waved at Jacob and Kay, who were making their way over.

"You two know how to throw a party." Jacob grinned at his wife. "I was telling Kay that at least our patio table set is being used. We've been so busy since getting home from our honeymoon, we haven't taken the time to sit outside and enjoy the summer."

"You can't let that continue," Lauren said. "No allowing a Washington summer to go by without spending as much time outdoors as possible."

"I know," Kay said. "Winter will be here before we know it."

"Banish the thought." Jacob mock-shivered. "Did Pete end up sticking around? The way he was talking, I thought he might change his mind."

"No. He's off to conquer the world. I hope the bad guys don't realize what's coming for them." Sarah fought to control her emotions. She wouldn't allow the cracks to show. Not tonight when so much joy filled the air.

"I'd hoped he would stay." Jacob's gaze met Sarah's. "I'm sorry."

"Don't be." Sarah widened her smile. "I'm made of tougher stuff than that."

He glanced away like he really didn't believe her.

"The band is starting up again." Kay took Jacob's hand. "Let's go." The two lovebirds strolled off hand in hand.

"I'm going to check on the food and see if anyone needs anything," Lauren said, but she didn't turn to leave. "Sarah, how are you…really."

"Really?" She felt the burn of tears. "I can't think about it. I'm sure eventually his absence will hit me, but right now I want to enjoy the fruits of our hard work. Check in on me in a couple of days, okay."

"I definitely will." Lauren left to talk with the man who'd supplied most of the food.

Sarah pulled out her cell phone to take videos of the event. She'd try her best to put together some decent video clips and post them on the rescue's social media. Moving off to the side, she recorded the square dancers and the musicians. She took another video that spanned the entire area to give the viewers the perspective of an attendee. Sarah zoomed in on Chloe as she swirled around with her skirt billowing around her legs—she'd save this video for herself. If only she could keep Chloe the carefree child she was right now. Someday, her daughter would be a teenager and fall in love. *Oh, my heart. Think about that another day.*

Exhaling a sigh, she opened up Instagram. All the notifications no longer startled her. There were always people liking, sharing and commenting on the posts. For a moment, she forgot how to upload a new video and went to the rescue's page. The sight of several posts of videos taken from the Hollow Hoedown produced confusion. Had Milton suddenly become tech savvy?

She clicked on the most recent. It showed a line of people filling their plates with steaming food. She closed that one and opened the next. Was that her? She continued watching as the focus of the video narrowed to Sarah. She stood alone, swinging back and forth to the music. The caption read "The most beautiful girl in the world." Lowering her phone, she glanced around, almost in a panic. She couldn't allow hope to rise. Pete wasn't here. He'd left hours ago.

In the distance, a figure approached, walking toward her across the field. Very reminiscent of Mr. Darcy's famous stroll but without the fog. And instead of breeches, a white shirt and full-length jacket, this man wore well-fitting dark jeans, a long-sleeved Western shirt made of crisp white fabric with blue and yellow embroidery over the chest and a broad cowboy hat. "Pete," she breathed out.

"Ma'am." He used his fingers to tip his hat. "I was hoping to find you here."

"What are you doing?" She studied him closely to make sure he wasn't a figment of her imagination.

"Hoping to make a dramatic entrance." He grinned. "How did I do?"

"I—I mean," she stuttered. "It was dramatic. You're supposed to be on your way to Phoenix."

"Changed my mind. It didn't take me long before I turned around." He took her hand in his and wove together their fingers. "I had to make a stop at the Blue Bar to get some square dance appropriate attire."

Sarah touched one of the mother-of-pearl–covered buttons that ran down the front of his shirt. "No vest?" She withheld her enthusiasm. Perhaps Pete didn't want to miss the dance he'd helped rescue, but he might leave again tomorrow. *No getting your hopes up. Been there. Done that.* She didn't like the hole in her chest the last bite of disappointment had produced.

"I decided to forgo the vest. I'm not really a rhinestone kind of guy."

He'd look handsome in anything. "I saw what you posted online." She showed her phone.

"Your videos are a million times better than mine."

"Only because you are in them." His playful demeanor turned serious. He raised their joined hands and he planted a kiss on her knuckles. "I know I said I'd never be happy living in a small town, working a job that wasn't full of action. I was wrong."

"What does that mean?" She feared his answer wasn't what she wished to hear. Her body began to tremble.

"It means, Sarah Carmella, that I'd like to stay, if you'll let me. I don't want to lose my second chance with the one woman I can't imagine living without."

"Stay?" Her voice squeaked. Did she want him to stay and move forward together? They'd both lived through experiences that changed them. Some for the better. Some made them stronger. Was she ready to let down her emotional barricade and take another chance on him?

"I understand." He dropped her hand and looked down. His posture seemed to crumple. "I'll go."

"No." She grabbed his arm and pulled him back, needing him close. "Dance with me."

"I don't know how to square dance."

"I don't want to square dance." She wrapped

her arms around his neck and waited while Pete encircled her waist. Her fingers brushed through the hair at the nape of his neck.

With his body close, they gently swayed to the melody of the collective sounds around them. A few birds still sang out from their hidden spots in bushes and trees. Music mixed with conversation, and laughter drifted in their direction.

Sarah rested her head against Pete's chest. "We're different people today than we were as teens. The timing back then wasn't right. We both had our own paths to journey, and I think what happened between us was for the best."

"It didn't feel like it at the time." Pete's hand stroked in a circle on her low back.

"No, it didn't," she agreed. "I thought the world was ending. But it didn't. You had a successful career in the army. I stayed where I belonged. If our marriage had lasted, I never would have had Mike in my life, and consequently never would have had Chloe. I couldn't imagine my life without her."

"She's the best."

The fact Pete adored her daughter made her verdict easier. "I believe in us now. I think we didn't work back then so we'd have this moment. I want you to stay, Pete. I want to start a new chapter with you." She could feel his smile as he rested the side of his face on top of her head.

"I believe in us too. Can we write an entire book together and not just a chapter?"

"A long book with pictures." She wiped happy tears off her cheeks. "My grandparents started the orchard and ranch with love—for the trees, animals and most importantly for each other. I'd like to make sure the land continues to be nourished by the same love my grandparents shared. Are you up for the challenge?"

"It will be my most cherished adventure." He lowered his head to kiss her, under the twilit sky and glow of lights from the nearby party.

Their past was already written. Their future was a blank page. "Come on, let's join the fun. Chloe can teach you to square dance."

"One more kiss." Pete stole another before looking into her eyes. "It took me a while, but I'm finally home."

Fern Hollow had gained a new resident. In its quirky way, the town had embraced Pete. She held his hand as they walked into the loving circle of friends who felt more like family. After an uncertain journey, Sarah and Pete were exactly where they needed to be—together.

EPILOGUE

THE DAY WAS PERFECT. Chloe skipped ahead down a path between rows of apple trees, while Sarah strolled contentedly beside Pete. Harvest season was just kicking off. Last weekend had been the apple orchard's first pick-your-own opportunity of the year. Families had flooded in, and some of the trees had been relieved of a good portion of their fruit. In another three weeks or so, the trees would stand free of apples. Those not selected by the public or set aside for the horses were sold to grocery stores or donated to be pressed into cider for the upcoming apple festival.

Pete's help had been deeply appreciated. He'd extended the lease on the house he had been renting. Every morning at dawn, rain or shine, he showed up with a smile and an eager attitude. She couldn't afford to pay him, with the exception of Mrs. Bryan's doughnuts, so he found a remote job. She still wasn't sure all what his job duties entailed but he was using his marketing skills to good use. A lot of computer work, which seemed strange given Pete wasn't fond of sitting still. But it was temporary and paid the bills.

"Come on," Chloe called out. She'd woven her way into the trees and was now out of sight.

"I guess we should pick up the pace." Pete swung Sarah into his arms and planted a firm kiss on her mouth. "You taste like apples."

"I had one before we left." She wiped at the corner of her mouth. "If the saying is true, then I'll never have to see the doctor."

Pete began walking again and hummed a merry tune.

She didn't recognize the melody, but she often caught Pete humming these days. Did that mean he was happy? Content? That he didn't regret turning down the job in Phoenix to live in Fern Hollow? While she occasionally worried that he would realize he'd made a mistake, Sarah's confidence in their relationship remained solid.

As they headed deeper into the orchard, the air grew sweeter. The scents of apples and earth filled her nose. It was a reminder she was where she was meant to be. Her connection to the land stayed as strong as a mother's love for her child.

Up ahead, Chloe waited by one of the orchard's original trees. "Is this right?" she asked.

"Yes." Pete replied.

"Yeah. Hurry." Jumping up and down, Chloe clapped her hands.

"What's the rush?" Sarah asked with a laugh. "Dinner isn't for another few hours."

She joined her daughter by the tree but was unable to go underneath the branches as Chloe had. Being short had its advantages.

"Do you know what tree this is?" Pete asked Sarah.

She studied it, searching her mind. "It's one of the few left from when Grandad inherited the land."

"You're right but that's not all. Giorgio took me out here one afternoon after a long day of horse training. He pointed to this very tree and told me that he'd proposed to Lucille right here." Pete pointed to the ground under his feet.

Sarah pressed a hand to her heart. "I should know that." How could she not? "I may have forgotten. I'm surprised you remember Grandad telling you." She turned her gaze from the tree to where Pete had been standing. Though he was no longer standing.

Pete knelt down in front of her with Chloe at his side. In his outstretched hand lay a shining gold band. "I made sure to ask Chloe's permission before doing this."

Chloe's eyes sparkled. "I said yes."

"Sarah Carmella. I've loved you since before I even knew what it was to love a girl. You've always accepted me. Never tried to change me. You offered me a place in your heart and in your family. Please do me the honor of being my wife?"

At a loss for words, Sarah looked from Pete to Chloe and then back to Pete. Her daughter was nodding very enthusiastically. Pete's smile faltered and the seconds passed without her response. Finally, something kicked in inside her head. "Yes." She covered his hand with hers. The cool metal of the ring pressed into her palm. "Yes, yes, yes."

Pete stood and slipped the ring on her left ring finger. He lifted Chloe into his arms to share a family hug. He kissed Chloe on the cheek and Sarah on the lips. "I love you both very much. Thank you for letting me join your awesome club."

"Can Horace be in the wedding?" Chloe asked. "He said he wants to."

"We'll see." Sarah stared into Pete's brown eyes and realized she was the happiest girl alive.

Pete set Chloe back down on her feet so she could run free. "It's my mom's ring." Setting his finger on the band, he twisted it lightly on her finger. "My dad gave it to me when I was down visiting. I know it's simple so you can pick something else to better suit you if you like. You wouldn't hurt my feelings."

"I love it." She gazed at the gold band, which was inset with five small diamonds. "I can't wear bulky jewelry while working on the ranch. And the fact this belonged to someone who loved you makes it extra special. It fits perfectly."

"You're a perfect fit." He stroked her chin and then down the side of her neck. "My dad offered it without my asking. I think he knew."

"How is he doing?"

"Fighting, as expected. Jean, his lady friend, is a big support. I never thought my dad would open his heart to anyone after Mom died."

"We all have the capacity to change. Even a tough navy man."

When Pete had gone down to San Diego to visit his father and his brother and family in August, Kenneth had sat everyone down and explained he'd been diagnosed with prostate cancer. They'd caught it relatively early so the outlook was good. Kenneth had known about the cancer during his trip up to Fern Hollow, which likely accounted for his softening. No more demands to go out into the world to prove one's worth. Pete had been discovering a new relationship with a man who'd always been very tough to get close to, and Sarah enjoyed witnessing the evolution.

"I'm glad you like the ring. And said yes." Pete kissed her again.

"I'm glad you asked me." She took his hand and headed in the direction Chloe had pranced off in. "I have a wedding to plan. Good thing I know a great place to have the reception."

"Are we really letting Horace be a part of the service?" The tip of Pete's boot caught on a root sticking up from the ground and he stumbled.

Sarah steadied him, much like he steadied her on many occasions, both emotionally and physically. "I feel like we are in for some heavy negotiations where the wedding is concerned. Not only will Chloe want a say but there's my mom. Emma will definitely have opinions." Sarah had barely survived her mom during the planning of her wedding to Mike. She'd once again insist on going the simple route. And if all else failed, she'd threaten to elope with Pete—again.

"I think I'm starting to win over your mom. She smiled at me at least twice the last time we were together."

"That's progress." Sarah stepped out of the grove of trees into an open field. The sky above was a sharp cerulean blue. Miles away, the tops of the Cascade mountains waited to be touched by approaching clouds. The scene, a combination of nature and love, was without fault.

Chloe twirled through grass and wildflowers almost as tall as her.

Resting her head on Pete's shoulder, Sarah inhaled deeply. Life's twists and turns were often unpredictable. Sorrow didn't last forever. Light always found a way back in. Sarah loved where she stood right now in her journey. She couldn't ask for more.

* * * * *

Be sure to look for Laurie Winter's next Harlequin Heartwarming book coming soon, wherever Harlequin books are sold!